"Eleanor!"

She turned, sweeping her gaze over all sides. The parking lot was devoid of another human being. The voice had come from the shadowed corner, from the air. From the lips of a dead man.

"I've been waiting a long, long time, Eleanor."

The voice seemed to penetrate her spine. Fear greater than any she'd ever known tingled through her.

"Where are you?" Her voice echoed eerily through the garage, striking the concrete walls and vibrating back to her.

"I'm here, Eleanor. Watching you." There was a deep, satisfied laugh.

"Carter!" The blood rushed to her heart, a pounding wave of denial. "No," she said. "No!" She held out her hand as if to ward off the vision. "You're dead!"

"No, Eleanor, I'm not." He stepped toward her, his face shadowed by the widebrimmed panama hat he always favored. "But you may be, if you don't give back what you took."

ABOUT THE AUTHOR

Animals have always added an extra dimension to the life of Caroline Burnes. She shares a home on Mobile Bay with three dogs and a cat. Active in many humane and wildlife organizations, Caroline urges all pet owners to vaccinate their animals and have them spayed or neutered.

Books by Caroline Burnes

HARLEQUIN INTRIGUE
86–A DEADLY BREED
100–MEASURE OF DECEIT
115–PHANTOM FILLY

Fear
Familiar
Caroline Burnes

Harlequin Books

TORONTO • NEW YORK • LONDON
AMSTERDAM • PARIS • SYDNEY • HAMBURG
STOCKHOLM • ATHENS • TOKYO • MILAN

This book is dedicated
to Cissy Jordan,
who knows a home isn't complete without a cat.

Harlequin Intrigue edition published March 1990

ISBN 0-373-22134-7

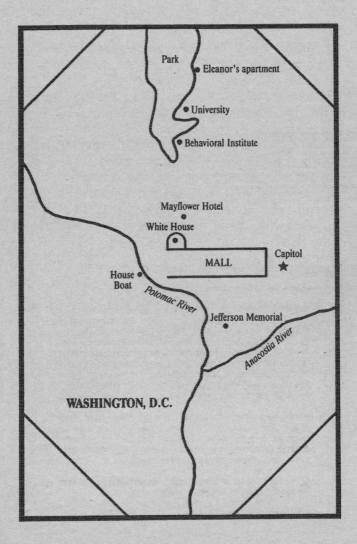

Park
● Eleanor's apartment

● University

● Behavioral Institute

Mayflower Hotel
●

White House
●

MALL

Capitol
★

House
Boat
●

Potomac River

Jefferson Memorial
●

Anacostia River

WASHINGTON, D.C.

CAST OF CHARACTERS

Familiar—Of all the characters in Eleanor Duncan's life, Familiar appeared to be the most innocent. But was he?

Eleanor Duncan—She wanted a quiet life after a turbulent marriage, but now she found herself in the middle of the action.

Peter Curry—He was best friend to animals, but his past had taught him that the most treacherous of all living creatures was man.

Carter Wells—He gambled with his wife, his fortune and his life—and he lost it all. The trouble with Carter was that he didn't want to stay dead.

Magdalena Caruso—Her bite was worse than her bark, and she knew how to bark loud and clear when it came to animal rights.

Charles Breck—A man with his ambitions knew how to bend the rules.

Alva Rousel—He was able to warn Eleanor about her past and terrify her about her future.

Cal Vrenner—He had a way with animals. Was it only for research, or something else?

Betty Gillette—She was Eleanor's friend and colleague, but by night she had another identity.

Congressman Sam Nottingham—Was he willing to push his authority to the maximum to achieve a personal goal?

Wessy—His door key was a convenience for too many people.

Chapter One

The dame is a real looker. She came out of the library with a stack of books that looked heavier than she did. Tall, slender, dark-haired, with that special sort of independent walk, she's just the one I've been watching for. Not a bad-looking woman, even if the horn-rimmed glasses do detract. Maybe a little too thin, from my perspective. You know the old adage: thin woman, empty pantry. But after all, it's a university campus, and what can I expect from an industry of pointy-heads? It's late, and she's leaving sans an escort. The odds are better than fifty-fifty that she lives alone. That means no cranky kids or irritable spouse, the things I've avoided in my single life. I've done my homework. Besides, I have to make something happen.

I've been on the run since the night before last, and my leg is killing me. Somehow I have to get the catheter out of it. The dame looks as though she can handle it. She looks as though she could handle a lot without freaking. Anyway, my time is running out. I know they're after me, and if I don't find a safe place quick, they'll have me.

Here goes! I limp toward her, partly because I'm in pain, and partly because I figure a sucker ploy like a limp won't hurt my chances. Not for the first time in my life, I'm perfectly accurate in reading a person. She's stopping, books ready to tumble and crush me. I hold her with my most appealing gaze, saying to myself the whole time, "Come on, baby, take a desperate fur ball home with you."

Uh-oh, she's starting to turn away. Time for the real dramatics. I make a sort of strangled noise and limp right up to her leg. The rub across her shin is calculated, but not half as bad as it could be. She smells great, and those legs of hers go straight to the sky. I mean if you have to give up newly won independence, even temporarily, this dame isn't a bad place to start. She's classy. One look into her dark eyes, and I knew she had a heart as big as Texas, as the old saying goes.

Well, I'll give her one more pitiful meow.

"You must be lost," she says.

Man, her voice is better than the sound of an electric can opener. I feel the old motor kick in my throat for the first time in months, and I purr.

She bends to touch me and carefully examines my leg. "What's this?" she asks, poking at the plastic catheter that's my Achilles heel. I have to get rid of that thing, and quick. There must be a million stray cats running around Washington, D.C., but none with plastic tubing hanging out of their limbs. It's a dead giveaway to my past.

"Meow," I answer, even more pitifully than before.

"Have you gotten away from a vet?" she asks. As she bends over me, a strand of her black hair brushes my whiskers. Before I can stop myself, I rub her chin with the back of my head. She is delicious. At this moment I realize how cruel fate has been. How did I wind up as a research animal when I could have been living with her?

For the first time in my short life I feel a pang of guilt. I'm a marked animal, and my life is in jeopardy. Now I've pushed my problems onto this dame, and there's no way I'll ever be able to make her understand, or even warn her.

THE CAT'S SLEEK FUR brushed across her face as she bent to examine the animal. Despite herself, Eleanor Duncan stroked it, gently examining the injured leg it had so pitifully displayed. An indwelling catheter had been inserted into the limb.

"Poor old guy," she said softly. "Where'd you come from?" Her hand moved up and down the cat, both examining and giving comfort. Except for the right front leg, the cat appeared to be in good condition. The soot-black coat was glossy, the animal well fed.

"Meow," the cat said, turning huge green eyes to stare directly into hers. "Meow," he continued, clearly asking her to take him home.

"I haven't had a pet since I was a little girl," she answered. Memories of her parents and the large, two-story house with the big yard in Tennessee came back to her. That had been a house for dogs and cats and lots of love. Her Washington apartment was a far cry from such an environment. "I don't think you'd fit into my life-style very well, boy."

She gave him a final pat and regathered the stack of books she'd dropped. "Good luck," she murmured and started toward her car.

"Meow!" the cat cried.

She walked faster, moving across the cherry tree-lined perimeter of the library grounds toward the parking lot.

"Meow! Aiowee!"

She glanced over her shoulder. The black cat was hobbling after her, barely able to walk. "Good grief!" she sighed, exasperated both with the animal and herself. "Con men, sick dogs and stray cats always want to follow me home." She dumped the books onto the grass and went back. The cat lifted his paw to her, steadily holding her with his intense gaze.

"Aeeow," he cried softly.

Eleanor Duncan swept him up into the warmth of her overcoat. He immediately snuggled down, popping his head out of the opening at her chest. "Mrrrow," he said, purring so loudly that he sounded like a motor.

"This is only temporary," she warned him. "We'll get that leg fixed up, and then we'll find you a good home. I can't have pets. I don't have time and I don't want to . . . get involved. Pets are notorious for running away, or getting run over, or doing some other stupid thing that always results in heartache. So I'll get you patched up, and then you're moving on."

The cat didn't bother to answer; he simply rubbed her chin with his head and purred.

With the cat tucked in her coat, Eleanor had both hands free to recover her books. When she was so heavily loaded that she almost couldn't see over the stack, she started to her car.

The parking lot was empty on the cold, mid-December night. Most of the elite University of Arts and Literature students were home for the holidays, tucked in among family and friends. Eleanor's life was the campus, her research, her work. With the students gone, the library was quieter, more suited to her linguistic pursuits. She loved teaching, but was more comfortable in the solitude of her research.

When she reached her small car, she balanced the books on the hood and searched her purse for the keys. Through all of the maneuverings, the stray cat lay cradled against her as if he'd been born to ride like a papoose. She scratched his ears as she slid the key into the lock. "You're pretty relaxed for a stray," she observed.

Iron fingers dug into her shoulder, throwing her around and slamming her into the side of the car.

"Hey!" she cried.

A hard slap cut the side of her nose and sent her glasses flying.

"You're going to pay for what you've done!" The threat was ground out in a tough, nasty voice. Even worse, the hideously ugly face seemed made of dough. "You can't provoke me like this!"

Eleanor stifled a scream; blearily she saw the stocking-distorted features of a large, angry man. Without her glasses she couldn't make out much else. She tried to duck, but his palm caught her again, striking so hard that her knees buckled, and she fell back against the fender of the car, scattering books everywhere.

"Who are you with?" the man asked, grabbing the lapel of her coat and roughly pulling her to her feet. He shook her so hard that her head snapped back and forth, the dark curls foaming over her face and shoulders. "Answer me!" he demanded as he pushed her backward. "Get in the car. We're going for a ride."

Eleanor felt the cat coil itself inside her coat. Just as the man drew back to slap her again, the animal launched itself from her chest and sprang, all claws extended, at the man's face.

Horrified and relieved, Eleanor saw the full weight of the cat drag down the man's face, ripping ribbons of blood into the stocking mask and the flesh beneath.

The man screamed, turning and striking at the cat with both arms. But the animal spit, snarled and clung, digging all four claws deeper and deeper. Then it suddenly sprang away and ran into the darkness.

Adrenaline pumping, Eleanor drew back one leg and kicked with all her might, catching the man first in one shin, then the other. Screaming, he fell to the ground and she opened the car door.

"Kitty, kitty!" she cried. A flying ball of fur propelled itself through the open door, across her lap and into the passenger seat. The car was skidding out of the parking lot before Eleanor even attempted to close her door. Unable to see clearly without her glasses, she hit a curb and lurched into the busy Washington traffic. As horns blared on all sides, she pumped the gas pedal and merged.

The shaking didn't get bad until she was in her cozy, ninth-floor apartment. The stray cat was happily slurping a bowl of warm milk and a can of tuna. She'd come in, locked the door, cared for the kitty, and finally gone into the bathroom to wash her face.

Her nose was cut where her glasses had been slammed into her face. Her right cheek was red and swollen from the slap, and she thought she looked as if she'd never recover from the shock of it all. Her skin, normally a milky white, was almost blue. Even her hair was standing out from her head like a woman from Bedlam.

That was when her body gave in to the delayed reaction and started shaking. Sinking onto the cold tile floor, she rested her forehead on her knees. She had to get up and call the police, but what in the world was she going to tell them? That she'd been attacked and beaten in a parking lot? So what! That happened every five minutes in a big city.

She could tell them that she was afraid! Big deal; she could at least afford to live in a pricey apartment with security and a doorman. The cops wouldn't have a lot of sympathy, and besides, she wasn't really hurt.

She sensed another presence and looked up. The black cat was standing in the doorway, watching her intently. He came over and sat down beside her.

"I almost got you killed," she said, remembering how she'd fallen against the car. She could have crushed him. "You know, big guy, you saved my life." She scratched behind his ears and under his chin. To her delight, he flopped onto his back and exposed his stomach. There wasn't a single white hair on his entire body.

"Back in old Salem, you'd have been burned as a witch's familiar," she said, stroking the cat's belly to his wriggling delight. "Familiar," she said. "I know I shouldn't name a pet I'm not going to keep, but until you go, how about that for a moniker?"

The cat flipped himself onto his feet and eyed her.

"Familiar," she said firmly.

"Meow," he answered, sitting down again. He gave her a full blast from his green eyes, then deliberately lifted one paw and began to lick it. He stopped, studied her again, then cleaned his face.

"Oh," she said, laughing softly. "I get the message. I should get up and wash my face, right?"

"Meow," he replied, walking out of the bathroom, his tail straight in the air.

She shook her head and got to her feet. One thing about her new roommate, he didn't have a shy bone in his body. He came in, ate, took over, and began issuing orders. It would only be for a short time, she reminded herself, but she couldn't help but notice that her comfortable apartment was even a little more comfortable with the cat around.

DR. PETER CURRY stroked the black cat on the examining table, but his attention was focused upon the striking woman who stood across from him. He could see a small, fresh gash on her nose and an obvious handprint on the side of her face. Someone had manhandled her, and in the not too distant past. He examined the cat's leg again. Was it just coincidence that a battered woman would show up at his clinic with a lab animal? He wasn't a great believer in coincidence, but he had a very healthy respect for frame-ups.

"How did you select my clinic?" he asked.

"You were the closest one," Eleanor answered. "I hope that doesn't offend you, but I haven't had a pet in years. I don't know a lot about the vets in Washington, so I got your address out of the phone book. The ad said small animals. Is there a problem?"

"And you found this cat?" He watched her eyes, looking for a trace of guilt or deception. The brown eyes shot with amber highlights gazed steadily back at him, completely unperturbed.

"Yes, I found him on the campus last night," Eleanor said. "He saved..." She stumbled on her explanation, not wanting to sound ridiculous. "The cat intervened and sort of saved my life," she finished lamely.

Dr. Curry bent to examine the animal, but looked up again surreptitiously at the woman. She was poised, controlled, not a likely victim for abuse from a spouse or boyfriend. Or for criminal theft. But it took all kinds. He'd learned that lesson well enough. It really wasn't his business where she got the cat. Unless... His gaze drifted back to her bruises. Hell, she was a grown woman. If she wanted to risk her neck, that was her affair. He tried to shrug it off, but still didn't like the idea of anyone slapping that ivory skin.

His practiced hands moved down the cat, ignoring the obvious injury to the leg. He checked out ribs, internal organs, eyes, teeth, everything. A tiny nodule, hard and self-contained, stopped him at the cat's belly. Without X rays there was no way to be certain what it was, but his best guess was a BB pellet. He saw far too many animals with lead implanted in their hides. In the loose skin of the belly it wasn't a critical issue. Lucky it wasn't near the eye, he thought before he turned back to the leg. With one expert movement that barely caused the animal to twitch, he removed the catheter. He held it in his palm.

It was a common device, but something made him look at it more closely. Blood surged to his brain, and for a moment he felt a cold fury he thought he'd left behind long ago. There was a tiny nick on the tubing, a mark. It was like a brand or an initial.

"Are there scientific research laboratories at your university?" He thought for certain she'd hear the cold anger in his voice, but she didn't seem to notice.

"None," Eleanor said. "We're arts only. No medicine. Why?"

"I believe this animal has somehow escaped from a research facility," Peter said. "This is a tube used to feed drugs, or whatever they're testing, directly into the bloodstream."

Arnold Evans.

The name shot through his brain, leaving behind a fiery trail of anger. If the woman was a plant, then she might well prove to be exactly the person he wanted to cultivate. He'd waited years for such an opportunity, and he couldn't afford to lose his temper now.

Arnold Evans! His hands tingled at the thought of putting them around the man's neck.

"The life of a research animal doesn't sound very pleasant," Eleanor said. Though she had always intended to return Familiar to his home, if she could find it, suddenly she changed her mind.

"Thousands of cats are used in all types of research." Peter Curry pretended to look at the cat as he spoke, but his attention was still focused on the woman. He'd seen it, that flash of subdued anger! Maybe Eleanor Duncan *was* more than the good Samaritan she pretended to be. He'd been expecting someone like her since Arnold Evans had resurfaced in Africa. The question was, which side of the line did she fall on?

"Can you tell what type of research he might have been used for?" Eleanor felt uncomfortable. The veterinarian was giving her what amounted to an in-depth visual examination, even though he was being very subtle about it.

"Impossible to tell," Peter said. "He's healthy in every way. My guess is that he was just started as a research animal. Are you having second thoughts about taking him in?" His generous mouth formed a thin line.

"I'm not giving him back." Eleanor surprised herself with the vehemence of her own words. The vet could like it or not. "This cat saved me from an attacker last night in the parking lot, and I owe him."

Peter was surprised by her outburst. She seemed to wear her emotions as plainly as the marks on her face. He walked around the table and stopped in front of her. His hand gently touched the cut on her nose. "I was wondering what happened to you. Looks like you could use a little antiseptic on that."

"I washed it well with soap and water, but I'm afraid my pantry was bare of medicines. Since I spend most of my time reading, I don't often need first-aid supplies." Eleanor couldn't help the huskiness in her voice. The last thing she'd expected was to find herself standing toe-to-toe with a veterinarian. With Peter Curry so close, she could see the thick fringe of lashes and the wrinkles at the corner of his eyes. His touch was gentle, confident.

Self-conscious, she dropped her gaze to the sea-blue flannel of his shirt. His chest was at eye level, and where the buttons began, she caught a glimpse of dark curls.

"I'm not a doctor, but I can clean that up for you," he offered. She was either ingeniously well rehearsed or really shy.

"What's good enough for Familiar is good enough for me," she said, glad for anything sensible to say. "I'd really appreciate it."

As Peter found clean cotton and a bottle of antiseptic, she glanced at her cat. Familiar sat on the examining table, watching both of them. He was more composed than she was.

"Here we go," Peter said as he held her chin firmly in one hand and stroked the cotton over the cut.

His touch was warm and the wet cotton cold. Eleanor found that she had no place to look except at his face. His hair was light brown with blond highlights; it was thick and a little in need of a cut. Two interesting scars crested the bone of his left cheek.

"I had a run-in with a wounded hawk," he explained, never looking away from her nose or stopping his work. "Maybe I should lie and say that I was injured in some adventure, some worthy cause."

"Not for my benefit," Eleanor said, and she could hear the stiffness that suddenly invaded her tone. "I'm not much impressed by adventurers or other romantic names for people who are incurably selfish."

"I'm glad I'm not Errol Flynn." Peter gave the cut one final dab and smiled. She was certainly not taking the bait he'd thrown to her. "For a lady who denies a yen for adventure, do you mind if I ask why someone attacked you in a parking lot?" He waited.

"That's the question of the week! It was late, and I had a stack of books from the library. I saw Familiar and picked him up, and was just about to get into my car when a guy with his face covered in a stocking grabbed me. I can assure you, I didn't do anything to provoke the attack. I have no secrets, no treasures, no money. Not even a great family recipe worth stealing. It was just a fluke, and my cat jumped on the attacker and drove him away."

Peter walked back to the table where the cat sat, obviously perfectly content, cleaning his back leg. Was she telling the truth? Eleanor Duncan wasn't exactly what he'd been expecting. But then neither was a lab cat with an Arnold Evans trademark.

"I'm impressed with old Familiar here," he said. "I've been doing a little study in animal communication. I've noticed the cat's ease with us, his confident and independent nature."

"He acts like he knows exactly what's going on," Eleanor agreed.

Peter laughed. "That's pretty standard for cats. They have a certain arrogance."

"Meow," Familiar said without looking up.

"His leg should heal without any trouble, Ms. Duncan." He stroked the cat. "If you keep him, we should start vaccinations. There's a growth or foreign object in the skin near his belly that should be removed. And then there's the matter of his reproductive future."

"Meow!" Familiar stood up, stiff-legged.

"Maybe we should spell," Eleanor said, her whole face brightening as she scratched his ears. "Familiar's too smart."

"Bring him back in a week, if you decide to keep him. And by the way, I heard you refer to him as 'my cat.'" He waited, expecting her to make another appointment. If she was working with a group, she'd want to return with another member. If she worked for Evans . . .

"Thanks, Doctor," Eleanor said as she gathered up the cat and went to the receptionist to pay.

THE WASHINGTON TRAFFIC was heavy at eleven in the morning. Eleanor stopped at the cleaners, her favorite deli, and returned to the campus. A quick stop at campus security yielded her books and glasses. The lenses were intact, but the frame was uncomfortably warped. As she put them on, they tugged painfully at her cut nose.

"At least I can see to drive a little better," she told the cat as she headed toward her apartment. "My luck has changed," she said, pulling into an open parking space directly in front of the door of her building. She much preferred the street to the garage.

Arms loaded and Familiar tucked comfortably inside her coat, she greeted John, the daytime doorman, and took the elevator to the ninth floor. The fear of the night before had worn away, but there was still a nagging concern. What had provoked the attack? She tried hard to remember the harsh questions the man had asked, but the whole incident was still a blur. She remembered the man, his large hands and hideous face. He'd threatened her, then asked something. Her brow furrowed with the effort to remember while she rummaged in her purse for the apartment key. But as she inserted it, the door swung open easily.

She stood in the hallway, mouth open. Slowly the books cascaded around her feet. Apparently startled by the noise, Familiar poked up his head near the collar of her coat.

The apartment was wrecked. Broken dishes were all over the floors. Pillows were slashed. Plants had been thrown against walls, leaving dirt scattered in all directions. Eleanor gasped and stumbled into the room. She slammed the door shut and leaned against it. A white-hot anger as jagged as a bolt of lightning buzzed down her spine.

Familiar eased himself out of her coat and took a quick survey of the scene.

"No!" Eleanor said, softly but with resolution. "No! I won't have this. I won't put up with it. Not ever again!" She leaned against the wooden door, fighting the anger until she felt the comfort of Familiar's insistent brushing against her leg.

The cat's touch brought her back to the moment, and she turned about to face the damage. The apartment was a mess. Whoever had trashed the place had been both malicious and very thorough. Walking resolutely to the telephone, she picked up the receiver, but her hand was shaking so badly that she had to put it back down. It was impossible to call the police. The scene before her was the worst of her nightmares revisited. She could hide out at a ritzy university, pretending that she was a scholar with a cool, impeccable life. She could wear subdued clothing and talk in a carefully modulated voice. She could deceive all of her new acquaintances. But this wasn't the first time Eleanor Duncan had faced a trashed apartment or violence in her life. Not on a bet!

"But that was the past!" she vowed out loud, picking up a pillow and pounding it with her fist. "That was Carter's life, not mine! Those were *his* gambling debts, not mine! And I won't have this!" She reached for the phone again, but this time her hand stopped halfway.

She'd built a safe, secure haven at the University of Arts and Literature, and there was no room in her life for scandal. She'd lived an immaculate life. She'd never been a day late in paying her utility bills. She'd never been the subject of a whisper. If she called the police, they'd make a report. There'd be inquiries, investigations, maybe even newspaper stories. Her hand fell to her side. It was too much to bear. Her life had been smeared across the scandal sheets once before in connection with gambling, gangsters' schemes and murder. She'd learned one good lesson from it all—*trust no one and keep your mouth shut*.

She turned and went to the door, carefully securing the lock. She didn't want anyone to see what had happened to her life. Her shoulders ached with tension as she went to the kitchen and got trash bags, a broom, a dustpan and gloves. She could clean it up. She'd done it before. That was the best way to handle it—alone.

With Familiar's presence to comfort her, she started in the kitchen, sweeping up flour, sugar, grits—pounds and pounds of ruined food. She was halfway through when Familiar sprang to the floor, his tail twitching in the air. He took two tentative steps toward the door, then paused.

"Meow," he said, alerting her.

Heart pumping, Eleanor rested the broom against the counter. She heard it, too, a tentative footstep outside her front door. Her hand moved to the kitchen drawer where the largest knife rested. Just as her fingers closed on the handle, she heard the knock.

Chapter Two

Peter Curry bounced the checkbook in his palm. He didn't need the excuse of returning it to see Eleanor Duncan again. He was quite capable of asking her out for dinner and dancing. He was just as certain, though, that a direct approach—such as asking for a date—would send the dark-haired professor scurrying to hide among her stack of books. If it was a game of cat and mouse she wanted, then he intended to turn the tables. She could spy on him while he pursued her!

Since she'd left his office, his thoughts had returned to her several times. He didn't believe in coincidences. When she walked into his office with a lab cat bearing the too recognizable mark of Arnold Evans, every one of his senses had hit red alert. But then she hadn't behaved as he'd expected. She was so open-acting and -looking. She was intelligent, well-spoken and humorous. All good qualities. And with that dark hair and ivory skin she was sexy as all get-out.

He sighed and knocked louder. If some animal liberators were trying to enlist his sympathetic assistance, they'd certainly used the best method of persuasion. He had to find out if that was what put Eleanor Duncan in his office, or if she was trying to set him up. He'd been unable to discern any trace of ulterior motive in her behavior. Maybe it was just his nerves working on him, or the magazine article on

Arnold Evans. He was overly sensitive about the man, but then he had a right to be.

Maybe it's because too much time has passed and Evans is still on the loose, and you feel guilty about it, he thought.

He knocked for the third time and looked at his watch. It was shortly after noon. He always closed his office after half a day on Saturdays. He'd hoped to spend some of the bright December afternoon in Eleanor's company.

"Who is it?"

The voice coming from behind the door was tense, wary. Peter's senses grew alert.

"Eleanor, it's Dr. Curry. I've come to return your checkbook. With your arms full of cat, you left it on the reception counter."

There was a long silence. "Just leave it in the hall," she finally said; there was a trace of anxiety in her tone.

"What's wrong?" he asked. "Are you hurt?"

He remembered the cut and bruises on her face. Maybe it wasn't the attack of a stranger. Maybe it was a boyfriend or spouse. Or worse. Maybe she really had stolen the cat from a laboratory. "Open the door, Eleanor. I'm not leaving until I know you're okay."

He heard the rattle of locks and bolts, and the door finally swung open a crack. She thrust her face at him. "I'm fine, Dr. Curry. I'm just not feeling well. Thanks for bringing the checkbook." Her hand reached for it.

A streak of black shot through the narrow space, ran between Peter's legs and hurried down the hall.

"Familiar!" Eleanor cried, now opening the door wide to chase the cat. Behind her, Peter saw the destruction of her apartment.

"What happened?" he asked.

A short distance away, Familiar stopped and sat do~
clean his front paws.

Realizing that Peter had seen the worst, Eleanor left the door open while she retrieved the cat. "Let's go inside," she suggested. "I don't want the whole building to know I've been...trashed."

"Were you robbed?" Peter closed the door behind him, still surveying the damage.

"Nothing I can find missing," Eleanor said. "There's not a lot of value, as I told you earlier. My books, some research. As you can see, the television and stereo are still here. I don't think robbery was the motive."

Peter picked up the cushions from the sofa and put the undamaged ones back. "If not robbery, what?"

Standing by the kitchen door, she stuck her hands into the pockets of her jeans. "I don't have the faintest idea." She shrugged. She'd pulled her hair back into a ponytail, and a curl had escaped to touch her cheek. "Last night that man. Today, this." Her lips tightened into an angry line as she brushed her face with the back of one hand. "I haven't done anything to anyone. I don't understand."

Peter squelched the urge to ask her directly what she was involved in. It wouldn't do a bit of good. If she was part of some illegal scheme, she'd never admit it. Not knowingly. Animal liberators were dedicated to the bone.

"I'm not much of a detective, but I am a darn good listener," he said. "How about I make some hot tea, grab a broom to help out, and you can tell me everything that's happened to you in the last week? Maybe you saw something or bought something in a store or checked out the wrong book at the library. Together there's a chance we can find out what's going on."

ether. The word seemed to echo in Eleanor's head. een alone for the last nine years. Completely on her very idea that someone might share her fears was en a little frightening. But Peter Curry already had her broom, and he was making a successful effort to gather up the feathers that covered the living-room floor.

"My life is as boring as reading a text on insomnia, but I'll try and remember the past week," she agreed. "You and Familiar are the only two unusual things that have happened to me in the last year! Except for the obvious, of course."

"A cat, a vet and sudden suspense," he said, leaning against the broom and giving her two raised eyebrows. "Diagnosis—you need more pets!"

Eleanor's laugh was soft, but heartfelt. The cloud of depression and fear began to lift. She put the water on to boil for tea and began helping Peter with the cleanup.

Two hours later they were sitting on the sofa in a rearranged living room. With the broken dishes, plants and trash cleaned away, the damage wasn't as bad as it had first appeared. In fact, Peter was taken with the muted mauves and aquas, the subtle but rich decor. Though he'd tried every possible approach, he'd been unable to link her directly with the cat's escape or any knowledge of Evans. He was beginning to wonder if he'd been completely off base with his suspicions. But he didn't believe in coincidences like the cat, her attack, and now her apartment.

Slightly uncomfortable with Peter's helpfulness, Eleanor had told of her life in Tennessee, her parents, her friends, the fun she'd had growing up near the Great Smoky Mountains. She'd carefully avoided all mention of her years with Carter Wells—her disastrous marriage to a gambler, gangster, liar and cheat. She'd played down the destruction of her apartment as another coincidence, another loop in a string of bizarre and unrelated experiences. She wasn't certain he believed her, but he was gentleman enough not to show too much doubt.

He was, in fact, a witty conversationalist who made it easy to talk and listen. He'd shared anecdotes from vet school with her and amusing stories about animals he owned and treated.

As he squeezed a lemon into another cup of hot tea, he continued with his easy banter. "While you were studying the fine points of language, I was up to my ears in fur, feathers and flea shampoo." He stood, stretching tall. "When I was a kid, I always thought I'd live a life of adventure. You know, James Bond, solving crucial secrets, that kind of stuff. Haven't you wanted to be involved in some secret mission?" He'd dangled the bait skillfully, he thought.

"Never." Eleanor looked up at him. Physically he could have passed as a superspy or professional athlete. He was lean but powerful, with the deadly grace of a man who knew how to control his body. He oozed charm. But it was tempered with compassion, and a genuine tenderness that extended to every creature he touched. She'd watched him work on Familiar. It had been her experience that men who lived lives of danger seldom had time to concern themselves with the needs or feelings of other creatures. "You probably would have made an excellent 007," she said, "but I'm glad you decided to be a vet. And so is Familiar."

"Meow!" Familiar remarked. He got up from his nap on top of the television set and went to the front door. He waited, tail twitching just at the tip.

"Company's coming," Peter said.

"I never have company," Eleanor pointed out. "Well, hardly ever."

"Familiar hears them," Peter said. "Cats, in fact most animals, have hearing more sensitive than ours. Or at least they employ it better." He gave Eleanor a hand and drew her to her feet. "Want to make a bet?"

The flash of pain that crossed Eleanor's eyes was almost undetectable, but Peter saw it.

"Did I say something wrong?"

"Not at all," she answered smoothly. "What are the stakes?"

"Dinner tonight?"

The tension changed, but never left her face. "Well, that seems pleasant enough. Okay, if someone comes to my door, I cook. If not, I take you out." She forestalled his complaint. "After all of this help I'd like to treat you to dinner."

"Agreed," Peter said, taking her hand for a shake just as the knock vibrated against the wood.

"I'm particularly fond of seafood," Peter whispered into her ear, letting her hand go so that she could answer the door.

"You probably arranged this," she challenged. But when she opened the door, she knew immediately that the woman who stood there was not an acquaintance of Peter Curry.

"I have a report on a cat in this apartment."

Eleanor stared at the short, red-headed woman who was glaring angrily at her. There was no masking the hostility in the green eyes, or the contempt she obviously felt for Eleanor.

"Excuse me," Eleanor said at last, "why are you here?"

"Magdalena Caruso, SPCA-ARSA. I got a report that you've been supplying cats for animal research. I'm here to confiscate any cats you have in your possession. Come, Bowser!"

An ancient white poodle emerged from the folds of the long black coat. "Aarrrf," he said, then ducked back again.

"Bowser, how can we stage a raid if you act like such a ninny!" She stooped and took the dog into her arms. "Well, do you have cats or not?" she demanded.

Eleanor cast a look behind her, but Familiar had vanished. Standing near the sofa, Peter waited with a blank expression.

"You're with the Society for Prevention of Cruelty to Animals?" Eleanor inquired.

"In a manner of speaking," the short woman answered. She brushed past Eleanor, bumped the door wide open with her hip and sailed into the apartment. "Cat, Bowser!" she commanded, putting the dog onto the floor.

"Hey!" Eleanor protested, but it was too late.

Tottering and snarling, the little poodle shot across the living room, down the hall and into her bedroom. A din of barking followed, then a yowl of pain.

"One way or the other, Bowser always gets his cat," the little woman said, hustling toward the bedroom.

Eleanor and Peter were close on her heels. At the bedroom door, Peter finally snared the woman's arm. "Mrs. Caruso, you can't come barging into someone's apartment and set your dog loose."

"You'd be surprised what I can do if it's necessary." Magdalena Caruso matched his look without flinching. The fire of a revolutionary burned in her eyes. "There's an animal here that's been reported as mistreated. I came to get it, and I mean to stay here until I do."

"Mistreated!" Eleanor felt her temper begin to flare. She turned on the bedroom light. Familiar was sitting on the end of the bed, perfectly poised. Bowser was cowering on the floor, whining. As soon as the cat looked away, the dog jumped and snapped. Familiar, with one graceful move, raked his claws down the dog's nose. Bowser howled and fell back.

"Get that dog out of my house," Eleanor told the intruder, iron in her voice. "If anything is mistreated, it's that stupid poodle."

"Oh, dear," Magdalena said, her breath coming in short gasps as she went after the quivering dog. "Poor Bowser. He can sniff the cats out, but he's never quite acquired the art of holding them at bay."

She scooped the poodle into her arms once more and stroked him until he stopped shivering. "That's the boy," she whispered. "Such a good sniffer. You found the kitty."

Eleanor's quick flash of temper disappeared at the sight of the little woman worrying over her poodle. Eleanor caught Peter's attention. "I owe you a dinner," she said, "and after this, I think even a homemade dessert should be included. I've never—"

"So you did have the cat," Magdalena interrupted rounding on her as soon as the dog was quiet. "My sources are never wrong."

"Ms. Duncan never denied that she had a cat," Peter interjected softly, "but as the animal's veterinarian, I can assure you that he's received only the best and kindest of care." Was Magdalena Caruso the person he needed to watch?

"You're a vet!" Mrs. Caruso looked him up and down. "Don't tell me you were here making a house call." Her voice was loaded with sarcasm.

"You, madam, are a hard case," Peter said, grabbing the older woman's arm again and propelling her out of the bedroom, down the hall and to the front door. "Leave immediately, or Ms. Duncan will press charges of unlawful entering, assault with . . . a deadly poodle, creating a public disturbance and whatever else it takes to get rid of you."

The short woman drew herself up indignantly. "I'm not afraid of the law—I've been arrested before. Sometimes when you believe in something, you have to pay a price. You haven't escaped without suffering, have you?" Her green eyes shot like a laser into Peter.

"You, lady, are a nut case," Peter said, easing her into the hallway. He had to get her out of here, there was an off chance that she might remember him. "Take your poodle and be gone. I have a lot of sympathy for the SPCA, but zealots can be very dangerous, no matter how worthy their cause."

"Are you really a vet?" Magdalena asked. There was a new hint of softness in her tone.

The suddenness of the question stopped Peter. "Yes," he said. "My clinic is over on Pitchton Road, about twelve blocks from here." He couldn't afford to appear ill at ease.

"And you guarantee that the cat isn't being injured?"

"Ms. Duncan found the cat with a catheter in his leg. She brought him in to my clinic this morning and had it removed. We believe the cat might have escaped from a research lab, but we have no intention of using him for any experiments."

The brightest of smiles touched Magdalena Caruso's face. "Once I saw the two of you, I couldn't believe that you'd use an animal inhumanely. I'm seldom wrong about people, you know. But I had to check it out. I must say, the cat looked fine and all. So glad when a mission turns out this way. God bless you!" She started down the hallway, her short, plump body moving with great speed and determination.

In the apartment again, Peter closed the door, leaning against it as he threw the lock. "Eleanor, you need a bodyguard." He couldn't swear that the little scene hadn't been deliberately constructed for his benefit, but had been unable to detect any hint of a relationship between the two women. He thought about confronting Eleanor with his questions outright, but decided that time was his best ally. If she was a member of a radical animal group that went around robbing labs and freeing animals, he'd find out soon enough. And if she had news of Arnold Evans, well, that would make his future that much easier. He had only to watch and wait.

Eleanor sank onto the sofa, a wry grin on her face. "My telephone never even rings. I swear it. Ever since that cat came into my life, I feel as if I've stepped into the middle of a circus.''

Peter looked up, eyes widened with anxiety. "How did that woman know you had a cat?" he asked suddenly. "Does she live in this building?"

"Not to my knowledge." Eleanor felt a sudden lurch in the pit of her stomach. "This is a big apartment complex. She could live somewhere around, but I've never seen her."

"How about the neighbors? Any of them know about Familiar?"

Eleanor shook her head. Each question was a little more frightening. "Peter, the two times I've brought Familiar into the building, he's been tucked in my coat. I'm sure no one noticed him."

"How did that woman know he was here?" He went into the kitchen and returned with a telephone directory. Looking under the *C*'s, he drew a blank. "There's not a single Caruso listed," he said. He flipped to the business section, then hurriedly dialed a number.

"SPCA?" Eleanor asked.

He nodded. "Yes," he said into the phone, "I'd like to speak with one of your workers, maybe a volunteer, Mrs. Magdalena Caruso."

There was a pause, and she saw him draw his eyebrows together. He replaced the receiver.

"She doesn't exist," Eleanor said weakly. The whole business was really beginning to frighten her. It wasn't just the strange little woman with her poodle, it was the whole thing. The attack, her apartment, the way her life had suddenly spun out of her control.

"Oh, yes," he answered, "she exists. She 'retired' from the SPCA two years ago, when she was arrested for dropping cans of paint onto the cars of research scientists. She's an activist against the use of animals in research with a group called the Animal Rescue Squad Arsenal. A radical group."

"How did she get my name?" Eleanor asked. "Who would have told her that I would hurt an animal?"

"I don't mean to frighten you, Eleanor, but there are some very strange things happening around you." If she was faking it, she deserved an Oscar.

"As if I couldn't tell that!" She stood up and began to pace the room. "Maybe she got my name from your files. I mean the cat was hurt and all, and I brought him in. Maybe..."

"I locked my office. My receptionist was gone." He paused. "I'm willing to bet anything that she didn't get the information from my office, but first thing Monday I'll talk with Lucille."

"And until then?" Eleanor felt her heart pounding in her chest. "I'm afraid to get in my car, afraid to leave my apartment. There's a whole crowd of people out there—" she swept out her hand "—who know more about what's going on in my life than I do."

"Before Monday, we need to have a little chat with Familiar," Peter said.

As if he'd expected a cue, the black cat strolled into the living room, dug his claws into the carpet and stretched, a perfectly glorious stretch.

"Meow," he said, heading for the kitchen. "Meow."

"I think your roommate wants dinner," Peter told her. "I have some errands to run. If you're okay, I think I'd better take care of them, so I can enjoy my hard-won dinner."

"Familiar and I will be fine," Eleanor assured him. "How about seven?"

"Perfect," he said, then lingered at the door. "Is there something I can bring?"

Their voices dropped to a mumble as they made plans for the evening. Yawning, Familiar padded toward the refrigerator.

BATTLING that frazzled white creature with bone breath gave me something of an appetite. I wonder if there's any of the cream left from this morning. Some cats are born with exquisite taste, and I'm one of those lucky ones. I mean, I made it pretty good in the neighborhood around Pennsylvania Avenue. Those politicos give a lot of parties, with a lot of leftovers. It wasn't until I was nabbed by the guys in the white lab coats that I ever saw those despicable pouches of processed food. Well, at least Eleanor knows how to set a proper table for a cat. I do believe seafood was mentioned as a possibility for later on. I could beg now, or wait. I'll think about it while I watch the effect Dr. Doolittle is having on the dame. Jeez, give a guy a little medical business and he moves right into your life.

The two of them together remind me of the sexy little Persian that lived at 1820 Roanoke. Clotilde! She had a walk that made my tail tingle. Yeow! It was in a fit of lovesickness for Clotilde that I let my guard down and got captured by the animal dealer. Three days in a cage without water or even a crust of bread, then sold for research. The only thing to sustain me was the thought of Clotilde. I could see her sitting in the bay window, fur all brushed and shiny. She'd be waiting for me to serenade her from her backyard fence. She liked a little calypso beat to her music. Yeah, she was a sweet little feline. Maybe one day I'll get a chance to go back and look her up. Watching the dame and Dr. Doolittle make cow eyes at each other gives me a real yearning for Clotilde.

It's strange how I'm here now, safe and secure. I was never so surprised in my life as when the Shadow opened my cage and let me out. The whole time she was liberating me and the other cats, I kept trying to get her to look in the back room at Zelda. But she wouldn't. Zelda was really top secret, and the Shadow was too busy herding all of us to freedom, I suppose. I'll probably never know how or why she came in, dressed all in black, and turned us loose. She was like some hero from a comic book, and at the time I didn't want to ask any questions, I just wanted to make a beeline for a dark alley and safety. I thought I could leave that hellhole behind me, but I can't! Living in the lap of luxury like I am, I can't get rid of the memories of that place! Of Zelda.

Maybe Dr. Doolittle can help me. He was pretty decent about removing that tube from my leg. He didn't say much, but I got the idea he's full of opinions about such things. If only there was some way I could get Doc and the dame to the lab. Boy! Then they'd get an eyeful. Dr. Frankenstein's workshop! And poor Zelda. They'll never give up on her. If she doesn't get out soon, it won't matter. She won't be able to remember anything but what they program her to know.

When we came home today and I saw the mess of this apartment, I knew Frankenstein was behind it. He left his stench everywhere. The dame and the doctor can't smell him, but I'd know it anywhere. Sort of a cheeseburger and cigarette odor—unmistakably his. And I was hoping maybe I'd done some permanent damage to his corneas last night. I gave it everything I had. Too bad. If anybody ever deserved to be laid up with an injury, it was him. The thought of him makes my tail fuzz. Who knows what he's done to Zelda by now? She never wanted to do anything but please. Hell's bells! Every time I start to think about something, it goes right back to Zelda.

I can't help it. Look at me. I'm free, I got this great dame who is knock-down gorgeous and looks out for me. Even Dr. Doolittle in there isn't so bad. I mean if you've got to have a physical, he's on the considerate side. But if I know anything about Frankenstein, even if I manage to put Zelda *out of my mind, he ain't going to forget us. He saw the dame in the parking lot with me. He knows she picked me up, and he came here and ripped her apartment to shreds. So he wants me back! I'm not too impressed with the plans he has for me. Well, since he came here and I was gone, maybe he'll give it up. He always struck me as a little on the lazy side.*

Really! Frankenstein and Bowser in one day! It's enough to drive a cat to clawing the furniture.

What's with Dr. Doolittle and the dame? They sure are taking a long time to make a few simple plans. The way he looks at her! I've seen a hungry tom show more discretion eyeing fresh fillet of salmon. Yessir, he's got that carnivorous gleam in his eyes. I just hope he understands that she's my dame. There's plenty of room for the two of us, as long as he doesn't push his luck. So now they've agreed on dinner, and he's out the door. What a relief. Now it's just me and my Eleanor.

"FAMILIAR, want a little snack?" Eleanor scratched the cat under his chin. "Maybe I shouldn't give you so much rich food. You did have a bowl of cream this morning, plus that ham."

"Meow," the cat answered, rubbing her legs, then playfully nipping her ankle.

"I guess you do want a snack. Well, okay. But it can't become a habit. If you get too fat, I'll have to borrow Bowser to come over and chase you around."

"Arrowow!" The black cat rolled on the floor, leaped to the counter, dashed on top of the refrigerator, took a flying leap into an open cupboard, sailed back to the counter, then jumped to the floor and rolled again.

"Familiar!" Eleanor said, laughing. "Are you trying to tell me that you get enough exercise on your own?"

"Meow," he said, scratching the refrigerator door with one paw.

"Great." She poured a small saucer of cream and left the cat lapping away. The apartment was clean, but there were still stacks of books and papers that had to be sorted. She went to the shelves and began to impose order. Most of her serious research was at the office on campus, but she'd been doing some of the lighter work at home.

As she shuffled through the papers, she found bits and pieces of projects she'd abandoned or incorporated into other work. Organization was one of her most effective weapons against the demands of academia, and she soon had the papers arranged and in proper order, with the exception of one missing file. She was just finishing when the cat sauntered into the room.

"Want to hear something strange, Familiar? Every single thing is here, except for a paper I did on the communication patterns of African apes. I'm sure you've heard of Dian Fossey and the breakthrough work she did with a tribe of apes. Well, I used some of her stuff to show similarities in all communication patterns. None of my research was original. Now why would anyone want to take that?"

Chapter Three

The white tapers were a troubling touch, but Eleanor left them. They gave the table a romantic formality that blended well with the small bouquet of fresh daisies. As Familiar walked round the table for the hundredth time, she patted him. "I already told you I'd save some snapper," she said.

Checking her preparations one last time, she felt an unfamiliar tingle in her stomach. How long had it been since she'd entertained a man with dinner? That question didn't bear answering. She couldn't compare the past with the present. It wasn't fair. Peter was awfully nice to help her so much, but it did arouse her suspicions, and she couldn't help that. Still, he seemed like a kind man.

The match made a soft, shushing sound as she struck it and lighted the candles. The scene took on a soft, intimate glow. The image was disconcerting. Leaning over to blow them out, she hesitated.

The doorbell rang as if on cue. Eleanor felt the bottom of her stomach drop away and opened the door with a fixed smile on her face.

Peter was almost hidden behind a mass of red roses. "They're a little traditional, but you looked like the classic American beauty to me. Sort of Snow White, with the dark hair and white skin." He handed her the flowers as he stepped inside. "Aren't you glad I couldn't find any red apples? Anyway, after the day you had, I thought you needed a surprise." A small degree of guilt had also entered into the purchase. What if she was exactly what she appeared, a kindhearted woman who helped an injured animal?

"I'm overwhelmed," she said. There were at least two dozen perfect blooms. She took them into the kitchen and found a vase, her hands suddenly awkward as she arranged them. "I was thinking earlier...it's been a long time since I've been treated to such a lovely bouquet of flowers. Thank you."

"How's my patient?" Peter asked, deftly turning the conversation to the cat that was patrolling the kitchen. He was acutely aware of Eleanor's discomfort and curious about it. Was she hiding something?

"Familiar is ready to gnaw the refrigerator down. He knows the fish is there and he wants it."

"For a stray cat, he sure has a lot of audacity," he said, his easy laugh lightening the mood.

"That's an understatement. How about some wine?"

She poured wine into two glasses and settled on the sofa, at the far end from Peter. "When I was finishing with the cleanup, I found that the person who trashed my apartment did steal something." She frowned into her glass. "It doesn't seem important, just strange."

"If something was taken, you have to call the police." Peter didn't emphasize the suggestion. One thing he didn't want was police meddling.

"I don't want to involve the police, Peter. The thing that was taken is some old research—not even original material. But it's just so odd. It was based on Dian Fossey's work with primates, their communication system. It doesn't have any bearing on anything I'm doing. I used the material for a speech."

"Animal communication. That's strange stuff to steal," Peter agreed. He couldn't help the quickening of his pulse. She'd brought up the subject of research again. "Still, even if it isn't valuable, I think you need to notify the authorities." He kept his tone cool and detached.

She shook her head. Her brown eyes were unfocused; her gaze never left her glass. "I really don't think there's any real danger. I suspect that someone from my past is trying to intimidate me. A long time ago, I was involved in something through my husband. This kind of thing—" she picked up a demolished pillow and threw it back to the floor "—became a part of my everyday life. I'd go to work and come home and find my things torn up and destroyed." A self-deprecating shrug lifted her shoulders.

"Even a spouse shouldn't be allowed to do this type of destruction." He spoke softly to hide his disappointment. The conversation had gotten off track again, and to make matters worse, she was married. "Did your husband leave after the quarrel?" He couldn't help the edge in his voice.

"Oh, no!" Now she looked at him. "It wasn't Carter who trashed my things. I'm sure it was his fault, but it wasn't him. He just neglected to tell me that he owed large sums of money to unsavory characters. All along I thought he was working on humanitarian projects."

A bitter smile gave her face a haunted look. "I was a little on the naive side, I guess you could say."

"So you think your husband may be running up bad debts again, and you're paying the price?"

She shook her head, causing her dark curls to shimmer. "My husband is...well, I've been single for nine years." She forestalled any sympathy with a steady look. "Don't say you're sorry, because I'm not. I took my maiden name back, I moved across the country and went to college. I've done everything I know to put the past behind me. And what I think is that someone has stumbled over me, and they're still a little mad at Carter. There's no limit to what he might have been involved in. But this is the end of it, I'm sure. One last act of revenge. That's just the kind of people my husband did business with."

"I'm sorry," Peter said, meaning it. He took her wineglass from her hand and put it onto the coffee table. He was sorry for a lot more than her past. He had a clear picture of what he was doing, and it wasn't very honorable. She seemed so damned open and vulnerable. His warm hands moved up her shoulders, drawing her to himself.

"Peter, I..."

"Relax a minute, Eleanor." Strong fingers found the knots of tension along her shoulders. "Just take a minute and calm down. There's nothing I can do to help, except maybe rub the tension from your neck." The bones beneath his hands were well-defined. She had one of the most extraordinary necks he'd ever seen. He could almost get lost in the soft whiteness of her skin.

"That does feel better," she said after a few moments. There was no insinuation in the massage, only a desire to relieve her stress, but she moved away from him nonetheless and turned to face him.

His smile was understanding. "I don't want you to think I'm strange when I say this, but I spend a lot of time with animals."

The shift in conversation caught her by surprise. He had a knack for treading around her wounds, shifting the focus just when she was feeling too raw. She gave him a wry smile. "Since you're a vet, it follows that you might spend some time that way."

"No wonder you professor types get a reputation for being arrogant," he teased. "Anyway, I watch animals. I study them, and I've discovered that they're far superior to people in some respects."

"Such as?"

"Well, take old Familiar. When he feels the need for some affection, he'll hop right up on your lap and demand it. Dogs are like that, too. I've watched dogs actually comfort each other after surgery, or when they're recuperating from an illness. One dog will go up and lick or help groom another. They understand how important it is to comfort and to be comforted." He gave her shoulder a slight squeeze. "No ulterior motives."

"It's no wonder that Familiar likes you so much," Eleanor answered.

Peter handed her glass to her. "We should have a fire," he said. "When I was a kid, I used to love it when my parents built a big fire. We'd sit around, talking, planning, dreaming." *Damn it all,* he found her far too easy to talk to. Next thing he knew, he'd be lying on her sofa, spilling his guts.

"We did that, too," Eleanor said, clearly unaware of his conflict. "We'd make popcorn or hot chocolate. It was perfect. But back then we lived in the country, with a big house, lots of firewood and someone to cut it."

"So, Eleanor, what are you going to do if this mercenary from your past continues to harass you?" Peter's voice was low. He had to keep his eye on his goal, to find out who'd sent Eleanor to his office. Who had finally decided to show the link to Arnold Evans?

"I don't know." Eleanor swirled the golden wine in her glass. "I've tried to believe it won't happen again. If it does, I guess I'm going to have to call the police, even if it means reopening a lot of ugly wounds."

"That's my girl," he said, unable to resist picking up her hand. Even her bone structure was elegant. "There's been no real damage, but I wouldn't want this thing to escalate. What about the other incident? I don't like the idea of some jerk mugging you in a parking lot. Do you think that's even related, or could it be the cat?"

"I don't know," she replied. "If I could only remember exactly what the man said. He told me to get in the car, and he said something about what I knew. I guess it's possible that someone thinks Carter has some money stashed away somewhere. That's dead wrong. In fact, it took me seven years to get my credit rating straight." She sighed and took a long breath. "Anyway, that's the past. We have some snapper marinating for the present, and this wine has made me hungry. Let me finish getting dinner ready."

Smothered in green onions, butter, garlic and lemon, the fish was perfect. The candlelight seemed to cast a warm mantle over the table, shutting out all unpleasantness. Peter proved a witty and facile conversationalist, and a man with a big appetite.

"It was hard, but I saved a little for Familiar," Peter said at the end of the meal. "He was very well behaved."

"If you believe that staring a hole through me was well behaved, you're a soft touch." Eleanor took the leftover fish to Familiar's plate.

"Meow," he said as he settled down to eat.

"He even knows how to say thank-you," Peter teased her. "How about we leave the articulate feline to his meal, and we take in a movie or some dancing? The cook deserves a treat." Even as he said them, the words sounded cheap and hollow. His grand plan didn't seem so great at the moment.

"I'd love it, Peter. I haven't been dancing in..." She laughed uncomfortably. She did love to dance, and it had been years, but she was also aware that dancing could be a very romantic occupation. "It doesn't matter how long," she finished lamely.

"Good, then," he said easily. "You won't mind if I'm a little rusty, too." Once he had her in the car, he could attempt another maneuver to get her to talk.

They'd barely left the apartment building behind when he slowed for a light. "Would you mind if I swung by a few research facilities?"

"To go inside?" Her tone held doubt.

"No, they won't be open tonight. Of course, we could make a raid on them and get a few more cats like Familiar." He pretended to adjust the rearview mirror, turning it so that he could watch her eyes.

"I never intended to keep him," Eleanor said. "I don't think I need another pet, Peter. Remember, you were the one who said a pet, a vet and suspense. I can't stand any more of it."

"I suppose you're right."

Gazing out the window at the traffic, Eleanor was completely composed. His plan to startle her with the suggestion of a trip to a lab was a dud. "Then why don't we skip the whole thing and simply go dancing?" For a moment he was distracted by the thought of her in his arms.

"Whatever you want to do," she said. She couldn't believe she was agreeing to such an idea. She hadn't danced in years, but Peter made her want to dance. "I wish it would snow. It isn't like the holidays without some of that white stuff."

Twenty minutes later they were dancing to a sexy alto sax in a small, dark club. Peter kept the conversation casual, and he felt Eleanor gradually relax, giving herself to the beat of the music. "I've never had the pleasure of dancing with someone so graceful." As he spoke, his face brushed her hair, loosening a burst of heady perfume.

"I love dancing," Eleanor admitted with an impish smile.

She moved like a dream in his arms. She was such a strange mixture of boldness and vulnerability. Bright, yet somehow tentative. Was it possible she was involved in raiding labs and bombing scientists? Could she be innocent and still know about his involvement with Evans?

"I know it's early, but we should go home," Eleanor said when the dance ended. "It's wonderful, but I've had a hectic day."

"Yes, you have." Peter held her on the dance floor a moment longer. "On the way home, we need to stop at a market," he said.

"What on earth for?"

"A big, fresh lobster. I think Familiar deserves a reward, for bringing you into my life." He felt as if he'd spoken the truth for the first time that evening.

THE TALL MAN stepped from the shadows of her building. He flashed a badge at her. "Eleanor Duncan, I'm Alva Rousel with the Central Intelligence Agency. May I have a word with you?" A strand of blond hair dipped and covered one eye. He appeared to be in his early forties, an imposing man with an aggressive attitude and a worried frown.

Preoccupied with thoughts about Peter and the past day, Eleanor was thrown off balance. She failed to respond immediately.

"What is this about?" Peter asked, taking Eleanor's arm. He was suddenly protective. If she was involved in raiding laboratories, the CIA was heavy-duty trouble.

"This doesn't involve you, Mr. . . ." The agent leveled a hard stare at Peter. "I need to speak with Ms. Duncan privately."

"My name is Peter Curry. And whatever involves Ms. Duncan, involves me."

"Peter, wait a minute." Eleanor recovered from the shock of having a badge thrust into her face. That seemed to be a pattern in her life, she thought bitterly, no matter how hard she tried to avoid it. "What can I do for you, Mr. Rousel?"

The agent turned to face her. "I have some questions for you, Ms. Duncan. Top secret," he added almost gently.

"May I have a few moments of your time? It's important, or we wouldn't bother you at this hour."

"It is late," Eleanor said. The suddenness of the man's appearance and the resurrection of past anxieties made her play for time. If Alva Rousel's questions involved Carter Wells, she didn't want to drag them out in front of Peter. "Can't this wait until morning? I'm really not prepared to answer any questions."

"Did I mention this involved a top secret project?" The agent's voice was loaded with concern. "If we could step into your apartment. Alone. It will only take a few moments."

Peter saw the flush of worry on Eleanor's face. If she was involved, she could be facing a serious jail term. He had to buy her some time and then make her tell him the truth. "Ms. Duncan has had a bad day. Call her tomorrow, after she's had a chance to get some rest." Taking Eleanor's arm, he started to the elevator.

"You can interfere in this now, Curry, but it might not be in Ms. Duncan's best interest. If she is implicated in an antigovernment plot, she may be sorry. When a suspect refuses to talk, it often looks worse."

"Antigovernment plot? Suspect?" Eleanor turned around. She ignored Peter's hand on her arm.

"We have reason to believe you've been involved, perhaps innocently, in something that could have a detrimental effect on national security. We'd like to ask a few questions." The agent walked with them into the lobby.

The accusation was ridiculous and frightening. Eleanor looked around for the doorman. Strangely enough, the post was empty. "What are you talking about? I don't understand."

"Maybe we could step up to your apartment." The agent was at her side, his expression worried. "I know you want to help in this matter. Just a few questions."

"I do want to help," Eleanor agreed. "What is this about?"

"You're involved with the study of communication skills, aren't you?" Rousel drew together his eyebrows in apparent concern. He, too, scanned the lobby. "I sent your doorman on an errand, but I would be more comfortable inside your apartment."

"I teach and study linguistics," Eleanor answered, aware that her tone betrayed her confusion. "My work is certainly not top secret, and I would think that it would be of minimal interest to most people, particularly the CIA."

"Friday night someone violated a federal . . . center. A project was jeopardized and some items were stolen." She saw him glance at Peter as he spoke to her.

"I don't know what you're referring to," Eleanor answered. "I had my own set of problems Friday night. Someone attacked me in the parking lot at my university."

"Why were you attacked, Ms. Duncan?" The agent's eyes darkened.

"That's the question I'd like answered," Eleanor replied, her voice rising slightly. "I was smacked in the face and threatened, and I don't have any idea why."

"This research you've been doing. Could it possibly provoke such an attack?"

"I don't see how," Eleanor answered.

"Something from your past?"

"No," Eleanor said, but her gaze turned swiftly to Peter. She tried to hide the expression of dread that briefly crossed her features. "I'm sorry, Mr. Rousel, but I feel sick. Could we possibly discuss this tomorrow?" She stumbled and took Peter's arm. "I need to go home."

"Just a few questions . . ." the agent said again.

"Call tomorrow after lunch," Peter told him, hurrying to the elevator with Eleanor. He was more than a little concerned. She'd turned gray before his eyes at the mention of her past.

As the door opened at the ninth floor, she was still silent, her full lips compressed. Peter offered the support of his arm and kept his advice to himself.

"So you've stumbled into a real hornet's nest, haven't you?" she said, striving for a light note. She fumbled for her keys to unlock the door. "You've been very kind to help me out with my cat and my apartment. As you can see, though, I'm a woman with a lot of problems."

"A woman who can stand her ground," he corrected her. "You handled the situation." He paused. "If there is a situation..."

"Living with Carter was a lesson in learning to hedge with law officers," she said. "As Carter's wife, I was questioned on more than one occasion. I tried to protect him, to be a good wife, but I could never lie." She finally found the right key and pushed the door open. Familiar was sitting on the sofa, looking at her with his large, intense eyes.

"You don't have to explain to me," Peter said softly. "By tomorrow you'll have time to think it all through and decide on exactly the right thing to say."

"I don't know what to do." Eleanor slumped onto the sofa, kicking off her shoes. "What's happened to my life? If one more strange thing—"

The buzz of the doorbell interrupted.

"I'll get it," Peter said. "If it's Rousel again, I'm going to strongly urge him to leave you alone until tomorrow. That guy just won't give up." He clenched his jaw and pulled the door open wide.

"Eleanor...Ms. Duncan?" A bewildered doorman stood in the hallway. "Excuse me. I didn't mean to interrupt, but someone left a package for Ms. Duncan while she was out. And since she's never out so late, I thought I'd stop by and leave it and make sure that she's okay. But I see she's fine, and I didn't mean to interrupt and..."

"Come in, Wessy," Eleanor said, rising from the sofa. "What package?"

The doorman reached inside his jacket and brought out a large manila envelope. "Right here."

"Thanks." Eleanor took it and gave the man a warm smile. "Thanks for checking on me. I'm fine."

"I worry about you, living here alone and all. I keep my eyes open, you know." He cast a suspicious look at Peter. "I think a lot of Eleanor," he added.

"That makes two of us," Peter said, shaking the man's hand. "Thanks."

Eleanor softly shut the door, her smile lingering. "He's a dear. If I come home in the rain and he's on duty, he meets me with an umbrella. If I have packages, he carries them. And not just for me, for all the women, young and old."

"Thank goodness for the Wessys of the world." Peter eyed the package curiously. "Research?"

"Hardly. I have no idea what this could be." She opened the flap and pulled out a picture. It was a black and white photograph of herself at the fish market a few blocks away.

"What in the devil?" she asked, handing the picture to Peter. "I was there just this afternoon, buying the snapper."

Peter flipped over the photo. On the back, a message was scrawled in black felt marker. "I'm watching you, my love!"

"Peter, what is this?" she asked, her eyes wide. "What's going on? Who's watching me?"

"I don't know." He dropped the photo onto the coffee table. "I'll be right back." He unlocked the door and dashed down the hall before she could stop him. He was back in less than ten minutes.

"The doorman's gone, and so is Mr. Rousel," he said when he returned, breathing hard. "Maybe after everything that's happened to you, it wouldn't be a bad idea to talk with the CIA." He had a chilling sensation that Eleanor was exactly what she appeared to be, and that somehow her life was in danger.

"Wessy will be back on duty tomorrow afternoon. I'm getting concerned," she admitted. She was curled up on the sofa, and Peter took a seat beside her. Very gently he took one of her hands and held it between his.

"Stay calm." Peter's voice was soothing. "Think about every project you've been working on at the university. We've never really talked about your work. Maybe there's something there, some reason that would draw an attacker or the CIA. There has to be some connection between you, the attacks, the CIA—and maybe that cat."

Peter's questions gave her something to focus her worries on. She quickly went over the past year's work, seeking anything that might interest the CIA—or anyone other than another academic.

She shook her head. "No matter how hard I try, I can't think of a single thing that would be sensitive or even controversial. The core of my research has been on cataloging colloquial expressions from the mountain regions where I grew up. My linguistics research is interesting, not crucial."

"If it isn't your work, it might be personal," Peter reasoned. "You've been single . . ."

"Nine years," Eleanor said, "and I can't believe that even Carter could have gotten himself messed up with national security. He was a gambler. And not a very good one."

"If someone thinks you know something," Peter pointed out, "they might be tailing you. A little intimidation. Someone followed you to that fish market." He was beginning to like the direction of the conversation less and less.

The thought of Eleanor alone, a stranger watching her every move, made him extremely uneasy.

"Peter! This is terrible! Someone might think I've seen something really important!"

"We have to figure this out, Eleanor," he said firmly. "It'll be light in another two hours, and by then, I promise you we'll have a plan."

"I don't want to play junior detective." Eleanor drew back and rubbed her tired eyes with the back of her hand. "I mean it. I'm not interested in solving a mystery or getting involved in this any further. I value my privacy, my sanity, my peace. I want this to end."

"You don't care why these things have happened?" Peter was amazed. "You're not even the least bit curious?"

"I'm not! And it suits me if I never know. All I want is for this to stop. I want to wake up to the sun shining, to a simple Sunday breakfast, complete with a good newspaper and fresh orange juice. Then I want to talk with that agent and get this straight."

"You're exhausted," Peter told her. "I'd like to stay the rest of the night, on the sofa. I'd sleep better if I knew you were okay."

"That isn't necessary." Eleanor felt her discomfort begin to build. Peter had become far too involved in her life—and her troubles. It would be better if he didn't stay.

"Maybe not for you, but it would certainly make me feel better," he pointed out. "I'm not moving into your life, I'm simply going to spend a few hours on your sofa. I'm not going to interfere."

"It's just that . . ."

"You don't have to explain, Eleanor." He took both of her hands and held them to his chest. "It's just that you've been attacked, and someone did break in here. Until we get to the bottom of this, *I'd* feel better if I knew you were safe." The truth of the matter was that if Eleanor was as innocent as she appeared, he might have jeopardized her!

"Peter, I don't—"

The telephone shrilled.

"I can't believe this," she said, picking up the receiver. "I've had more phone calls and visitors the last twenty-four hours than I've had all year. Hello." She spoke crisply.

"Bad mood, darling?"

It was a confident, familiar voice. She'd heard those words so many times before, spoken with just that same tone of arrogance. She tried to reply, but no words came out.

"Come on, Eleanor. Don't play games. We have a lot to talk about. So much has happened. To both of us."

"Who is this?" she demanded.

"Take a guess. Or better yet, want to make a bet?" Rich laughter spilled into the earpiece of her telephone. "You were never one to gamble, were you?"

Eleanor slammed down the phone as hard as possible.

Chapter Four

Eleanor awoke to a strange sense of warmth at the small of her back. Bad dreams of a threatening and well-remembered voice had kept her tossing and turning most of the night. She knew the voice. She'd obeyed it, though unwillingly, but she couldn't place whom it belonged to. Lying on her right side, she opened her eyes. Something warm and heavy was pressed against her.

"Familiar!" she guessed.

"Meowww," came the sleepy reply.

"So now you've invaded my bed! What next?" She turned to pet the sleepy cat and then quietly slid from beneath the covers. "It's obvious that you believe you belong here," she said, slipping into a floor-length robe that matched her purple gown.

She opened the blinds to a beautiful morning, such a contrast to the dark fears she'd fought all night. Peter hadn't believed her when she'd tried to convince him that the midnight call had been a practical joke. Her fear had been too audible in her voice, she knew. But how could she tell him that the voice sounded like...a dead man? The answer to that was simple. She wasn't going to tell him. Carter Wells was dead. The phone call was someone's idea of a practical joke, or at worst, a little scene of revenge for one of Carter's past sins. Like wrecking her apartment and frightening her with the photograph. When the joker got tired, it would all be over.

Taking care to be quiet, she padded down the hall. She could tell by the way the sun came through the window that it was late morning. At the entrance to the living room she paused. Peter was sound asleep on the sofa, one leg dangling from beneath the blanket. His brown hair was rumpled, his lips full and sensual in sleep. She tiptoed past him into the kitchen to make coffee.

As the aroma of the rich Columbian brew wafted through the small kitchen, she tried to order her thoughts. How much would she tell the CIA agent? It wouldn't take a Sherlock Holmes to reopen her past. But what was the purpose? When she was married to Carter, she'd known virtually nothing of his business. Now she had left even those shreds behind. And no matter how she tried, she couldn't visualize her dead husband as some counter-espionage person involved in treason. To be sure, Carter had always been an opportunist, but a traitor? Never.

Familiar strolled into the kitchen. His paw grazed the refrigerator door, but he refrained from his morning yowling.

Eleanor absently gave him the last of the snapper she'd saved, stroking his back as he ate. All her life she'd been softhearted, developing strong attachments to loved ones and pets. Out of the mess her life had become in the last forty-eight hours, Familiar was the good part. And Familiar had brought Peter into her life. Eleanor frowned. She still wasn't certain if that part was good or bad.

She poured a cup of coffee and started back to her bedroom, then remembered the morning paper. She loved Sunday's *Washington Post*. Her colleagues would laugh at her, but she took a positive delight in the horoscopes and advice columns. She cracked the front door and reached out a hand.

"Ms. Duncan?"

The unexpected voice nearly scared her to death. "Mr. Rousel?" She saw the agent standing across the hallway, his gray suit as immaculately pressed as if he'd just come from the cleaners. "You startled me." She stepped into the hall, suddenly too aware of Peter's sleeping body on her sofa.

"Could we step inside?" He nodded toward her apartment. "My questions are somewhat delicate."

"No, I'm afraid we can't," she said. She could have given him a very good reason—Peter—but didn't. "I honestly don't have any information that could help you. There's nothing in *my* past that would interest the CIA."

"There's nothing you want to tell me?" he asked. "If you're an accomplice..."

The word triggered a strong reaction in Eleanor. "I've assisted no one in any crime, Mr. Rousel. Not this year, not nine years ago when my husband was killed. There's nothing I can help you with."

"I didn't mean to upset you," he said softly. "We're only interested in protecting you. Your husband was involved in some very serious things in Colorado. A project, maybe you've heard of it. Code One Orange?" He watched her intently as he spoke.

Eleanor shook her head. The man's accusations were ridiculous. "Carter gambled, he lied and he cheated at every opportunity, but I can't believe he was involved in covert activities," she said.

"If an agent couldn't hide his work, he wouldn't be a very good agent, now would he?" Rousel countered softly. "Believe me, he was definitely involved. And that involvement has extended through the years. Until now."

The fear that struck Eleanor was so sudden and so intense that she couldn't respond at all. What had Carter been doing? And did the CIA actually suspect her of criminal behavior, of working against the government?

"Do you have any pets, say a guard dog, to look out for you?"

Eleanor's burst of temper was gone, and his question made her stomach twist. "The building doesn't allow pets."

"Not even cats?" he pressed.

A sense of dread crept over her. "Not even cats are allowed. I've never heard that they're good guard animals, anyway." Her fingertips began to tingle.

"I guess I just have cats on my mind. Several cats were stolen from the research lab. One of them was black. We'd like to get him back."

"What type of research was the cat involved in?" She felt sick. If Alva Rousel found out about Familiar, he'd take him back.

"Psychological." He stared at her.

"I thought that type of testing was more effective with people?"

"I'm not a psychologist." He smiled, taking the sting from his words. "During the break-in, one of the lab workers was seriously injured. His eyes. He thought it was a woman who attacked him."

"I'm sorry," Eleanor said. "But I can't help you with any of that. In fact—" she picked up the paper "I haven't even had a chance to read about it in the *Post*."

"If I've done my job properly, it won't be in the newspaper," he countered. "I'm not overstating the issue when I say that the research I'm investigating is of the most vital kind. Interference, from anyone, could be viewed as an act of... treason." He softened the words with another smile. "I know you're not that type of person, Ms. Duncan. I don't want to intimate that you are." His smile widened further, revealing white teeth. "I don't even believe you're an accomplice. But I do want you to understand the seriousness of this business."

"I'm not the type of person who breaks into buildings," Eleanor said, her fingers wrapping the newspaper into a tighter bundle. "I don't speed, I don't litter. I don't have friends who do those things. In fact, I'm a model citizen. I don't even cheat on my taxes. I can't help you." She opened the door and started inside.

"We're not the only people looking for the stolen items."

Rousel's quiet words stopped her cold. She turned back, feeling herself grow pale as she spoke. "What?"

"I don't want to frighten you unnecessarily, but you should know that dangerous elements are involved in this case. We suspect a faction of a terrorist organization, ruthless people, completely without conscience. Some of them with a long past. Some of them you might know." He stared directly into her eyes.

"I can't help you," Eleanor repeated.

"They may have infiltrated an animal rights organization to use the group to obtain their own goals. I'd hate to see an innocent woman caught up in something tragic." He rubbed the barely visible stubble on his face and gave her a sheepish grin. "I slept outside so I could watch your building. It wasn't all that comfortable, but I had the feeling that you might be in danger."

"What kind of danger?" She couldn't completely cover the panic she felt growing. She was on the verge of telling the man about her midnight phone call and the photograph.

"I can't tell you, ma'am. I shouldn't have told you as much as I did. If I seemed pushy, it was because I was worried. This is a big case, top level."

"Thank you," she murmured, feeling a need to get inside her door, to turn the lock and seek the safety of her small apartment. The lesson learned at the feet of Carter Wells, came back to her—*trust no one.*

"I'll keep an eye on you, at least for a while," he said, giving her a reassuring smile. "Just in case."

She hurried inside, forcing herself to breath deeply, calmly, to fight the panic that threatened to turn her knees to Jell-O. An employee of the CIA had clearly implied that she was in grave danger.

"Your coffee got cold." Peter came out of the kitchen, his hair still tousled. "I poured you a fresh cup." He held the steaming mug toward her.

"Thanks," she managed. She knew her face was pale and she could still feel her heart beating a mile a minute. "That CIA agent was waiting in the hall to talk with me."

"What did Rousel have to say so early in the morning?" Peter sipped his coffee and unobtrusively watched her. She was frightened again.

"He said someone broke into a research lab and stole Familiar and some other cats, and that whoever did it was dangerous. He said I could be in danger."

Eleanor looked down at the floor as she talked, and Peter knew it was because she wanted to hide her fears. He could see it in the way her chin trembled slightly. In her hands as she clutched the coffee cup.

"Does he know who broke into the lab?" This could be the information he had to get, if she wasn't the one.

"I think he thinks I did." Her brown eyes were round with concern.

"How about a Denver omelet for breakfast?" he suggested. "I found some oranges in the fridge and squeezed them, because it seems to me that last night you made reference to a nice tall glass of juice and—" he pointed to the newspaper under her arm "—some reading material." He could question her later. She was too upset, too close to snapping.

"You have a really miraculous way of rescuing me from painful conversations," she said softly. "You always know the perfect moment to change the subject."

"Hey, I was just getting hungry," he said with a grin. "And I do have to brag a little. I'm pretty handy in the kitchen."

The knife-edge of fear had begun to diminish with Peter's easy bantering. She filled him in on most of Rousel's questions. "I know it's crazy, but somehow I think this cat is mixed up in all of this. I didn't exactly tell Mr. Rousel about Familiar," she admitted, following him into the kitchen.

"He asked about the cat?" Peter's interest stirred. That cat held a direct link with Arnold Evans. The catheter proved it.

"Well, he asked about a black cat. He said one was stolen from the lab, one that was being used in psychological testing. He didn't seem that interested in getting the cat back." She held her breath through the lie—she didn't want Peter to pressure her into giving Familiar back. It was better if he didn't think along those lines. "I got the impression Mr. Rousel was more interested in finding who broke into the lab."

"That would make sense. If a lab was broken into, then I suppose a federal law enforcement agency would be interested in apprehending the criminals," Peter said, cracking four eggs into a bowl. "As I said earlier, Familiar doesn't look any the worse for wear. A lot of those animals are terribly...abused. Maybe he isn't important in the research. Maybe when they find out who broke in, they'll forget about him."

Eleanor took a knife from the drawer and started to cut up green peppers for the omelet. "But Rousel implied that someone else might be interested in the cat." She swallowed. "He even went so far as to say a faction of a terrorist organization." And implied that her dead husband had some connection with the group! The phone call came back to her and the knife slipped through the pepper, missing her finger by a hair. At least it made sense now why someone was pretending to be Carter.

Peter dropped the whisk into the eggs. "Eleanor!" He took the knife from her hand and put it onto the counter. "Terrorist organization?" This was a little more than he'd bargained for.

"That's what he said."

"Well, I wouldn't let this get out of hand in your imagination, Eleanor. Rousel may be a federal agent, but he could also have a tendency to exaggerate."

"That's true," she agreed, slightly relieved. "Why would a terrorist group liberate a black tom cat?"

"Now that's the sanest comment I've heard this morning," he said. "Let's just enjoy breakfast and hope by Monday morning all of this has been resolved." He forced a smile, but felt his anger boiling beneath the surface. The CIA agent must be an idiot to talk to her in such a way.

"I hope my past hasn't come back to haunt me," she said as she took silverware from another drawer; there was definitely a haunted look on her face, he observed.

"No, I'm sure it hasn't."

As Peter poured the eggs into the pan, Eleanor set the table. In a few moments they were ready to eat.

"The juice is great." She took another long drink from the chilled glass. "And the omelet, too."

"What's on your schedule for this afternoon?" he asked.

Eleanor grinned apologetically. "Actually, I often spend Sunday afternoon in the library or in my office. Betty Gillette, a colleague of mine, and I usually wind up working. Boring, huh?"

"Yes," he said without hesitation. "How about some Christmas shopping?" After all that had happened, Peter wanted to keep her in sight as much as possible. She didn't think her research was related to the recent attacks, but he wasn't so sure now. In fact he wasn't sure of anything—

except that he had to find Evans. That particular chore was looming larger and larger in his mind.

"I haven't even begun to buy my gifts," Eleanor confessed. "It wouldn't hurt me to pick up some things and get them in the mail."

"Good, then it's settled. We'll give Saint Nick a hand with the gift list. Maybe we'll even pick up a little something for that black fur ball on the sofa."

"Yeah," Eleanor agreed. "An alarm clock. I refuse to let him sleep all day while I have to work."

THE STORES were crowded and the lines long, but in Peter's company, Eleanor didn't mind the inconveniences. They picked up several items for respective family members and then sauntered through a pet supply shop.

"How about a red collar for Familiar?" she asked, holding up an item with an abundance of rhinestones.

Peter shook his head. "I don't think Familiar's the kind of cat who would appreciate such a gift. Catnip might be more up his alley. Or maybe even his own alley, if you're feeling plush."

Eleanor laughed out loud. Peter was delightful. "I suppose you're right. Catnip it is."

While she stood in the checkout line, Peter went to look at a display of magazines. Eleanor was drawing her billfold from her purse when she felt someone staring at her back. She forced herself to turn slowly, casually. Not twenty feet away across the crowded store was Alva Rousel. He was engrossed in a wind-up toy of a jumping cat, but Eleanor knew he'd been watching her.

She felt like abandoning her purchases, but instead put them onto the counter. The routine checkout seemed to take hours. Bag in hand, she hurried through the store until she found Peter.

"The man from the CIA was here, watching me," she told him. She couldn't help rushing her words together; her heart was pounding.

"He said he was going to keep an eye on you." Peter was completely unruffled. "I'm glad to see he's actually doing it. I hope he's better at watching than he is at keeping his mouth shut." He grinned. "Don't you feel better, knowing that the CIA is protecting you?"

"You're right," she said, pulling herself together at his casual tone. "But I was buying all of these cat toys—after I said cats weren't allowed in my building."

"Eleanor, my dear," Peter said patiently, "the truth is, you could have fifteen pet cats. Or you could be purchasing the toys for someone else's cat. Or you could be a seriously kinky lady with a passion for catnip and stuffed birds on elastic strings."

Eleanor laughed and the last of the tension was blown away. "I've never known anyone like you," she said. "You're immune to panic."

"Don't count on it. It's just that I—" he touched the top of her nose "—don't have a guilty conscience about lying to the CIA. How about an ice cream?"

She followed him out of the shop onto the brisk Washington street. "No ice cream for me. It's freezing! Besides, I can't wait to get home and give Familiar his presents."

"I do need to spend some time at the clinic," Peter said. "I like to check all of the animals, just to be on the safe side."

"I like that," Eleanor said. "I like it that you care."

"Then I'll drop you off at your place, and I'll take care of my work. Would I be pushing my luck if I asked you to a movie? We could find one we want to see or rent one."

Eleanor didn't feel pushed at all. She'd had a few misgivings about spending the evening alone, and Peter was a fun companion. "An old black and white with Cary Grant in it?"

"The Bishop's Wife?"

"Perfect. And I'll make some hot chocolate and popcorn, and maybe we could even build a fire."

Peter pulled in the car at the curb before her building. "See you about eight, then?"

"Eight," she said as she got out. Leaning toward the window, she smiled and waved before she ran to her building.

"Are you okay, Ms. Duncan?" Wessy stepped out and pulled open the door for her. "I hope I didn't intrude last night."

"Things were a little hectic yesterday, Wessy, but I'm much better now. I'll tell you a little secret, if you promise not to tell anyone else."

Her excitement kindled a fire in Wessy's eyes. "What?"

"I have a pet, Wessy. A cat."

The older man grinned. "I think that's a fine thing, Ms. Duncan. You've been alone too long. A pet can make all the difference in the world."

"I don't think pets are allowed in the building, though," Eleanor probed gently.

"Well, what the management don't know won't hurt 'em," Wessy said. "Cats don't make a lot of noise and they don't make a mess. So I don't see how anyone could complain, right?"

"Right," Eleanor agreed. "Now that we've settled this issue, could I ask you about the man who left the manila envelope for me?"

"I didn't see him," Wessy said. "I was taking Mrs. Porter up some medicine the all-night pharmacy delivered. Her arthritis has been bad lately, so I left the door for a few moments. When I came back, the envelope was there with your name on it."

"You didn't see anyone?"

"No, I thought it must surely be a Christmas card or something from a friend. Maybe even a special letter." He nodded at her. "I used to send my wife special delivery letters back when we were courting. She loved it."

"Because you're a special man, Wessy," Eleanor said.

He shook his head, slightly embarrassed. "Then if it wasn't a letter, what was it?"

"Actually it was a photograph... of me shopping. I was just sort of curious about who sent it."

"There wasn't a name?"

"No." Eleanor shook her head and forced a smile.

"So, the university professor has a secret admirer." Wessy grinned. "I just hope it isn't one of your students helplessly in love. That's hard on a young fellow."

"I hope not, too," Eleanor said. "I'd better go check on the newest resident in my apartment. And thanks for looking out for me."

"My pleasure," Wessy said, returning to his post by the door.

PETER WAS AWARE of something the moment he unlocked his clinic door. Looking around the waiting room and reception area, he couldn't put his finger on it, but something was wrong. Damn! He was in a hurry to check on the animals, and then get to Eleanor's university office. Maybe there was something in her research that might tip him off.

His gaze swept the large room, roving back to the filing area behind the desk. Several of the files were pulled out, as if someone in a hurry hadn't taken the time to put them away properly. He felt the hair on his nape of his neck begin to rise. Lucille, his receptionist, was a fiend for neatness. He carefully examined the door lock, but there was no sign of forced entry.

Treading as silently as possible, he moved into the examining rooms to the left of the reception area. The office was quiet, too quiet. The normal cacophony of barking dogs and meowing cats was missing, and Peter felt his nerves grow even tauter. Whoever had broken in might still be in the kennel portion of the building.

Step-by-step he moved toward the cages where boarded animals and those recovering from treatments were kept. The unnatural quiet grew more and more ominous. At the green door that led to the indoor kennels he paused. He had no weapon, didn't keep one. From one of the examining rooms he took a squirt bottle of diluted ammonia. If worst came to worst, he could try to spray it into the eyes of anyone who threatening him. It was sometimes an effective way to keep a bad dog from attacking.

Fingers gently gripping the knob, he turned and pushed at the same time. The door flew open and before he could step into the room, he was partially blinded. Something flew at his face and he felt a razor-sharp grip on one shoulder.

Massive wings beat about his face, talons dug deeper and deeper into his flesh. He felt as if his shoulder were being torn apart, and knew that only the thickness of his coat protected him from severe injury.

It took only a split second for him to remember the great horned owl that someone had brought in, stunned by a car. He ducked and rolled, forcing the bird to loosen its grip. In another maneuver, he was on his feet and facing the bird. The owl had settled on the floor, enormous yellow eyes watching his every move. Peter was effectively trapped in the kennel, and now he knew why all of the dogs and cats had been so quiet. A great horned owl was big enough to make off with a full-grown cat. Even safe in their cages, the animals were smart enough not to agitate the big bird. He looked quickly to the right. The door of the owl's cage swung open, unlatched.

"Come on, bird," he muttered. "Back in your cage."
Who would know the potential hazards of a trapped owl?
A trace of ugly memory came back to him. Vet school, a
first-term student who'd never seen the work of a preda-
tor's talons. The student had required a hundred stitches
down his arm. He was lucky. And standing right in the
middle of it all had been Arnold Evans.

Peter tried to move toward the door, but the bird spread
its enormous wings and puffed its chest feathers in the first
warning of attack. But Peter could clearly see that the bird
favored one wing and appeared to be in pain.

"You're going to have to let me by," he said softly. "No
help for it." He shifted forward slightly. The bird made no
noise, but it was plainly bracing itself for an attack. It would
come talons extended, ready to hold and twist. The beak
was a secondary attack weapon, and it was strong enough
to inflict nasty wounds.

Moving very slowly, Peter took off his jacket. The owl
was dangerous because it was hurt and frightened. In normal conditions it would never attack a human. If he could
get the jacket over it and carefully fold down its wings, he'd
stand a chance of getting it back into a cage without hurt-
ing it further.

"Steady, fella," he said, advancing with the jacket. When
the bird feinted, he followed and quickly enfolded it in the
jacket. In a matter of a few seconds, he had it back in the
cage.

"Someone was hoping you'd do some damage to me,
weren't they, Cornelius?" he said, still speaking gently to the
bird. "Well, whoever pulled this prank is going to be very
disappointed." How had Evans learned that he had begun
hunting for him? He'd told no one.

As soon as he was certain the owl had suffered no serious
damage, he went back to the reception area. As he'd sus-

pected, the files that were disordered were those surrounding Eleanor Duncan's name.

He went back to his office, Eleanor's file in hand. As he flipped it open, he saw the potential for trouble. Her address and Familiar's brief but damning history were all on one page.

He picked up the telephone and dialed Eleanor's number. On the seventh ring he started to get worried. By the fifteenth, he was standing and reaching into his pocket for his keys. He should have walked her into the building. He should have made sure that her apartment was safe. He ran out of his office and into the parking lot. At the sight of his car he stopped. All four tires were flat. He walked toward it, examining the left front one. Several holes had been jabbed into the sidewall. A flutter of paper on the rear tire caught his eye. He saw the note, then the surgical scalpel that had been used to slash the tire and hold the note.

"Mind your own business," he read aloud.

Chapter Five

Eleanor stood at the gate that led to the small house and took a deep breath. It had taken a tremendous amount of wheedling to get the address of Magdalena Caruso from the SPCA. The organization had been reluctant to admit to any dealings with the woman. She was an avowed radical, and they wanted no connection with her, present or past. But persistence had paid off, and they'd finally relented enough to yield her address.

She opened the gate and stepped along the sidewalk, which was bordered on either side by a variety of plants. The small house with its tiny front garden was exquisite. It was obvious that Magdalena Caruso was as fanatical about plants as she was about animals.

Eleanor took her time inspecting the neat flower bed. She could imagine how bright the yard would be in summer. She could picture the marigolds, petunias and the vivid zinnias.

Standing silent, she let the recent events stew in her head like some roiling gumbo. Out popped the name of Magdalena Caruso. If anyone could shed light on "terrorist" behavior, it was her.

"Ms. Duncan!"

Eleanor's head snapped up from her inspection of the flowers to find the small, rotund woman standing on the front step. "How nice of you to pay a call. Come in."

Bowser's head ducked out behind her legs and he issued a short bark of welcome.

Eleanor didn't know how she'd expected to be greeted, but it certainly wasn't so warmly.

"How's that cat of yours?" Magdalena asked. "You did a very generous thing, taking care of him. Not many people are willing to help animals from labs. They don't want to get involved. I won't ask how you got him."

"Familiar is fine," Eleanor said, stepping over the threshold. Now wasn't the time to explain to the woman that she hadn't "gotten" Familiar. If anything, he'd "gotten" her.

As the door shut behind her, she stopped dead in her tracks. At least fifteen cats were perched, posed and positioned on different pieces of furniture in the living room. Totally oblivious to the feline population, Bowser went to a small rug and settled down for a nap.

"Let me make some introductions," Magdalena said. "You've met Bowser, so that's Garp, Slugger, Minnie the Moocher, Zazu, Squeaky, Whiskers, Lord Byron, Adolph, Mister Mitts, Jones, Tiger, McDonald, Cochise, Asia, Calico, Mozart, Smokey, Stay Puff, Yoda, Pitter, Van Gogh and Faulkner. That last one has defied my ability to come up with a name, so we call it Boo Boo Kitty. Cats, this is Eleanor Duncan, new cat owner." She waved Eleanor to an empty chair.

"How many are there?" Eleanor asked. She felt as if the room could burst into motion at any second.

"Too many," Magdalena said cheerfully. "But they needed a home, and I had one with a wonderfully enclosed garden in the back. What brings you to this part of town?"

"I want to know more about ARSA," Eleanor told her.

"Why, my dear? You'll forgive me if I say you don't seem to be the type to want to get involved in what will inevitably be a dirty fight. Now that veterinarian friend of yours, he looks like a good candidate." Her green eyes were intense. "Is he?"

"I don't know about Peter. I don't want to be in a fight at all, dirty or clean," Eleanor said with emphasis. "But I'm already involved. I didn't steal Familiar, but when he came into my life, a lot of things changed. I'm not exactly certain how, but I've begun to think that maybe some of the changes might relate to that cat. Did your group break into any labs recently?"

"The Animal Rescue Squad Arsenal hasn't officially been active since last summer."

"This isn't a real answer," Eleanor pressed.

"It's the only answer I'm prepared to give," Magdalena said. There was a no-nonsense look in her green eyes now.

"Last Friday night there was a break-in. A man was seriously injured." Eleanor took a deep breath and met the direct gaze of the woman who sat across from her. "I have been questioned by the CIA, and I think my cat was stolen from there."

"I see." Magdalena was clearly evaluating something. "When I got the report about you and the cat, I was led to believe you were supplying experimental animals. There seems to be a great deal of confusion here, and I'm wondering how that might be. How about a cup of tea?"

"I could use one," Eleanor said. She was more nervous than she'd anticipated, but Magdalena Caruso was surprisingly easy to talk to. "If ARSA didn't rob the lab, who did?"

Magdalena rose. "Excuse me while I brew the tea. If I talk very loud, you can hear me." She continued to talk over the clatter of cups and the whistling of the teakettle. "ARSA has been officially inactive since last summer, when I was arrested on a fur protest and subsequently injured in the local jail. I haven't lost my heart for the work, but it has taken my ankle a bit longer to heal than I expected." She popped her head around the door. "This lab that was broken into, what was taken?"

"I don't know for certain," Eleanor said. If the ARSA leader didn't know about the break-in, who did? Or it could be that Magdalena was playing the innocent? She made rapid calculations as she talked. "A cat that was being used in psychological experiments was taken, and I think that cat is Familiar."

"Was ARSA's name mentioned?"

"No. The CIA agent who questioned me didn't say what organization. It's just that you were the only person I knew who did animal rights work, and I thought this was as good a place to start as any. You have to admit, it's more than coincidental that Familiar arrives at my house and you show up not a day later."

Magdalena returned with the spiced tea. "Yes, I do agree that more than coincidence is at work. Tell me everything," she said.

An hour later, Eleanor gathered her gloves and keys. If Magdalena Caruso had been involved in the lab break-in, she was a very convincing liar. Eleanor had told her everything—except for the business with her dead husband. "Before I go, would you tell me how you first got my name?"

"I've been thinking about that myself," the woman said. "I got a call from Charles Breck."

"Breck? Is that the Charles Breck who's in the news every night? The man who's waiting for confirmation to head the CIA?"

"Waiting and hoping. There is another candidate, you know, that Bueler man. Anyway, Charles doesn't publicly support my work. He can't afford to do that. In fact, I'd say he more than likely hates me because I hold his feet to the fire. But he has a good heart, and he gives me a lot of undercover support, such as leaking me the names of animal suppliers. He actually thought you were selling cats. Whoever gave him his information must have been confused." Magdalena let her head drop to one shoulder. "Or else old Charles is trying to use me for some gain. This is all interesting, and I think that maybe a meeting with Charles will clarify a lot of things. Are you game?"

"Sure," Eleanor agreed. "At least this explains how the CIA got my name," she said. "This is beginning to make a little more sense."

"I'll arrange a meeting," Magdalena promised. "I'll be back in touch."

"Thanks." Eleanor hurried down the bordered walk to her car.

"And one more thing," Magdalena called out.

Eleanor's hand was on the gate. "What?"

"Be very careful. I'd like to know what kind of research has got the CIA so concerned."

"I just want them to leave me alone." Her face was grim as she got into her car.

Flipping over the issue again and again in her mind as she drove home, she could find no solid answers. No matter how she linked the events of her life, she could not make a triangular connection between Familiar, the frightening phone call and herself. The business with her apartment and Carter had to be some nasty practical joke that was unrelated to anything else. Magdalena's warning was still on her mind, but her biggest sensation was one of relief.

As she approached her apartment building, she was still engrossed in her thoughts. The winter night had fallen swiftly, and she noticed with a disappointed groan that all of the parking spaces on the street were filled. The afternoon wind, already brisk and cutting, had turned into a howling evening terror, and she shivered in anticipation of the damp chill that lurked in the parking garage. She cheered herself with an image of Familiar and a cozy fire as she spiraled down the ramp into the garage.

The parking lot was subterranean, but it had never bothered her before. She didn't care for the sense of being buried but wasn't afraid of the perpetual murkiness. At least she hadn't been. Now, as if her imagination were being deliberately perverse, she remembered the phone call from the night before. The cruelty of it made her angry again. She'd cut her ties with Carter and his past. No one had the right to use her dead husband as a scare tactic. No one.

The voice had sounded more than a little like Carter. Or at least it had sounded like she remembered Carter's voice. Nine years was a long time, especially for a memory she didn't particularly relish. If she found out who was practicing such ugly jokes, she'd certainly press criminal charges.

She slipped from behind the wheel and gathered her purchases. The grocery package was light, and she was anxious to get inside the warm building. As she dropped the keys into her purse, she heard the scuffing of leather on the concrete floor. It was a small sound that rang through her head like an alarm. She held herself perfectly still to listen better. Only the emptiness of the parking lot came back to her.

"I'm letting my imagination get away with me," she said out loud, realizing even as she spoke that she was imitating the young boy who whistled in the graveyard. All of her senses were vitally alert. There was something about the garage that didn't strike her as right. It was too silent, too dark. She started toward the elevator.

Her footsteps echoed emptily on the concrete, a steady, comforting sound. She walked faster, unable to stop herself from glancing between the cars. The elevator was only a hundred yards away.

"Eleanor!"

Her whispered name seemed to echo around the concrete columns. She froze.

"Eleanor!"

She turned, swinging her gaze in a 360-degree sweep on all sides. The parking lot was completely devoid of other human beings. There wasn't even the sound of an idling motor. The voice had come from the shadowed corners, from the air. From the lips of a dead man.

"I've been waiting a long, long time, Eleanor."

The voice penetrated her spine. Fear deeper than any she'd ever known tingled through her muscles.

"Who are you?"

"How cute, still the innocent little Eleanor."

The voice! She knew it for certain now! She knew that teasing note, the edge of familiarity.

"Where are you?" Her own voice echoed eerily through the garage, striking the concrete walls and vibrating back to her.

"I'm here, Eleanor. Watching you." There was a deep, satisfied laugh. "You thought I was gone forever. Glad to see my car at the bottom of the cliff, weren't you? I messed up your neat little life."

"Carter!" The word was barely a whisper as it came from Eleanor's throat. "Carter, is it you?"

"Oh, yes, it's me. Back from the dead. Back to claim my wife."

"I'm not your wife anymore." She swirled suddenly, hoping to find him behind her. But the garage was as empty as it had been the last time she looked. "Quit playing stupid games, Carter, and come out."

"Come out, come out, wherever you are," he mocked her. "Did you mourn me when I died, Eleanor? I don't think so. You packed up and left Colorado. You didn't even tell our friends goodbye."

"Your friends, Carter." She turned on her heel and started to walk away, wobbling slightly. The garage had become a landscape for a nightmare. She had to escape, to get away from the sound of his voice so that she could think clearly. She started to run.

Carter Wells was dead. Dead and buried, and she was standing in the garage of her building having a conversation with her imagination. Or maybe her guilty conscience. She hadn't allowed herself to feel anything for a man...until Peter. And now that she was beginning to warm to a spark of interest, her mind had opened up to give her the ugly reminders of Carter. There was nothing real in the voice she heard, only her own repressed guilt.

"Hey! I've come a long way to see you."

She turned suddenly and looked back at her car. Her knees began to buckle. Lounging against the fender was Carter Wells. He was smoking a cigarette, the gesture casual and perfect, as always.

The blood rushed to her heart, a pounding tide of denial. "No," she said. "No!" She held out a hand as if to ward off the vision. "You're dead!"

"No, Eleanor, I'm not." He stepped toward her, his face shadowed by the wide-brimmed hat he'd always favored. "But you may be, if you don't give back what you took."

PETER WAS FRANTIC as he waited for Wessy to open Eleanor's apartment door. He didn't speculate on what he might find, but he was afraid she was injured. At last the door swung open and he and the doorman rushed inside. There was no sign of Eleanor, but Familiar gave them a half-interested greeting.

Peter checked all the closets before he was completely satisfied, and then he left with the doorman, his own plans still indefinite. He had to find Eleanor, but where could she have gone?

"Ms. Duncan might be shopping," Wessy offered.

"Of course." Peter didn't want to reveal how deeply worried he was. "I'll call back later, and thanks for opening the door."

"Is she in some type of trouble?"

Peter closely scrutinized the old man. Wessy was obviously fond of Eleanor, but was there something else behind his question? He'd delivered a threatening photo, and he'd conveniently been away from his duty post when it was left.

"No, she isn't in any trouble, Wessy. Why do you ask?"

"Well, you're looking for her with a worried face, and that friend of hers, Dr. Betty Gillette, came by earlier and asked for her. She looked worried, too. Even Eleanor seemed nervous when I was teasing her about a secret admirer."

"Who is this Betty Gillette?" Peter asked.

"Some professor out at the university. She and Ms. Duncan work together."

Peter remembered the name. Eleanor had said she often worked with the woman on Sunday afternoons. "Probably some business thing," he said, "but I'll tell Eleanor when I find her." He didn't wait for a reply but hurried toward the elevator.

Instead of heading for the lobby, he pressed the button for Parking. There were three levels, and he intended to walk the entire garage until he found Eleanor's car—if it was parked. She might be shopping, as Wessy had mentioned, but he wouldn't rest easy until he knew for certain.

He walked the first level, looking for the bright red import. He spiraled to the second level, his eyes growing more and more accustomed to the gloom. Parking garages! How he hated them. It was like being in a cave that worked its way slowly and inexorably into the heart of the earth. He turned a corner, walking gradually downhill.

Long, slender legs seemed to protrude from the rear of a car. He saw them but didn't believe his eyes. Even as his brain refused the image, his own legs began to pump. He ran.

He recognized the skirt, the jacket, the ivory skin and hair.

"Eleanor!" She was sitting on the bumper of a car, her face in her arms. "What's going on?" When she didn't respond, he gently touched her shoulder. "Eleanor?"

Her breathing had steadied at last, and Eleanor lifted her face to Peter's worried gaze. "I had a dizzy spell," she said. There was no way she was going to try and convince him she'd had a confrontation with Carter Wells. She wasn't sure she believed it herself.

"Eleanor, what happened down here? You're pasty-looking, as if you'd seen a ghost."

She managed a feeble smile. "Only a linguistics professor could appreciate that comment," she said. She had to pull herself together. Whatever was going on, she wanted Peter out of the path of danger. Carter Wells had never been a tolerant man, and dead or alive, she didn't think he'd mellowed much in the last nine years. He'd made his threat and then calmly walked out of the garage, hands in his pockets, hat cocked to one side. He'd never even turned around. No, she didn't want Peter mixed up in the mess her life had become.

"Can you stand?" Peter gave assistance as he spoke.

Knees still wobbly, Eleanor got to her feet. When she almost stumbled, Peter held her against his chest. "Easy now. Was it something you ate?"

"That would be my guess," she said. "Peter, I want to get out of here."

"Yeah, I hate these places, too." Peter's strong hand on her elbow guided her to the elevator.

"Maybe it would be best if I went upstairs and tried to rest." She had to make him leave, but without arousing his suspicions.

"Not on your life," he answered as he punched the button.

"I'm not really feeling well enough for company," she insisted.

"I won't leave you alone until I'm certain you're okay."

There was no arguing with him once his mind was made up, she realized and relented. "Maybe a cup of hot tea would do us both good." The worst thing she could do was make him wonder what had happened in the garage.

I THOUGHT I could escape them, but maybe it isn't going to be so easy. Looking at the dame, with her face all white and her eyes so scared, I feel like hell. If it weren't for me, she'd be sitting at the university in front of her computer, looking up the roots of words like "fetch" and "latch". I can only wonder how Dr. Frankenstein figures into this little drama. It's easy enough for a cat to see that the dame's hiding something from the good doctor, and I'll bet that something involves my good friend from the laboratory. I know the dame isn't schizy, so she had to see something in that garage. Something really scary. I may have to put my old alley cat abilities to work and sneak down for some personal snooping of my own. If Dr. Doolittle is good, I might even let him go with me. That is, if he can give the dame a rest for a few minutes. He's got more than a medical interest in her health, even if he's too stubborn to admit it to himself.

I can't help but think this all tracks back to my old laboratory home and those wonderful humanoids who tried to use me for some of their experiments. I wasn't exactly cooperative. Whoever would have thought they'd be so desperate to get me back that they'd terrify the dame? They seemed so much more involved with Zelda and her pro-

gress. I was foolish enough to think they really wouldn't miss me.

Poor Zelda. What are they doing to her now? Whenever I think about her brown eyes, and the eagerness with which she tried to please, I don't know if I can ever appreciate my freedom. If there were only some way I could get Dr. Doolittle to take a look into that place, he might be able to get the muscle to shut them down. That crazy broad with the poodle, Magdalena Caruso, may even be my last hope. To think that I'd have to appeal to a dog lover to save Zelda! It makes me shudder to think about what they might be doing to her, though. I guess I'd sell my soul to save Zelda. And that means doing whatever it takes, even appealing to a canine woman.

Maybe it's foolish of me to think anyone would help. When that bigwig with the CIA showed up, I thought he'd clamp down on that little romper room of horrors. But Charles Breck never dirtied his three-piece suit with a snoop into how experiments were performed. He only looked at Zelda and remarked on how cute she was, and what an absolutely perfect little gift she'd be. He didn't even notice the burns. He never even really looked closely. I was so mad that day I could have popped. But Zelda may be right. What's a prisoner to do except escape? And maybe that's the only hope for Zelda. As for me, I think I have some chores to attend to with the dame. Dr. Doolittle looks about ready to jump into her lap, and I'm going to stake my territory first.

"HEY!" Peter laughed as he pushed the tom cat down. "I think your cat is worried about you."

Eleanor scooped Familiar into her arms. "I'm much better now," she said. "Peter, would you mind if I canceled our movie tonight? I think I'd like to try and sleep." She burrowed her face into Familiar's fur.

"You've been under a lot of pressure, Eleanor. Maybe it would be best if you could rest. Are you sure you want to be alone, though?"

"I'll have Familiar to protect me. He saved me once." She stroked the purring cat and scratched him under the chin. It wasn't all a nightmare. Familiar was proof of that. Carter Wells wasn't a hallucination. And neither was the fact that someone destructive was back in her life. Maybe it wasn't Carter, but it was someone who had known him well enough to pull off a very good imitation.

"Are you keeping something from me?" Peter asked. In the short hours of their separation, Eleanor had somehow grown distant.

"I'm just tired, that's all." She pressed her hand against his shoulder and was surprised by the way he pulled back. "What is it?"

"I seem to have bad luck with predatory birds. Someone broke into my office and let a great horned owl out of a cage. The bird was injured and frightened. When I went back into the kennels, he attacked."

"How bad is it?" Her own worries were momentarily pushed aside.

"Just a bruise, really. His talons were weakened and I had on a thick coat. I'm fine, but my jacket was a total loss." He looked at her. She'd had enough for one night. He decided against telling her about the damage to his car. But he did have to tell her about the files. The dreadful sensation that perhaps he'd involved her in his troubled life had been gnawing at him all evening. "What isn't fine is that whoever broke in, broke in to get your file."

They both turned and looked at the cat.

"Why Familiar?" Eleanor breathed. "What is it that he could have been involved in?"

"That question grows more and more important," Peter said.

"And more dangerous," she added.

Chapter Six

The dark walls of the garage closed around Peter. He was on the second level, not fifteen feet from where he'd found Eleanor slumped on the bumper of the car. He felt a surge of anger at the memory. Something had happened to her in the garage, something so frightening that she didn't trust herself to share it with him. Was it Evans? Had he frightened her?

Locked in her apartment with Familiar on guard and Wessy alerted, she was reasonably safe. For the moment. But he wanted an explanation of what was happening in her life. In the last few hours, he'd gotten the distinct impression that she wasn't telling him the whole truth.

He paced the area where she'd been sitting, but there was not a trace of anything. The concrete floor was clean of even a scrap of litter. He moved to her car. Someone could have been hiding in her back seat. He pushed the image from his mind and examined her tires.

There was no sign of anything amiss. The only thing he saw at all was a cigarette butt. He nudged it with his toe. The brand was Dunhill, a trademark he didn't recognize. He locked the car doors and headed back to the ground level. If there had been anything else in the parking garage, it was gone now.

He left through the street exit, his mind still full of Eleanor. He'd taken a cab after his car was crippled, but he felt as if he needed the clarifying feel of the wind on his face now, so he walked. The night air carried the smell of snow.

Washington was often thought of as a city of lights. Along the Potomac, the yellow brilliants were reflected again and again in the river and the pools before the many monuments. But on this night, Peter felt as if a dark hand had clutched the city and was slowly choking off the power. As he rounded the block and crossed an almost empty street, he realized that his sense of gloom came from his worries about Eleanor.

Was it possible that she was involved in some sensitive research? Something so sensitive that the CIA could be concerned? Had Familiar actually strayed up to her as she'd said, or was there more to the story?

He cut across a side street and headed into a small, neighborhood park. Almost fifty acres in size, it was typical of Washington's insistence on greenery in the midst of progress. In the spring, when the border of trees leafed out, it would be a tiny patch of paradise.

It was in the brittle leaves that had collected under a tenacious sycamore that he heard the distinct sound of someone else's footsteps.

He slowed his pace and the footsteps slowed. He walked faster, and they increased. Peter forced himself not to turn around, but to continue walking at a steady rate.

The choice of entering the park had been a poor one, especially on a blustery winter night. As he quickly scanned the area, he saw that except for the follower, he was alone. There were floodlights in the park around the swings and games, but the periphery was in dark shadow. Peter kept walking, hoping to emerge on the park's outer rim before the person behind him drew any closer. He cast a quick glance backward. An overcoat-clad figure was a hundred yards behind him.

Unable to tell if the figure was armed, Peter decided against a confrontation. The attack by the owl could have been lethal, and it had been an effective warning of intent. If he maintained his distance and kept moving, he might luck into a policeman. He walked faster.

The footsteps behind him increased in tempo, too.

He was two-thirds of the way across the park, following a narrow bicycle path that flashed back and forth among shrubs and trees. It was the perfect place for an ambush, and Peter was aware of his vulnerability.

Turning for another look, he saw again the dark figure behind him, inexorably following at the same distance as before. It was as if fate had magically linked them.

At last Peter broke free of the trees and found himself on the outer edge of the park. Directly ahead was a well-lighted sidewalk; people were milling about the front door of a restaurant. He crossed the street quickly and stopped at the restaurant. The door opened and a young couple came out, laughter bouncing on the walls and pavement as they waited for their cab.

Peter turned back to face the park. His gaze found the overcoat-clad figure. Backlighted by a street lamp, the man's head was covered with a wide-brimmed hat. As Peter watched, the figure inhaled on a cigarette and blew a cloud of smoke in his direction.

A city bus cut between them. When it passed, Peter scanned the edge of the park again, but the figure was gone, as if it had vanished into the night.

"So, you took a weekend off," Betty Gillette said as she fell into step with Eleanor on the way to the English department. "If you keep up that kind of behavior, I'm going to get the faculty grant I've been coveting for so long."

Eleanor smiled at her red-haired friend. Betty was more competitive than anyone had a right to be, and she was direct as hell about it. Since Eleanor had come to the English department two years ago, her research had won the grant offered to the university faculty. Betty wanted that grant, and she didn't mind letting Eleanor know.

"Cheer up, Betty. Maybe next year the faculty will view your work as more deserving of notice. Lord knows, I'm interested. But I keep telling you, the problem with your research is that it isn't exactly the thing universities lust after. It's more psychological, or even sociological."

Betty made a wry face. "That's the bureaucratic line, for sure. But if we fully understood the modes of communication between all species, we'd have a better idea of how important the written word is. My work isn't that far afield from linguistics. It's all part of the same ball game."

"You're preaching to the choir, Betty." Eleanor picked up her pace.

Betty laughed and shook her head. "I missed you yesterday. I stopped by your apartment and talked with your doorman. He assured me that you were fine. Why did I get the impression that he was worried about you?"

Eleanor hesitated. She was tired, worn out from the weekend, but eager for a friendly ear. "It's been the wildest time," she said. She started to say more, but the sight of a solitary student running across the green alerted her to the time. "Let's have some lunch and talk."

"Is it a man?" Betty's blue eyes were dancing. "Did the studious Dr. Duncan spend the weekend with a man?"

Eleanor laughed. Betty was also incorrigibly nosy. "Not in the way you think, but I did spend the weekend with a man. And a cat. And an attacker. And a woman from a radical animal rights group." Her voice lost its touch of humor. "And the ghost of my dead husband."

"Where did you put all of those people in such a tiny apartment?" Betty asked.

Eleanor laughed. "We'll talk at lunch."

"I can't wait," Betty agreed as she waved Eleanor toward the classrooms. "I don't know whether to ask about the cat, the man or the ghost. Meet you in your office."

Eleanor knew that she barely had time to rush into her office and grab the papers she'd left, already graded, on Friday afternoon. She felt a short note of panic. Even after two years, teaching was sometimes difficult, especially student conferences. With classes out for the holidays, she was surprised when several of her pupils scheduled meetings. Now she felt ill-prepared, especially after skipping her normal Sunday afternoon work session. She was out of kilter with her job. She smiled at the expression, one she'd often heard her grandmother use, and hurried down the maze of halls to her door.

"Dr. Duncan?"

The unexpected voice almost made her scream. She whipped around, sending her hair flying in a black circle about her head.

"Joey," she exclaimed, trying to breathe and talk simultaneously. "You scared me nearly to death. Hasn't anyone ever told you it's rude to sneak up on people?"

"I didn't sneak up," he said. "I just wanted to talk with you a minute. I was worried about that paper I turned in before break." Joey Knight shrugged and looked at the toes of his high-top sneakers. "I always try harder in your class. It's important to me that I do well."

Feeling as if she'd overreacted, Eleanor managed a smile. "You really did startle me, but I'm glad you came by. I'm surprised that you aren't home for the holidays. I thought your folks lived pretty close to here." Seeing the hurt expression that passed swiftly across his face, she rushed on. "What can I do for you?"

"How was that paper?" he asked. He was a good six inches taller than her, but stood there like a small boy.

"I have to tell you that I wasn't very impressed. I got the feeling that maybe you wrote it between television programs." She smiled. "You can do better work." She unlocked her office. "Just a minute and let me grab some papers. We can walk to the mezzanine together. I have an appointment with Tina."

She pushed open the door and flipped on the light.

"Oh, no." The soft whisper of words escaped her.

"What is it?" Joey pressed behind her. At the sight he grasped her shoulders, pulling her from the office. "Somebody wrecked the place," he said. "I'll get campus security."

He was halfway down the narrow hallway before Eleanor was able to stop him.

"Wait, Joey," she called. "Hold on a minute."

He turned, disbelief on his young face. "Why? The sooner they get here, the sooner they'll catch whoever did this. They'll have to take fingerprints and all."

She held up both hands. "Hold on. If it's a case of student vandalism, we'll get security. But I want a chance to see what damage has been done, okay?"

"If you go in there tampering with things, it'll destroy evidence." He walked toward her. "You could get hurt, Dr. Duncan." His hand touched her shoulder. "I'm worried about you."

"I'm fine, Joey," she reassured him, moving away from his touch. He was a sincere student, a hardworking one. His concern was slightly unnerving, though. "I'll take care of this, if you'll help me by going to meet Tina. Just tell her that something came up and I won't make it. Tell her we'll meet at the same time tomorrow."

Joey turned and started to rush down the hall again, but she called him back.

"Joey, I have to ask a favor of you."

"Anything," he answered.

"Don't tell anyone about this. No one at all. Not another student or faculty member. Just let me handle it, okay?"

Understanding registered on his face. "Is there something else wrong?"

"A few odd things have happened to me lately," Eleanor answered. "Nothing I can't handle, but I want it managed in a certain way, if you get my meaning."

"Whatever you say, Dr. Duncan. You have my word. I won't tell a soul."

"Thanks, Joey."

She watched him hurry away with a sinking feeling. How long would it be before the whole English department learned of the destruction? She had to make a report, but she wanted a few moments alone to see what damage had been done.

Walking into the office, she shut and locked the door behind herself. Despair mingled with anger as she took in the books that had been tumbled from the shelves. Her desk drawers were upturned and flung about the room. Her desk top had been swept clean of everything; it had all been pushed onto the floor. Even the trash can had been upended.

"Wanton vandalism?" she asked herself. "Or is there method to the madness?" She wouldn't be able to tell until she sorted through her things, and she couldn't do that until a report had been filed with security. She could only probe a little.

The clamor of the telephone almost made her jump. She picked it up automatically. The receiver was at her ear before she realized that her hand was shaking. What if it was Carter's voice?

"Hello." She almost choked on the word.

"Eleanor, are you okay?"

Peter's warm voice seemed to free her emotions. She felt a tide of relief and a desire to see him.

"I'm fine, Peter, but someone destroyed my office at the university. I'm standing in the middle of it now, trying to get up my nerve to call security."

"So you're going to report this incident?"

"I don't have a choice. The university's computer is on the floor, and I'd say the repair bill is going to be high."

"I'm not all that busy this morning. Would you like me to come over and help?" He'd wanted to get into her office, but it sounded as if someone had beaten him to the punch. "Could you hold off calling security until I get a chance to look around?"

Something in his voice made her withdraw. "You shouldn't get involved in this any further, Peter. I thought it would simply stop, but it hasn't."

"Have you found anything important disturbed?" he pressed.

"Yeah, two years' worth of work and a lifetime of accumulated office junk. You're nice to offer to help, but I think I'd better handle this alone." She replaced the receiver, her emotions in complete turmoil. Why was Peter so consistently interested?

She righted her desk chair and sat down, a weary sigh escaping her.

"So, here we are again," she said aloud. "More destruction." She decided to heed Peter's warnings and to check out what was missing before she filed a report.

She bent to the pile of papers at her feet and began the long process of reordering her work. Fifteen minutes later she was sitting on the floor when she heard a knock.

"Litter patrol!" Peter's voice came through the wooden door.

She scrambled up and unlocked the door. She let him in and then relocked it.

"Looks like the same story as your apartment," he commented.

"Yeah, just more papers. I'd like to find the creep who did this." She picked up a sheaf of papers and put them onto her desk. "I'll never get all of this sorted in time for my eleven o'clock meeting with Rhonda."

Peter went to the bookshelves. The destruction appeared to be random. Entire shelves had been swept to the floor, while others were virtually untouched.

Something about Peter's intense interest unnerved Eleanor. She made the call to security with the telephone scrunched against her shoulder as she reordered another stack of papers with her hands.

While she talked, Peter walked the office. He picked up her coffee cup and desk calendar, her clock and an empty pencil container. Under the pile of rubble he noticed a printed flyer. The pitiful picture of a dog on an examining table caught his eye. It was a flyer from an underground animal rights group. His eyes flashed to Eleanor. She was either a very good liar, or she was being framed.

"Is it possible some student had it in for you?" he asked, slipping the paper into the pocket of his coat.

"I don't think so. All teachers have students who dislike them, and I'm no exception. But I don't remember any student who violently disliked me. Not to this extent." She waved her hand around the room.

"I'm not making light of it, but we can't rule out the possibility that it might have been student orchestrated."

"I wish I could believe that." Eleanor dropped the papers onto her desk and attacked another pile. "My students aren't vicious."

"It could be a student with a crush." Peter remembered the photograph of her at the fish market. It had been signed with the words 'my love.' And Wessy had mentioned the possibility of a student infatuation.

"I don't think so," Eleanor argued. She felt her temper begin to rise. "Normal kids don't react to a crush with destructive tendencies."

"No, and normal dogs don't bite. But you have to allow the possibility that it might happen." He was surprised by her adamant denial. She was certainly protective of her students. Maybe that was the link! A student activist group. He remembered his college days, the idealism. And Arnold Evans!

"Why are you so certain it's a student?" she asked irritably. She knew he was trying to be calm, to find a reasonable explanation. And she knew she should be grateful to him for coming up with something that was far less scary than the conclusions that had been tumbling around in her mind. "You're right, Peter. It's something we should consider."

"Just keep the thought in mind," he said.

His thoughts were interrupted by the arrival of the security team. The officers were clearly aggravated by the sight of Eleanor and himself muddling through the mess. Their questions were cursory and hurried before they began to dust for fingerprints.

"Let's grab some coffee while they do their job," Peter suggested. "There must be a student hangout around here somewhere."

"The Hub," Eleanor agreed. "Good coffee and that never-changing atmosphere of college." She looked at her watch. "I guess I missed my eleven o'clock appointment. It's nearly noon."

"Then I'll buy you lunch," Peter said.

"Will you be available for questions?" one of the officers asked. He gave them a disapproving glance. "It might be better if you stayed around."

"We'll be at The Hub," Eleanor told him.

The walk across campus put them into the weak winter sunlight that brightened the bare campus, but the sun's rays did little to boost Eleanor's mood.

"I could stand some snow," Eleanor commented. "It doesn't seem like it's getting close to Christmas without some of that white stuff to slip and slid in."

"So, you prefer the traditional image of Christmas, white lawns, big fires, wassail. A lot of single people go to the islands during the break."

She shook her head. "No. I've never been one to do that. If I could go anywhere, I'd go back to the Smokies. My dad's asthma forced them to move out to Arizona, so there's no home there now, but I love the mountains more than anything, especially during Christmas."

They entered the student hangout, a tall building with high, Corinthian arches. There was a small gift shop, the coffee shop cum cafeteria, and the student mailboxes.

"Nice place," he said, nodding toward the art display that was one of the features of the building.

"The students do a great job of using the space for their art shows and posters. It's their building, and they also manage the cafeteria. Everything they serve is fattening and delicious. They have the very best malteds in the world, and their hamburgers aren't far from being ideal."

"You've just made my order," Peter said. "Can I get the same for you?"

"Sure. I'll get us a seat."

She found a table in the back where they could talk in some degree of privacy. The cafeteria was relatively quiet, compared to the normal roar when classes were in session, Eleanor reflected.

"Most of the students are home," she reminded him. "During the regular session, this place is loud, wild, chaotic and rather comforting. It's good to know the savage beast still roams free in the youth of today."

"At times," he agreed. "Was there something in your office that anyone would want?"

"I don't have a clue." She thanked the student who brought over their burgers and malts. "It could be a student, as you suggested," she said, but her tone lacked conviction. "It could be the same person that broke into the research lab." Her brown eyes were suddenly worried. "Peter, it could be anyone."

"I want you to make a list. Put down the name of everyone who might wish you harm. Everyone. From petty jealousy to real dislike." With that list he could begin his own private search. Someone on it would undoubtably lead him to Evans.

"I hate this," she said, sipping the shake.

"I see you got a better offer for lunch." Betty Gillette was standing behind a rack of greeting cards near the table. She moved around it, coming to stand in front of them.

"Oh, Betty!" Eleanor flushed crimson. "I completely forgot. My office was vandalized and Peter, Dr. Curry, came over unexpectedly. In all the confusion I forgot about our lunch."

Betty shook her head. "Don't worry about it. If I had an offer from Dr. Curry, I'd have lunch with him rather than you, too." She looked at Peter. "Are you a doctor on staff, or another type of doctor?"

"Veterinarian," he answered, standing and pulling out a chair for her. "Join us."

"Not on your life," Betty said. "Eleanor and I were going to have a gab session. She said something this morning about an exciting weekend, including a visitation from—" The look of panic on Eleanor's face stopped her.

"Including what?" Peter asked. He looked from one woman to the other. Something had passed between them, some unspoken signal to withhold.

"Oh, it was a long list of things, one of them being an exciting, attractive man. I presume that was you."

"Betty, I didn't say that!" Eleanor felt her discomfort level rise sharply. She didn't need Betty's prodding to appreciate Peter's qualities, and she didn't need Peter thinking she gossiped so about him behind his back.

"I'm prone to exaggeration," Betty said.

"What exactly did Eleanor say?" he asked.

"She said she had a chaotic weekend involving a man, a cat, an attack.... That's all I remember."

Eleanor silently sighed. She'd been certain Betty was going to mention the visit from her dead husband, but she had to give the woman credit for sensitivity.

"And now an office vandalization," Betty mused. "What was it this time, a kid with a crush or a kid with an F?"

"Neither, I think," Eleanor said. "Peter made the same comment, but I can't think of any of my students who would do such a thing."

"Face it, Eleanor, you have the only students who stay at school during the Christmas holidays just to get a private appointment. That Joey kid is always bird-dogging you."

"Joey's parents are divorced, Betty. I don't suppose he really has anywhere he wants to go during the holidays."

"Deny that he has a crush on you." Betty looked at Peter. "He's no competition, but he's a nice-looking kid. And he dotes on Eleanor. He'd spend all of his time slaving at her feet, if she only gave him a wink of encouragement. But she doesn't. In fact, she doesn't even see how bad he has it for her."

"Joey finds security in talking with me," Eleanor said. "He's a decent kid with a lot of troubles. There's nothing else to it. And just to set the record straight, he was with me this morning when I found my office in such a mess, and he was as shocked as I was.''

"Okay, okay." Betty backed away from the table. "I rest my case, Eleanor. You'll go to your grave defending that kid. And you're probably right. But just remember, all of our little clients aren't decent children from loving homes. Some of them are the same people who grow up to be criminals and weirdos.''

"Are you sure you won't join us for lunch?" Peter asked. He felt the tension between the women and wanted a chance to explore it.

"Listen, you guys, I'd love to stay, but I have an appointment. Some guy named Rousel has been bugging me for two days to find time to talk with him.''

"Rousel?" Eleanor repeated, looking at Peter.

"Yeah. And I'm going to meet him. I've finally found someone who's interested in talking to me about my work.''

"What does he do for a living?" Eleanor asked.

"You know, it seems like he said, but I don't remember. Why? Do you know him?''

"Maybe," Eleanor answered. She hesitated, then added, "He may be with the CIA, if he's the same man.''

Betty grew so pale that her freckles stood out like measles, Eleanor noted. "The CIA? Why would he want to talk with me?''

"There was a break-in at a laboratory around here somewhere." Eleanor spoke carefully. She didn't want to frighten her friend needlessly, but did want her to be alert. "A cat was stolen. And before you ask, it may be the cat I have, Familiar. I'm not giving him back." She met Betty's gaze.

"I don't know a damn thing about any cats," Betty said quickly. "That's your business. But why would he want to talk to me?" she asked as her color returned.

"He may ask you some questions about Eleanor," Peter said.

"Yes, it seems I may be a suspect in a case of something very close to treason."

Chapter Seven

Eleanor bent to the waist and rewrapped the towel around her damp hair. The hot bath had soaked away some of the tension that knotted her shoulders, but it was returning now. She dialed the number for the third time in an hour.

Betty Gillette didn't answer—hadn't answered all afternoon. Eleanor felt a vague sense of unrest. Betty had gone to talk to Alva Rousel and seemed to have dropped off the face of the earth.

Picking up the receiver again, Eleanor started to dial, then stopped midway. She depressed the switch and held the receiver to her ear. She'd debated the wisdom of cracking open the wounds of her past, had indeed fought against taking such action. Now it was time. She dialed long-distance information. The vision of her ex-husband in the parking garage had goaded her into formulating a plan.

In the light of afternoon she didn't believe her husband had returned from the dead, but she was going to find out whatever was going on with Carter Wells or his memory—without involving Peter. Carter's friends had always been rough. Far too rough.

"*Denver Post Chronicle*, please," she responded to the operator's inquiry.

"That number is 555-6968," a recorded voice informed her.

She wrote the number on a pad. Her hand was shaking as she replaced the phone. She tried to block out the next memory, but it filled her mind. A puddle of fluid on the carport floor. It was after Carter's car had gone over the side of the mountain that the police had found the brake fluid leak.

"A tiny nick in the line. The fluid leaking out drop by drop..." She could still hear the officer's voice, so calm, so rational. She shook her hair free of the towel and began to brush it out. With each long stroke she tried to put the past behind her.

Was there a future with Peter? She pulled the bristles through her hair and focused on him. He was someone who cared. There was an undeniable attraction between them. She felt it every time he stepped into the room, each time she thought about him. She responded to him with awakening desire. With his touch he'd rekindled the old fire that smoldered just beneath her skin.

Pushing her wet hair away from her face, she dialed the Colorado number and asked for the news desk. At first her voice faltered, but as she continued to talk, she grew more self-possessed. The reporter on the other end listened attentively, and with no small degree of sympathy, as far as she could tell.

"I remember the case," Adeline Valentino said. "It was my opinion that the police didn't try very hard to solve the murder."

"Carter's death wasn't exactly a blow to the social fabric of the nation," Eleanor said, unable to cover the bitterness. "I know it's an odd request, but could you send me copies of the clippings involving the car crash?"

"We really aren't supposed to do that," the reporter said, "but I'll do it this afternoon, on my time. But first you have to answer a question."

"Okay?"

"Is there some reason I might be interested in these clips myself?"

Eleanor paused. "Not at this time. But you have my word, if it turns out that you might be interested, I'll give you a call."

"It's a deal," Adeline said. "I'll post them to you overnight."

"Thanks." Eleanor replaced the phone. She never would have believed she'd want to read the newspaper accounts of her husband's death and subsequent exposure as a gambling crook. When she'd left Colorado nine years before, she'd burned every scrap of paper, every item that might link her to her ex-husband.

With the small victory at the newspaper behind her, Eleanor got the number for the Denver police. She'd talked to a Sergeant Kleaton on the day her husband died. So when the phone was answered, she asked for him.

"Kleaton here," he answered, sounding just as bored and routine as he had nine years before.

Eleanor explained her call. "Would it be possible for me to get a copy of the death certificate?"

"Let me check," he said.

As the minutes ticked by, Eleanor's sense of accomplishment began to slip from her. Something was wrong. The sergeant was taking far too long.

"The state granted a death certificate on Carter Brett Wells, but there was no actual coroner's examination of the body."

"I know," Eleanor responded. "But there was proof that he died. Solid proof. Right?"

"The car at the bottom of a ravine, the explosion. That's pretty solid, but all circumstantial. It's like the air disasters. When there's no way to reclaim the bodies, the presumption of death is based on circumstantial evidence."

There was a pause. "Nine years is a long time to wait to get curious about your husband's death, isn't it?"

"Sergeant, did you ever suspect that Carter might be involved in something more than gambling?"

There was a longer pause. "Mrs. Wells, I don't know what you're trying to imply. Maybe it would be better if you brought your questions here in person, or had your local police department call me."

She could hear the suspicion in his voice and tried to allay it. "There's really nothing to investigate. It's just that I—thought I saw someone who looked exactly like my dead husband. I guess my imagination got away with me and I started thinking. I never saw a body. I just wanted to be sure."

"Well, if Carter Wells was in that car, you can be sure that he's a dead man. No one could have survived that crash. No one. And looking at the file here, the searchers did find a shoe you positively identified as your husband's." There was a note of pity in the policeman's voice. "Listen, Mrs. Wells, take my advice and put this behind you. I remember you. Just a kid. Your husband wasn't the nicest guy in the world. No point rattling bones where he's concerned."

"You're right," Eleanor said. "But just the same, I'd like a copy of the death certificate."

Sergeant Kleaton chuckled. "You said you were a college professor now, eh. Well, that sounds like thorough research. I'll see if I can't arrange to have one mailed to you." He took down her address. "By the way, what type of trouble was your husband supposed to be hooked up with?"

Eleanor hesitated. The CIA agent had spoken in strictest confidence. But was telling another law officer a violation? Certainly not after nine years.

"Something called Code One Orange."

"Never heard of it," Kleaton said. "But then working a homicide beat, I'm not often thrown into activities with official code names. Mostly I get the day-to-day criminals."

"Thanks for your help," Eleanor said. As she replaced the receiver, she didn't know if she felt relieved or more concerned. Sergeant Kleaton seemed to have no doubt that Carter had died. *If he was in the car.*

In all of the time that had passed, she'd never doubted that. Now she couldn't leave it alone.

Her hair was almost dry now, as she stroked the brush through it several times until it fell in a soft tumble of curls to her shoulders. Still feeling bleak, she picked up her address book and turned to the back page. There were two numbers listed, both without names beside them. She discounted the first, her parents', and finally dialed the second. Rayburn Smith. Carter's best friend from grammar school. When she and Carter had moved to Colorado, Rayburn had moved with them. He and Carter had been inseparable.

"Rayburn Smith, Sundial Sales."

The familiar voice sent a pang through Eleanor. She'd never been close to Rayburn, but his friendship with Carter had been one of the few instances where she'd seen her husband demonstrate any lasting integrity. He and Rayburn had stuck together through thick and thin. Mostly thin, and mostly slightly illegal schemes.

"Rayburn, this is Eleanor."

"Eleanor?" Rayburn's voice rose an octave. "Of all the people I expected to hear from, you'd never be one."

"I know. I'm calling to ask you a few questions, if you don't mind."

"After nine years, what could I mind about?" Rayburn said, "Unless you've decided to work for the IRS. Then I might get a little anxious. How are you?"

"I'm fine. I've started a new life and things are going well for me."

"I don't guess you could say that when you were with Carter. He never did treat you right, Eleanor. I told him, more than once. It was something I never understood about him. He was a good friend to me, but a terrible husband."

"He was a good friend to you. It's one of the best things I remember about him," Eleanor agreed.

"What kind of questions did you want to ask?"

She couldn't be certain, but there seemed to be complete openness in Rayburn's voice.

"Did you know any of Carter's associates in the last few weeks of his life? I mean, some of the people he might have had business with?"

"You mean who wanted to cut his brake line and kill him? I never thought finding out that information was very important to you."

"It wasn't. Until now." She was shocked that Rayburn had thought of Carter's death as a murder all of these years. She'd never considered it. The leak had always been accidental—in *her* mind.

"Carter had a lot of irons in the fire. He was getting in over his head in some areas. He had his gambling business, which was bad enough, but in the months before he died, he got in a little deeper with some other guys."

"Code One Orange?" Eleanor asked.

The gasp on the other end was very audible.

"Carter told me never to say that name out loud." Rayburn's voice was panicky now.

"Why?" Eleanor pressed. She could feel her skin beginning to prickle. So Alva Rousel wasn't far off track. Carter had been involved in something other than gambling schemes.

"Eleanor, you've got to believe me. Carter never told me much. He would drink a little too heavily and say something about how his ship was really going to come in. He talked about his contacts, but he was always careful never to reveal any names. And to be honest, I didn't want to know. When he talked about that stuff, I tuned him out. I had my little sales scam going with the mobile homes and I was content. I tried to get Carter to come into a partnership, but I was too small-time. I tried to get him to..."

"I know that, Rayburn. You did. I heard you talk to Carter again and again. As you said, he wanted to make the big league. But I have to find out about Code One Orange. I have to!"

"I wish I could help."

Now there was a distance in Rayburn's voice. Eleanor knew she would have to fight to pull any further information from him. But one thing she'd learned without asking. If Carter was alive, he hadn't contacted Rayburn. Rayburn spoke of him as dead, as only a friend who truly grieved could speak.

"Did this Code One Orange have anything to do with the Indians?" she asked, trying to jog his memory and grasping at straws.

"Hell, no! You were the one worried about the Indians. Carter used to, well, laugh at you behind your back. I liked what you were trying to do, but Carter thought you were ridiculous with your books and dreams of education."

Even nine years later, Eleanor could still feel the sting of her husband's disdain.

"You're right!" Her mind jumped forward again. "Was Code One Orange about animals?" She couldn't control the excitement in her voice.

"Animals?" Rayburn was shocked. "Hardly! If you have to know, it was about some bombing in Central America. Now, take that and put it away. Let it drop, Eleanor. I'm serious. When Carter talked about that stuff, it gave me the willies."

Eleanor felt her firm grasp on the clues begin to slip away. "Rayburn, you have to tell me the rest. What about the bombing? I have to know." She was more confused than ever. What could this have to do with Familiar and herself?

"Why? That's the question I should have asked. Why after all this time do you have to know this?"

"Because someone is impersonating Carter and trying to scare me, and the CIA is questioning me about Code One Orange."

"Holy cow!" Rayburn whistled. "Why?"

"I don't know. I honest to God don't know. I picked up this stray cat, and my life began to disintegrate."

"Code One Orange had to do with a plan to blow up the Mexican Embassy in San Gabriel. The idea was to blame the government of San Gabriel and throw the two countries into open fighting. Carter was supposed to train the guerillas in the Colorado mountains. He did, but the plan went wrong and some people working with Carter got in big trouble about it. That's all I know."

"What went wrong?"

"I never knew for certain. The wrong people got blown up."

"And they thought Carter did it deliberately." She was taking broad guesses, but knew she was getting closer and closer to the target.

"Carter and his associates."

"What associates, Rayburn?" She could hear the strain in her voice.

"I don't remember their names. Bingington or something like that. Anyway, he was some big cheese in Central America at the time."

"How long was this before Carter's accident?"

"Two weeks or so."

"So it wasn't gambling debts." A cold chill raced down her spine. "It wasn't anything nearly that simple and clean.

It was this other. Code One Orange. And Carter had to die because he knew too much.''

"That's your assumption, not mine. Listen, I got a customer waiting here. Since I've become an honest car salesman, I got to service my clients. I haven't got time to gab all day on the phone.''

"Rayburn!'' Eleanor felt a sudden attack of panic close in. "If you had seen Carter, you'd tell me, wouldn't you?''

"He's dead, Eleanor. I accepted that a long time ago. You should, too. And bury the past, or it'll eat you alive. Got to go.'' There was a click and then the sound of static on the line.

CATS HAVE an extraordinary sense of direction. Better than dogs, though most people don't know it. I'm not great on estimating distances, but I can tell you that if I traveled due south, I'd eventually run into the prison where Zelda is confined. It's a fair distance, but that isn't really the drawback. It's all of these damn cars! I mean, think about confronting a highway from my perspective—wheel level. And not a single vehicle willing to slow down and let me across. Getting to Zelda is going to be an exercise in futility, but I've got to try. And I've got to do something to protect my Eleanor. She was terribly distressed when she came home from work. She didn't say a word, but it was all over her. That woman is strung as tight as a piano wire. I'm no rocket scientist, but I can predict that something awful happened to her at the university.

Let's see, now, this is the second level of the garage. Not a lot of animal traffic through here. There's not even the scent of another cat. Too bad. Since I left the laboratory, I haven't had a single conversation with one of my peers. I love Eleanor, and Peter's okay, but I crave my own people. Maybe next escape, I'll try for a park or an alley. But now it's down to work.

Here's Eleanor's car. Nothing unusual about it. No current odor of Dr. Frankenstein, at least. In fact, there's not one interesting smell in this whole place. Maybe I'd better go topside and check out the street.

There must be a way to get from here to the lab. Or some way to get Dr. Doolittle over there. The dame is great, but he's the one with the muscle—and, I suspect, the big interest. The dame is the kind of person who never even thinks of cruelty because it's alien to her nature. That's why she makes such a perfect target. I've been putting together the tidbits I hear, and it's clear to me that Eleanor's in for some serious trouble. She's part of a plan, a tiny cog in a big gizmo of destruction.

Well, here's the street. Traffic is mad in Washington. I'd be one big, greasy spot if I tried to make a dash across this four-lane. It's not even safe to sit on the street. The dogcatcher will be down on me and before I know it, I'll end up sold for research again, and believe me, that's a fate I can miss without shedding a tear.

But look! There's that tall blond guy. Mr. CIA with the gray suit and the debonair smile. Yeah, he's sitting in that car across the street. If he's protection, then I'd rather buy a German shepherd. It seems like he should be showing a little interest in who comes and goes in the dame's building. He obviously thinks his job is to watch her. Great! Now that's human logic. Why isn't he out trying to find a criminal?

Well, enough people-gazing. I'd better get back in the apartment before the dame realizes I'm gone and has a catniption—hey, hey, that's pretty clever, if I do say so myself.

PETER CLOSED his office door and pulled the photocopied flyer from his pocket. He hadn't wanted to read it in Eleanor's company. Now he studied it carefully. There was the gruesome picture of a dog in some experiment, then a brief paragraph of copy calling for action against animal abuse.

"There will be a rally of the Action for Animals at 7:00 p.m., Wednesday night at Pier 27," he read aloud. He knew the area, a small section of houseboats on the Potomac. It was the perfect meeting place for a radical group. Especially one planning some new aggressive action. Would Eleanor be there? There was only one way to find out.

He slid the note into the middle drawer of his desk and locked it. He had one other task to accomplish before the afternoon slipped away. That was a visit with Magdalena Caruso. Just as soon as he finished with his afternoon patients.

It was nearly five, with traffic turning thick and irritating, when he pulled up in front of Magdalena's house. He expected Bowser, but the cats were something of a surprise.

"I have two more left at my kennels. The owners decided it was too much trouble or too expensive to care for them. Would you like them?" Peter asked her as she showed him into her crowded living room.

"Not necessarily. But I'll take them."

Peter couldn't conceal his smile. His visit wasn't one of pleasure, but he couldn't deny that he felt a lot of respect for the short woman who bustled about, making room for him on her sofa. She put her money where her mouth was. She didn't simply criticize the way other people treated animals. She took care of them herself.

"You've come to talk about Eleanor, haven't you?" she asked, taking a seat across from him.

"Is she a member of ARSA?" There was no point evading the issue.

"No, Peter, but I'd like for you both to be."

"I'm a vet," he said, looking deep into her green eyes.

"We could use a good vet. Some of the animals we get are in pretty bad shape." She smoothed her skirt. "We've tried several vets in the area. Some will help, but not if it's obvious what we're doing."

"They're afraid of losing their license. You know that."

"I do. But something tells me you wouldn't necessarily be afraid. Why is it, Peter, that you look so familiar to me?"

"I look like a million other guys with brown hair and hazel eyes. We aren't exactly unusual." He smiled his crooked smile.

"It'll come to me. I'll have to think about it, but it'll come. So what do you want to know about Eleanor?"

"Just after her office was destroyed, I found a flyer for a rally. The Action for Animals group."

"AFA?" Magdalena paused. "I didn't know they were in the area. They must have been the group that staged the raid that has everyone so worked up. Eleanor had a flyer?"

"It was in her office, but the thought has crossed my mind that it could have been planted. That's the thing. People are breaking in not to steal, but to leave incriminating evidence behind. I'm beginning to wonder what was left in her apartment."

"It wouldn't be the first time that maneuver worked," Magdalena said. "That's an old but effective trick."

"What can we do about it?"

Magdalena smiled. "If you won't save animals, at least you're willing to save Eleanor. Well, what we can do is arrange a meeting for Dr. Duncan and Charles Breck. Once Breck takes a look at Eleanor, he'll see she isn't capable of violent actions."

"Can you arrange it?"

"Yes. I'll call Eleanor tonight. You just make certain that she agrees to come."

"I'll take care of it."

"And Peter, I'll remember where I know you from. Eventually."

"Maybe I was your vet in another lifetime." He laughed as he stood to leave.

On the drive back to Eleanor's, he tried to frame a reason for barging in on her evening. At last he remembered the movie date they'd broken. He stopped at a video store and picked up a tape of *The Bishop's Wife* and hurried to Eleanor's building.

"Want to check out Cary Grant in action?" he asked, holding out the tape when she opened the door.

"Peter." She was surprised. She'd thought of him repeatedly during the afternoon, but had never expected him to materialize at her door. She touched her hair and remembered she was completely without makeup.

"You look fresh and scrubbed and very much like a girl who needs a good movie," he said, as if reading her thoughts. "How about that popcorn?" He edged past her into the apartment.

"Well, I hadn't made any plans." She hesitated. What would it hurt to watch a movie? "Okay." Her nerves were still raw from her talk with Rayburn. The truth was, she was more than glad to see Peter. He could make her feel secure when no one else could.

Peter built a blazing fire while she listened to the sound of popping kernels in the microwave. "Old-time popcorn was so much harder, and I don't think it tastes any better," she said. "You'd be hard put to get me to admit to modern improvements in a lot of traditions, but microwave popcorn is a definite step forward for mankind."

Peter put the fire screen back into place. He settled down on the sofa and took a large handful of the buttery corn. "I won't argue that point." Picking up the remote control, he flipped on the movie. "So let's relax."

The credits had barely finished when the telephone rang.

"Tell them to call back," he teased her, but watched her alertly as she took the call.

"I will," she promised, lifting the receiver, "after this call."

"Why, Magdalena, how are you?" She raised her eyebrows at Peter, and he flicked the movie to Mute.

"Tomorrow evening? Yes, I could manage that. Charles Breck has agreed to meet with me. Of course, I'll tell Peter," she said. She replaced the receiver before she looked at him.

"As you heard, I have an appointment with Breck tomorrow. Magdalena Caruso arranged it. He thinks I'm some undercover animal rights radical." There was no amusement, only worry on her face.

"Where's the meeting?" Peter asked.

"I don't know. I'm to go over to Magdalena's, and she'll take me from there. She asked me to tell you. And she said if we aren't back by eight, that you should—" She stopped.

"I should what?"

Eleanor looked up. For the first time, Peter saw the depth of her worry in her eyes and felt a nasty twinge of guilt.

"That you should notify the authorities and find us a very good lawyer. She said we'd need one."

Chapter Eight

Eleanor wiped her palms on her wool slacks. A lingering, unpleasant odor came from the empty cages all around her.

"The research here was vital," Charles Breck was saying. "The break-in and violation of federal security is intolerable." He looked directly at Magdalena Caruso as he spoke.

"Prove it, Breck," she responded, not the least bit ruffled. "I've got a doctor's certificate that says I can't walk long distances or run. I'd be a fool to break into a research lab in my physical condition."

"Your ability to act the fool has never ceased to amaze me." Breck's tone was severe, as was his expression.

"What type of research was conducted here?" Eleanor asked. She felt completely at odds with her surroundings, and in contrast to her expectations, Breck acted as if she were one of Magdalena's associates. He acted as if she might be armed and violent, and Magdalena was doing nothing to counteract that impression!

"We weren't really engaged in research," Cal Vrenner, the white-coated scientist, said smoothly. "At the stage of the break-in, we were really more of a training center. Obedience." He smiled at her.

"Dogs and cats?" she asked. Familiar was at the back of her mind, and she could hardly look at the cages with the mesh wire bottoms. For an animal with padded feet that type of cage would be sheer torture.

"A little more sophisticated," Vrenner said.

"You seem proud of your work, Vrenner. Maybe we could see a little demonstration of what you're training." Magdalena's voice held only contempt. "What's the penalty for disobedience? A slap? A kick? Maybe an injection of drain cleaner?"

"That's enough of that, Magdalena," Breck told her. "Cal has been involved in a small project that we at the CIA are very interested in seeing happily completed. And you'll be glad to know that it involves no cruelty."

"I don't believe it."

Magdalena's gaze challenged Vrenner, and Eleanor felt a new appreciation of the short woman. She had once said she was capable of anything to save an animal, and Eleanor now understood how far that meant she'd go. Magdalena hated Vrenner. She hated him with a raw passion that could turn into violence. She must have despised him the first minute she'd laid eyes on him.

"Get the ape," Breck said, breaking the tension that flowed between Magdalena and Vrenner. He straightened the coat of his dark suit.

"Of course," Vrenner agreed with a modest amount of deference. "I'll be right back."

As soon as he was out of the room, Breck rounded on Magdalena. "Watch your step," he warned her. "Vrenner is a dedicated scientist, but he has a temper. You could push him too far."

"I'd love to be on the other end of an assault charge from that man," Magdalena fumed. "And if you're implying he'd slug a woman, what must he do to these animals when there's no one around to control him!"

Vrenner returned before Breck could respond. He led a small female orangutan on a silver leash. The collar around her neck was jeweled.

"Curtsy," Vrenner commanded.

The ape executed a perfect curtsy, sweeping her head almost to the floor in front of Magdalena.

"Kiss hand," Vrenner said.

Magdalena's hand was clutched by the monkey and kissed.

The plump woman grasped the ape's hand and held it, turning it over to reveal a series of sores, some of them heavily scabbed.

"What is this?" Magdalena demanded.

"Unfortunately, in trying to give the ape some freedom from her cage, she was left unsupervised. She decided to play with a Bunsen burner that was lighted. The burns weren't deep. We've made sure she had veterinary care," Vrenner said. There was no apology in his voice, but rather a note of careful pride. "We take care of our animals, Mrs. Caruso, whether you want to believe that or not."

"I don't believe it," she said flatly. "My guess is that you burned the monkey, administering some sort of reprimand."

"Prove it!" Vrenner challenged her.

"I wish I could," Magdalena answered.

"How is the ape's training coming along?" Breck interjected.

"Beautifully. She'll be ready for the ceremony day."

"I'm delighted," he said. Turning to Magdalena, he explained further. "She's a gift to a foreign leader, a man known for his fondness of apes and his kind treatment. An old friend of mine, Frederick Nottingham, wanted to give the ape as a gift, and I agreed to help him find suitable training. She's going to be a surprise, and if her training continues successfully, maybe an asset. What with the curtsy and all, I think she'll be a smash success, don't you agree?''

"I don't agree with anything that goes on in this building," Magdalena said. "If I had my way, I'd take the ape with me to some reputable trainer."

"Are you implying that I'm not reputable?" Vrenner demanded.

"I'm not implying anything," Magdalena answered coolly. "I'm saying it outright. You're scum, Vrenner. I know your reputation, even if Charles is too thickheaded to look at the facts. I despise you and your cohorts, and whenever I get the chance, however it comes, I intend to destroy your little business. Proper training doesn't require physical pain. I know you."

The tension in the room was electric. For a wild moment, Eleanor thought Magdalena might pull out a gun and shoot the scientist. Or vice versa.

Breck stepped between the two. "Enough. I thought I could show you and your associate—" he stared at Eleanor "—some positive work. I can see now that the effort was wasted. We'd better leave."

"What about the ape?" The words were out of Eleanor's mouth before she could stop herself. Breck's cold look told her that she was damned in his eyes.

"She's perfectly fine." Breck's tone was harsh; he put a hand onto Eleanor's shoulder and started to push. "I hoped you'd at least understand the necessity of animal use. After all, you've done your own research with communications."

Eleanor balked. "What are you talking about?"

Breck looked at Vrenner. The scientist shook his head. "Excuse me, I misspoke. The car is waiting."

"Where are the rest of the animals?" Eleanor pointed to the empty cages. "You don't keep cats or dogs in this type of cage, do you? The mesh hurts their paws."

"I knew you had it in you," Magdalena said, nodding approval.

"I don't have anything in me. I'm not on anybody's side in this, but some things aren't to be tolerated." She shook herself free of Breck's hand. "And I'm not to be pushed around like some criminal element."

"Out of here!" Breck commanded. "Both of you! Magdalena, this is the last time. Don't call me, don't expect any advice or assistance. I'm finished with you. I'm sure now that you are responsible for the break-in here, and I believe Dr. Duncan was also involved."

"Believe what you want to," Eleanor retorted. Now her own temper had risen to a dangerous level. "The lab is funded by federal monies, I suppose. Well, maybe this is something the taxpayers should look into."

Breck propelled both women out the door.

The car tore out of the parking lot with loose gravel spinning from beneath the wheels. Eleanor looked through the back window. The Behavioral Institute was a redbrick building tucked away in a small nook of isolation. It wasn't that far from her university, but it seemed like another planet.

"There's not even a tree nearby," she said aloud.

"To some people, trees aren't important. Cal Vrenner and his ilk are that type."

"What will happen to the monkey?" Eleanor asked.

"Not a damn thing!" Breck said, turning to them over the front seat. "I'm serving you both with a strong warning. If anything goes amiss at that lab again, I'm holding you responsible. Got it? It may take several weeks of interrogation before anyone decides that you have certain civil rights."

"That's a dire threat, Charles," Magdalena said. There wasn't a trace of concern in her voice. "As a former resident of the Washington city jail, I can only hope the federal facilities have a higher standard of cleanliness."

"You can be cute all you want to, Magdalena. But if you get in trouble again, it's your hide. Don't call me."

Magdalena started to respond, but Eleanor touched her hand and restrained her. There was no point in pushing the conversation any further. Breck was seething, and Magdalena was clearly itching for more hot words.

"Let us out at Brenniton's," Eleanor said suddenly. "I think I'd like to treat Mrs. Caruso to dinner."

"Eat hearty," Breck said; the car pulled to the curb in front of the busy restaurant. "And stay away from Vrenner," he warned as they exited.

"I do what I have to do," Magdalena answered. She slammed the door with unnecessary force.

"He's really angry with us now," Eleanor said to the older woman as they made their way to the maître d'. For the moment, she held back her own frustration with Magdalena.

"Not nearly as much as I am with him," Magdalena answered. "There was a time when I thought Charles might actually have a little soul in him. I can't believe he's paying Cal Vrenner for any type of governmental work. I'm not exaggerating, Eleanor. If Vrenner's the man I think he is, his reputation is so disgusting that even the larger chemical companies won't hire him. There was a fire about fifteen years ago at International Chem-Co." She stopped suddenly.

"And what happened?" Eleanor prompted. Magdalena looked shocked.

"A man who looked an awful lot like Vrenner was running the lab there. An assistant was implicated, and in a major fire many animals died. Nothing was ever proven." Magdalena's voice had lost its tone of conviction. She seemed to be thinking of something else as she talked. "It's a complex story."

"That's horrible," Eleanor said. "What happened to the assistant?"

"I don't know. He disappeared. I'm sure he never got another job in research. But that Vrenner person has continued, and now that I know he's here and working under federal contract, I intend to stop him."

The maître d' led them to a table near the window. Eleanor couldn't stop herself. She leaned over and took Magdalena's hand. "Be careful. Vrenner isn't a man to tamper with."

"I don't tamper. When I strike, I intend for it to be a fatal blow." Magdalena flipped her napkin and effectively changed the subject. "Especially now." She looked up with a quick smile. "What do you know about AFA?"

The acronym drew a complete blank. "Nothing. What is it?"

"Another animal group. I thought you might be a member."

Eleanor shook her head. "I have my own set of personal worries, one of which is that you set me up with Breck. You made no effort to make him believe I wasn't a member of your group."

Magdalena shrugged. "He already had his mind made up. There really wasn't anything I could do."

"Then why did I meet with him?"

"You never know." Magdalena shrugged. "How are the desserts here?"

"Maybe we shouldn't have come on so strong. I mean, how did you know the ape was injured by Vrenner? She could have burned herself, as he said."

"She could have," Magdalena agreed, "but I don't buy it. As I told you earlier, Vrenner's reputation precedes him."

Eleanor let the subject drop and ordered a glass of white wine and a light salad. "Excuse me," she said, rising. "I'm going to find a phone. I promised Peter I'd check in."

"Tell him to meet us here," Magdalena said, then smiled. "I don't think you'll have to twist his arm."

Eleanor shook her head and chuckled as she walked away. She had to hand it to Magdalena; she was a sharp cookie.

The restaurant was crowded, and she wove her way around the tables. That was a wonderful thing about Washington. She could go to the busiest places and never see a familiar face. It was such a contrast to the small mountain community where she'd grown up. Anonymity was a very comforting sensation.

As she turned right to find the ladies' room and a pay phone, she saw the tall, tailored body of Alva Rousel. The CIA agent was sitting alone at a small table at the window, his face hidden in a newspaper. The obvious attempt at concealment was so pathetic that Eleanor smiled. The man was tailing her, and everywhere she went, she caught on to him. Her first impulse was to go over and talk with him, but she stopped herself. She didn't want to confront the issue of Carter's past. But she was dying to find Betty Gillette and see what the two of them had talked about during Betty's question session.

One more thing to do tomorrow, she reminded herself as she turned into the ladies' room. A pay phone in the small alcove was available, and she made the call to Peter. He quickly offered to come to the restaurant and drive her and Magdalena home.

They'd finished dinner and were having coffee by the time Peter arrived, eager for an account of the evening's meeting.

"Eleanor was brilliant," Magdalena gushed. "She tried to make those rascals accountable for their conduct."

"I didn't," Eleanor protested. "I only asked a few questions. The place was, well, disreputable."

Peter raised his eyebrows. "Meaning?"

"There wasn't even a single tree," she said, realizing she sounded ridiculous. "And the orangutan had these sores on her hands." She didn't want to get into the business about Vrenner.

"Electric shock?" he asked. When he saw Eleanor's startled look, he regretted his sudden question.

Magdalena nodded. Her green eyes were sharp as a cat's, he noted.

"How did you know?" Eleanor asked Peter.

"Standard operating procedure for some labs and other so-called training facilities." He shrugged it off.

"The Behavioral Institute," Magdalena said. "The cages were empty. I didn't get much of a chance to tour the place. Typical setup, mesh cages on top of each other, that type of thing."

"I know it only too well," Peter said, shaking his head. He stood up. "I'd better get you ladies home. It's late."

He assisted Magdalena to her feet. Outside the restaurant, a sheen of ice had touched the sidewalks. The wind sang around Eleanor's ears with a new bitterness as she slipped into the car. Something had transpired at the lab that she'd missed—something between Magdalena and Vrenner—and possibly Breck.

Magdalena made an issue of giving Peter her address as they moved into the traffic. Their eyes met and held in the rearview mirror for a moment.

"Hey, isn't that your friend from the university?" Peter pointed to the corner window seat.

Eleanor strained to catch a glimpse of the red-haired woman who sat at the table with Alva Rousel, but couldn't be certain if it was Betty or not. Traffic forced their car forward before Eleanor could get a good look.

"I couldn't tell if it was Betty, but I'm certain the man was Alva Rousel," Eleanor said, and for some reason the idea of the two of them dining together unnerved her. "I saw him earlier when I went to the ladies' room. He was hiding behind a newspaper, as if he'd been sent to tail me and needed a crummy disguise."

"Maybe he was just having dinner," Peter said. "That isn't an unreasonable assumption. Betty is an attractive woman, and from all I could gather, she's single."

"I suppose you're right," Eleanor agreed.

"But you don't like it, do you?" Magdalena asked from the back seat.

"No, I don't," Eleanor admitted, chuckling at her own irrationality. "And I don't know why."

"Woman's intuition," Magdalena said. "It's the best reason, and the only one you can't ever explain."

TUESDAY MORNING rain pelted Eleanor's bedroom window. She pulled the covers over her head and sighed. Only Familiar's insistent kneading convinced her that she had to get up. She checked the bedside clock and found that it was nearly nine.

"Ten days until Christmas," she said, awed by the reality. "I'd better do some serious shopping today."

Looking out the window, she knew she'd go instead to the university. She didn't have the fortitude to confront millions of shoppers on such a dreary day. She needed the comfort of her research, and she was dying to talk with Betty.

Peter had walked her to her door the night before, but she'd declined his offer to act as watchdog. There were things she needed to tell him, but last night hadn't been the proper occasion. She was still up in the air about her own feelings.

"I'll talk with Peter about it in a day or two," she told Familiar as she opened a can of salmon for him. "I owe him an explanation."

"Meoww!" Familiar answered, then tucked into the food.

Eleanor took her time selecting warm clothes and getting ready for work. She dressed casually, in a long, flowing wool skirt and a turtleneck sweater that accentuated her willowy grace. With her hair pulled back in a ribbon and the dark frames of her glasses, she looked very young and studious.

As she walked across the lobby to the desk, she recognized Alva Rousel sitting in one of the lobby chairs. Once again a newspaper concealed most of his face.

"You must be up on current events," she said, stopping in front of him.

"I try to keep alert," he said. His smile was boyish, charming. "Did you enjoy your dinner last night?"

"Very much."

"I can't say as much for the company you keep," he added, still smiling.

"Which one, the woman or the man?"

"Both," he said, then smiled again. "The CIA isn't interested in your romantic life. Is that the role Peter Curry is playing?"

"In a manner of speaking," Eleanor said, fighting her inclination to become defensive. "I have a few personal questions for you. Was that Betty Gillette you had dinner with?"

Rousel grinned, breaking the tension. "She's a fascinating woman."

"I couldn't agree more," Eleanor said. "Even if you haven't found a good reason to lock me up, at least you discovered a nice woman to date."

"Fate has a way of rewarding the deserving," he said. A worried frown replaced his smile. "I don't want you to have something you don't deserve happen to you."

Eleanor felt the rush of blood through her veins. "What are you talking about?" she asked.

"Your background. Your husband had a lot of irons in the fire. He was a man with many interests, and I'd guess at least ninety percent of them were illegal."

"I can't defend Carter, and I don't intend to try," Eleanor said. "But he's dead, and I wasn't responsible for what he did."

"When federal authorities asked you to testify against him, you refused. Isn't that correct?"

Eleanor's anger moved up a notch. "Yes, that's true. I was married to him, and whether you understand it or not, I took my vows seriously. For better or worse, in sickness and in health. Those little words meant everything to me. I couldn't testify against my husband. Even if I wanted to, I didn't know anything about Code One Orange until you told me. I didn't even believe you until yesterday, when I talked with his old friend."

"I'm not always at liberty to reveal details." Rousel's blue eyes hardened. "Who did you talk with?"

"Rayburn Smith. Carter's best pal."

"He's still alive?"

"Very much. He wasn't involved in the Central American thing. Rayburn was a petty criminal. He had no ambitions like Carter."

"Few men had the ambitions of your husband," Rousel said. He folded the newspaper and held it in his lap. "Eleanor, is there any chance that Carter...might have survived his automobile wreck?"

The room seemed to dim slightly, and Eleanor saw her hand reach out and clutch the arm of Rousel's chair. He stood quickly and assisted her by grasping her elbow. Cool sweat covered her back and forehead, and she thought for a moment she might be physically ill. Rousel helped her into the chair.

"Was it something I said?" he asked, concern wrinkling his forehead.

"What makes you ask if Carter might be alive?" Her heart was pounding so violently against her ribs that she thought Rousel would surely see her distress. He was watching her eyes, after all.

"No real evidence, just a hunch."

"The officer who investigated Carter's accident had no reserve about declaring him dead. He said no one could have survived that crash. Why are you asking so many questions about Carter? What does he have to do with the break-in at a laboratory?" This was the link that completely eluded her. She was completely confused.

"If Carter was in that car," Rousel said, biting his lower lip. "If he was in that car . . ."

"He couldn't have escaped." She knew she was sounding desperate, but couldn't stop herself. "Nine years have passed. It doesn't make any sense that Carter would come around now. If there was the chance Carter was alive, don't you think he would have contacted his wife?"

"Maybe he did, Eleanor. Maybe he will again."

Chapter Nine

Eleanor's legs were steady, but her blood rushed from the surge of adrenaline Alva Rousel's words had created. Carter, alive! It wasn't possible. But a CIA agent had given the nightmare thought some daytime credence. There were so many questions. Why now, after all these years, would Carter suddenly reappear if he were alive? She stumbled out of the elevator and into the dank parking garage. As soon as the elevator doors closed behind her, she felt an attack of fear.

She swept the garage with a long, slow gaze. The rows of cars seemed somehow sinister. The dark shadows and trapped fumes created a gruesome atmosphere straight from her childhood fantasies of hell. Taking a deep breath, she thought about getting back into the elevator and calling a cab to take her to the university.

"No," she said aloud. Carter Wells had effectively ruined her past. He wasn't going to get control of her present and future. If he was lurking around parking lots trying to scare her, she'd confront him. She'd ask him right out what he wanted. All of her obligations to him had been erased. She owed him nothing. She owed herself the courage to confront her past and end it, once and for all. She had to do it. For herself and for Peter. If her feelings for Peter were to grow and develop, Carter had to be laid to rest.

Her booted footsteps echoed in the empty garage as she walked down the line of cars. She could see the bumper of her own and walked toward it, never looking left or right. Her spine tingled as she listened for an unnatural sound, for some half-expected warning.

"I'm too old for such foolishness," she told herself. "I'm spooked like a silly teenager."

The walk seemed to take forever. With each step forward, she seemed to fall two steps back. The sensation was like a nightmare. The longer she moved toward the car, the farther away it seemed.

She picked up her pace, still refusing to look to either side.

Out of the darkness her nightmare was reborn. Behind her came the sound of footsteps.

Panic struggled to release itself in a scream, but she held it back. It wasn't Carter. It couldn't be. The talk with the CIA agent had simply rubbed her nerves raw. There were hundreds of cars in the garage. That meant hundreds of owners would be coming in and out, getting and parking their cars.

She cast a quick glance over her shoulder. Someone darted into the shadow of a column. Someone tall and masculine.

She started to run, fumbling in her purse for her keys. The footsteps came after her.

She knew better than to look back. The figure was gaining, drawing closer as she clumsily searched her purse and tried to run in the high-heeled boots. Her breath came in gasps, the fumes of the garage tearing at her throat and lungs.

She flung herself at the car, finally pulling the keys free of the purse. The doors were locked, and she cursed as she struggled to insert the key into the lock. She heard the footsteps behind her, coming at a steady but rapid pace.

At last the door lock clicked and she threw herself inside the car. Simultaneously pulling the door closed and cranking the motor, she jerked the car into Reverse and hit the gas. Cold, the motor stalled, then fell into gear with a roar. The car shot out of the parking spot.

"Hey!" the figure called to her. She heard a thud and punched the car into First. Whoever was behind her was flesh and blood! With a squeal of tires, she drove away. In the rearview mirror, she saw a man struggle up from the pavement.

She'd hit him! She'd actually struck a human being with her car! The panic began to clear and she slowed. The figure in the rearview mirror was standing upright and limping. He held up a hand to her, a hand of...pleading? Her hands gripping the steering wheel were numb, but her foot slid from the gas to the brake. The figure was coming toward her, one leg dragging. Whoever it was, it wasn't Carter!

She turned off the ignition, struggling with the key. Clumsy fingers fumbled again and again. It was as if all the messages from her brain had somehow been garbled. Time hung suspended.

"Dr. Duncan?" Joey Knight rapped on the window.

Eleanor's head snapped up. Her student was standing at the side of the car, pain etched across his young features.

"Are you okay, Dr. Duncan?" he asked.

"Joey!" She rolled down the window. "Joey, are you hurt?" Her voice shook. "What were you doing in the parking garage?" She opened the door and got out. A wet stain of blood was soaking through the leg of his jeans.

"I was worried about you after the break-in at your office. I came over to ride to the university with you. Some guy in the lobby said you'd just left. He said he thought you might be in the garage." The young man shrugged his shoulders. "When I got down here, I felt like a fool, so I started sneaking around behind you."

"Oh, Joey!" Eleanor helped him to the passenger side of the car and put him inside. "We're going to the hospital and have some X rays. Were you hit hard?"

"I sort of rolled over the back of the car and fell," he said. "I'm not hurt, I just scraped my leg. I thought for a moment that you were trying to kill me." His voice was shaky.

"Not you, Joey. I thought you were someone else."

"I guess I scared you, following you," he said.

Eleanor slipped behind the wheel and started out of the garage. "More than scared me. You terrified me."

"It wasn't such a bright idea, now that I think about it," he reflected ruefully.

"No, it wasn't bright. But that isn't important now. We'll get you fixed up at the hospital and see how bad the damage is."

"No hospital," he said. "It's only a scrape and a few bruises. I promise. If you'll take me back to my dorm room, I'll put some bandages on it and get some clean jeans."

Eleanor looked doubtfully at the red spot on Joey's thigh that was growing larger and larger. "I think you should see a doctor."

"No, I can't," Joey told her. "If my mom finds out about this, and she will, if I have to put it on the insurance, she'll have a fit. She'll call Dad and fight with him long-distance, and he'll be in trouble, because I was supposed to be with him over the holidays. I can't," he said. The misery on his face convinced Eleanor.

"Okay," she agreed. "I have a secondary plan. Medical attention, but no doctor. On the condition that you promise to go to the hospital, if Dr. Curry says so."

"Dr. Curry?" Joey looked at her as the car burst from the garage into the rain.

"A veterinarian."

Joey grinned. "Cool! I don't mind going to a vet."

"I only hope Peter doesn't mind me bringing you," she said.

The waiting room at the clinic was filled with pet owners and their animals, but as soon as Eleanor gave her name, she was ushered back to Peter's office.

Startled by the receptionist's description of Eleanor and a bloody young man, Peter rushed into the office. He took one look at Joey, who was sitting in the chair, clearly doing his best to mask his pain, and his hands went to Eleanor's shoulders. "Are you okay?" The sight of the blood and the whiteness of her face struck him with a sudden terror. She was at risk. There was a spot of blood on her skirt and her hands were smeared.

The same anger he'd felt the first day he saw her with her face cut and bruised came back to him, only much stronger. "Who did this?"

"I'm fine." She fought to control her shaking, offering a tentative smile. In Peter's angry reaction she saw his concern. A tiny pop, like the opening of a bottle of exquisite champagne, sounded in her heart. No one had ever cared about her the way Peter did. It was written all over his face. Taking a deep breath, she explained about the accident. "Would you look at Joey's leg?" she asked.

By the time she finished, Peter was much calmer. She wasn't hurt, and his heartbeat had returned to a reasonable pace. "I'm not a doctor," he reminded her. "I don't mind treating a bruise or scrape, but I . . ."

"Joey's promised to go to the hospital, if you say so."

"Okay," Peter agreed. "If you promise me that *you* aren't injured." The tenderness was fading from his eyes, but it was still audible in his voice.

"I promise, and I'll wait outside." Eleanor excused herself while Peter tended to Joey's injuries.

She washed her hands and rinsed the blood from her skirt in the rest room. After she'd found a seat in the waiting room, she hid behind a magazine, avoiding the curious stares of Peter's patients. But there was nothing she could do to avoid the thoughts that tumbled through her mind. Peter's unguarded concern for her was like a warm, healing touch. Safe behind the covers of a pet care magazine, she marveled at the fusion she'd felt with him. The emotion was deep, strong, a sense of connection with purpose.

She pushed the thoughts away, more than a little frightened by their implications. Focusing on the magazine, she read an article about poachers and African elephants.

"Thank goodness I don't own any ivory," she mumbled. She flipped the pages, scanning the winning entries in a pet photo contest and an article on cosmetic experimentation. A small black and white photograph circled several times in black ink at the bottom of the page caught her eye. A handcuffed man was being led away by two uniformed policemen.

Something about the picture was familiar, and she stared at the grainy photo. The caption explained that the photo date was 1977, and there was only a short blurb. The man in the photo, Arnold Evans, had been arrested on charges of animal abuse. He'd skipped bail and was still at large thirteen years later. The story was an update, noting that Evans had last been seen in May 1988 on a safari in Kenya.

The story meant nothing to Eleanor, but she was strangely drawn to the photograph. She studied it carefully and finally smiled. The man bore a strange resemblance to someone she knew or had met.

It was nearly half an hour later when Peter called her back into the his office.

"Is he hurt?" she asked.

"He's young—and lucky. Nothing worse than a scrape. I gave him some Betadine to wash his leg and some bandages. And a long lecture about hanging out in parking garages." Peter smiled, relief evident in his face. "He'll be healed in a matter of days."

"Thanks, Peter," she said. "I was so scared in the parking lot. I was terrified. I heard him following me, and I saw him behind me, and I lost it. I knew I hit him, but I couldn't stop immediately." As she recounted the experience, her voice rose. She felt her legs begin to tremble again.

"Why were you so afraid, Eleanor?" Peter brushed a hand across her forehead. "Did something else happen in the garage?"

Peter's question caught her off guard, and she knew that now she was ready to confide in him. "I need to talk with you, Peter. Tonight. Could you meet me about seven, or as soon as you finish here?"

"Of course." He stroked her hair, pushing it back from her face. With a gentle finger he lifted her chin so that their gazes met. "I've been waiting for you to tell me." Her dark gaze promised so much that it was all he could do to keep from pulling her into his arms.

"I know," she said, and her voice was throaty. "I wanted to tell you, but it's so complicated. And it's going to sound crazy."

He shook his head. "Not to me."

"Doc, how long will it be before I'm completely well?" Joey asked. He hobbled over to them at the doorway.

Peter's hand dropped from Eleanor's face and he took a step back. "Oh, three to five days of stiffness, then a few more days for the scrape to completely heal. Just protect it and you'll be fine."

"Thanks." Joey took Eleanor's elbow. "Could you take me back to school now? I have a science project I need to work on."

"Of course." Eleanor answered. She exchanged a look with Peter and received a knowing smile. The young man took her arm for assistance as they went through the lobby and to the car.

Watching him as she drove, she saw the determined jut of his chin.

"Is something bothering you?" she asked. "Do you need to stop for some medicine or anything?"

"No," he shook his head and turned to gaze out the window. "You're involved with that vet, aren't you?"

"Joey!" Eleanor was shocked by the question.

"You are. I can tell by the way he looks at you."

"My relationship with Dr. Curry shouldn't concern you." Eleanor slowed down to turn onto the campus. Before she could say anything else, Joey opened the car door and jumped onto the grassy curb. He slammed the door with force and limped away, his shoulders squared and stiff.

"Good grief," she murmured as she drove toward her parking space. "This is all I need." Joey was upset and too emotional. She didn't give any credence to what he'd said, but the fact that he was so distraught was terribly upsetting.

Instead of going to her own office, Eleanor went to Betty Gillette's cluttered habitat. The red-haired professor was hidden behind a stack of books, but Eleanor heard her singing.

"Knock, knock," she said at the open door.

"Eleanor!" Betty whirled and stood up. "I've been trying to call you. I had the most interesting chat with Mr. Rousel."

"And a nice dinner, I assume?" Eleanor grinned.

"How did you know?"

"I saw you. At Brenniton's. Or at least the woman looked a lot like you. Was it business or pleasure?" The question was unnecessary, because she could tell by her friend's face that the evening had been delightful.

"Well, it started out as business, but when he asked me out to eat, I began to suspect that he had ulterior motives. And I was right!"

"Congratulations," Eleanor said. "He's an attractive man. I just hope he appreciates how lucky he is that you'd spare your research time to consume food with him. I've already told him as much."

"Quit teasing me. I really like him," Betty said. "We had the best time, and believe it or not, he was interested in my research."

"I'll bet that wasn't all he was interested in," Eleanor added with raised eyebrows. "I'm delighted. It's time you had some fun."

"We're going to dinner again tonight. Alva knows this wonderful place in Virginia, and we're going to make a real evening of it. I feel like my first date."

She laughed, and Eleanor noticed that she looked like a teenager.

"I'm glad to know that having my apartment and my office trashed served some purpose. Do you mind if I ask what Rousel wanted to know about me?"

Betty's expression sobered, and Eleanor saw a cautious light touch her eyes. "Not really that much. He asked about your work. He wanted to know about your background. I couldn't help him much with that. I never realized it until he started asking questions, but I don't know anything about you, Eleanor. You grew up in Tennessee, and that's about the extent of it."

"You knew I was married," Eleanor said. Discomfort made her tuck her hands into the pockets of her skirt.

"Yes, you mentioned that. A bad marriage, as I recall."

"A fatal marriage. My husband was killed." Eleanor wasn't sure if she said that to test her own reactions or Betty's.

Remembrance lightened Betty's expression. "Now I remember. Car wreck in the mountains. I thought it was interesting that you grew up in the Smokies and lived in the Rockies and finally ended up in Washington."

"What else did Rousel ask?"

"Alva wanted to know if you were maintaining an active social life and—" she lifted both hands "—if you were an animal nut. I told him no to both questions. He did imply that he thought you'd been mixed up in some break-in at a lab, but I set him straight on that. I've never met a more law-abiding person, I told him that very clearly."

"Thanks," Eleanor said. She felt a slight turbulence in her stomach. At least Rousel hadn't gone into the sordid details of her past with Carter.

"What was that you said to me the other day about a visit from your dead husband?" Betty straightened a stack of books on her desk. "You sounded frightened."

"Someone in the parking garage startled me. I had this insane feeling that it was Carter, my ex. He talked like him, he acted like him. I must have been delirious. Carter's been dead nine years. It was just my imagination." Now Eleanor regretted blurting out that tidbit the day before, especially in view of the new relationship between Betty and Alva Rousel.

"Are you sure?" Betty probed.

"Yes, you can tell Mr. Rousel that I thought I saw a ghost, but it must have been my poor eyesight or an overactive imagination." She smiled. "Just tell Mr. Rousel that contrary to popular belief, the past is dead and buried."

Betty's brow furrowed. "Whatever that means."

"And have a wonderful evening. I'd better get busy on my own work, or you'll surely snatch that grant from under my nose."

Eleanor spent the rest of the day sorting through her office and rearranging the shelves. Although there were several expensive ceramic pieces, nothing of value appeared to be missing. She called campus security to check on the progress of the investigation, but they had no news for her. The intruder had worn gloves of some type. Without her computer it was difficult to actually work, so she finished the cleanup and prepared to go home.

The event with Joey Knight continued to nag at her. She'd never suspected the young man would have a personal interest in her. She sighed. There were times when even with the best intentions, she took the wrong course of action.

With all of the unpleasant happenings, it was good to see Betty so happy. In the two years they'd known each other, Betty had often commented on her desire for a serious relationship. Now it looked as if that wish might be coming true.

And what of her own romantic desires? The memory of Peter's concern was like an intimacy, very delicate and treasured. In that moment of magic, much had changed between them. Now the future depended on her ability to trust him enough to tell the whole truth. Trust No One was a motto she'd have to learn to discard.

She walked slowly to the parking lot, half expecting to run into an apologetic Joey. The kid was confused, and she felt a spark of guilt. Everyone but herself had seen it coming. She'd allowed the young man to spend extra time with her. She'd never realized he was developing a painful and unresolvable crush. I should have been more observant, she thought as she drove home.

To her delight, there were three empty parking spaces on the curb. No garage scenes for her. She whipped into one and hurried into the building.

"Eleanor!" Wessy called to her when she stopped at the desk to check her mail. "Come here." He motioned her into a small alcove near the door, then glanced furtively around the lobby to make sure no one could hear them.

"What is it?" she asked, an uneasy feeling creeping over her skin.

"Dr. Curry called and left a message. He didn't want anyone to hear it but you."

Eleanor's suspicions grew. Peter would never give an important message to Wessy. He didn't trust the doorman.

"When did he call?" Eleanor asked.

"About ten minutes ago. He must have missed you at the university. But he said it was urgent. He said that Magdalena Caruso had been attacked and injured. He wanted you to come to her house immediately."

"Are you sure?" Eleanor clutched her purse. Magdalena's house was across town.

"Positive. He said it was urgent."

"I'd better call," Eleanor said, hurrying to the telephone on the desk. She dumped her purse's contents onto the marble countertop and looked until she found the number Magdalena had written out for her. She dialed and got a busy signal. After three tries, she called an operator.

"The number is out of service," the operator said.

"Can you tell me why?"

"I'm sorry, but there's no way for me to tell."

"Thanks." She hung up, reassembled her purse and started out the front door.

"Be careful," Wessy called after her.

"I have to be," Eleanor shot back. She rushed back into the street, aware that the night was turning bitter once again. Even the Santa walking down the street had a sinister appearance. Everything that had once been familiar now seemed filled with fear.

THE FOUR PATROL CARS parked outside Magdalena's small house, blue lights still flashing, made Eleanor doubly upset. A burly patrolman stopped her at the door, but Peter soon persuaded him to let her inside.

"Magdalena was asking for you," Peter explained. "She was almost in shock when I found her."

"Wessy said for me to come right away." She looked at him in bewilderment. "I tried to call, but the phone was out of service."

"The attacker jerked it from the wall. I had to go next door to call you. I had no choice but to leave the message with Wessy."

The house was completely wrecked. Broken china was all over the floor, and the teapot had been smashed against the hearth. Magdalena had enjoyed that pot. Eleanor felt a lump swelling in her throat.

"How is she?" she whispered.

"The paramedics are with her. They didn't want to move her," Peter said. "Hey—" he gave her a smile "—it isn't going to be fatal. I think I'm more worried about you."

The first tear slipped down Eleanor's face. "Are you sure she's okay?"

"A hundred percent. She's hurt, but not too bad. She's a tough old lady. Remember?"

"I feel so responsible," Eleanor said. "Look at this place. And what about the cats?"

"They escaped into the backyard. I think I've rounded up most of them in the kitchen, but only Magdalena will be able to tell. There are over two dozen. All spayed and neutered." He wiped the tear from Eleanor's cheek. "She's a remarkable lady."

"I know," Eleanor said. "We have to stop all of this. I have to tell you something really important. About the parking garage. About me."

"It can wait until we get home," he said. "You're upset and worried, and now isn't the time." She looked on the verge of snapping. As much as he wanted to hear what she had to say, it would have to wait.

"Why was Magdalena attacked?" Eleanor asked.

"We haven't been able to discover a reason. Why don't we go talk to her?" He put his arm around her back for support and led her to the door.

Eleanor cautiously approached the bedroom. Magdalena was sitting propped up in bed, two paramedics in attendance. Her face was wan, but she smiled warmly at Eleanor. "*Entrez*, my half-molded young radical. I'm slightly battered but not really harmed."

"What happened?" Eleanor asked as she and Peter slipped into the room.

"I was in the kitchen, preparing dinner for my furry friends, when I heard something in the living room." She waved the paramedic away when he tried to slip a blood pressure cuff onto her arm. "I thought it was one of the cats, roaming around for his spot to sleep, but it didn't sound like a cat. Felines are so careful. They can walk through an entire collection of glass and never budge a piece, unless they want to make a mess. I knew it wasn't a cat, because I heard something break."

"Her pulse is normal, no sign of concussion," the paramedic said into his radio. "Bruises, cuts, and a large lump on her head from the blow, but no serious injury."

"Ten four," the answer crackled back. "Since she refuses transfer to a hospital, bring yourselves home."

"Ten four and out," the paramedic responded.

"Young man, I'm trying to tell these people what happened," Magdalena said huffily.

"Yes, ma'am," he answered, repacking his black case as he talked.

"I keep several weapons in the house, and I found my little .22 pistol in the kitchen drawer. I know it isn't the most effective weapon in the world, but it would discourage a burglar, wouldn't it?" She didn't wait for an answer.

Eleanor took a seat on the bed. There was a goose egg-sized lump on the side of Magdalena's forehead, but other than that, she seemed to enjoy being the center of attention.

"I took my pistol and started into the living room. Then wham! The kitchen door flew right into me and knocked me back. Then this big man rushed through. I'd fallen to the floor, and he raised his arm. I can't remember what he was holding, some trophy or something, and he crashed it down on my head. That was it. I didn't have time to fire a single shot. And when I came to, I was still lying on the kitchen floor and the back door was open. All of the cats were milling around, and I knew I had to get up and close the door before they got out into the street."

"The cats are fine," Eleanor reassured her. "Peter put them in the kitchen. He thinks he's got them all, but he needs you for a head count when you feel better."

"I'd feel better if I could get that guy who hit me. Is anything missing?"

Eleanor shook her head. "I can't really tell, but it looks more like vandalism than burglary. My apartment and my office have both been broken into and ransacked."

"My dear!" For the first time Magdalena looked as if she were taking the break-in to heart. "What's going on?"

"I was hoping you could tell me," Eleanor said. "Did you get a look at the man?"

"The police have questioned me over and over again. He was tall, big shoulders, dark suit."

"That's it?" Eleanor couldn't hide her disappointment.

"There was something else. He said the strangest thing to me. It doesn't make a bit of sense, even though I remember it clearly."

"What?" Peter asked.

"He said, 'Tell my wife she's going to die.' I was almost unconscious, but I remember the words very clearly. It was almost as if he'd broken in here to deliver that message. But there's not a soul I can tell that message to, since I know all of my married friends' husbands.'' She looked at Peter. ''It was so strange. Just the memory makes my skin crawl. His eyes. I seem to remember the way his eyes were focused on me. 'Tell my wife she's going to die.' Terrible!''

Chapter Ten

In the floating light of passing cars, Peter examined Eleanor's face. She hadn't spoken a word since they left Magdalena's house. The strange and threatening message delivered by the older woman had had a paralyzing effect on her.

A million questions rose in his mind, but he kept his mouth closed. What was her involvement? He was beginning to strongly doubt that she knew anything about the lab break-in, Magdalena, Evans or anything else.

On the spur of the moment, he decided a simple test was in order.

"How about a moonlight drive?"

"What?" She turned to him, her ivory skin luminous in the passing headlights of the cars.

"I said how about a drive along the river? I know a nice, quiet place where we can talk. You said you had something to tell me."

"A drive would be fine." She looked away from him, lost in her own thoughts again.

"Pier 27 has a wonderful view of the city from the river. I have a friend with a houseboat."

"That's nice. I've never been on the river." She spoke like an automaton.

"Pier 27 is a great place." He was pushing her to make the connection.

She looked at him. "Then let's go."

Her reaction was completely innocent. He turned toward the river, hoping that he wasn't making a serious miscalculation. He wanted to check out the AFA rally. He'd wanted to find a branch of that organization for a long time. The AFA was intensely secret, and for good cause. Their activities had devastated a number of different research groups. If Eleanor was as innocent as she pretended, she was the perfect spy to send inside. The flyer was essentially an invitation. They'd be waiting, watching. Peter's spine tingled. He couldn't go because he might be recognized; Magdalena had almost remembered. But Eleanor was perfect.

"Peter, if a woman started seeing her dead ex-husband behind every bush and trash can, would you say that she might be having a nervous breakdown?"

Eleanor's question drew him from the tangle of his own thoughts. She was troubled; he hadn't realized the extent. "I don't know, Eleanor." He smiled at her, reaching over and pulling her against him. "I think you need a little species-to-species comforting."

In the darkness she smiled for the first time. "I think I do, too. But it isn't going to make what's happening around me go away. Today I called the newspaper and the police in Colorado. I had to ask them to make certain that Carter was dead."

Peter's shock was evident in the way he turned to face her, hands tightening on the steering wheel. "Why?"

"They assured me he was dead. Absolutely dead." Her voice began to tremble. "Even Carter's best friend believes he's dead."

"And you don't?"

"I did. Until he appeared in the apartment building parking garage."

"What are you saying?" He swerved to miss a car that had slowed.

"He was waiting for me. He came out of the shadows and he threatened me. He said he wasn't dead and that I had something he wanted."

"So that's why you freaked out and nearly ran over Joey." Understanding touched his face. His arm around her tightened slightly, giving a squeeze of reassurance. "Why didn't you say something before?"

Eleanor shook her head. "Because it sounded so crazy. I mean, listen to the things I've told you. Everything I say reverts to Carter. I sound obsessed. Even to myself. And now I'm claiming to see a dead man in a parking garage. That sounds crazy, even to me."

Peter wasn't certain what he thought, but he was certain how he felt. Eleanor Duncan was one of the sanest people he'd ever met.

"I don't think for a minute that you have a crazy bone in your body."

"That business with Magdalena. I think it was Carter, and I think the message was meant for me. He intends to kill me."

Peter pulled his car to the side of the road and cut the engine. Eleanor's fears were too big, too intense. He had to do something to alleviate her suffering. For the moment Pier 27 was forgotten.

"Why, Eleanor? Why would Carter want to do anything to hurt you? Why after nine years?"

"I've asked myself that question a million times."

"And?"

"And I get the same answer. I don't know. In the garage he said I'd taken something and he wanted it back."

"A deed, something like that?"

Eleanor shook her head. Peter's arm was the only comfort she had. Instead of talking, she wanted to burrow against his chest and rest. "There was nothing. Absolutely nothing. I've racked my brain."

Peter turned so that he could hold her in both arms. For a moment he cradled her against his chest. If this was the secret she'd been hiding, it certainly wasn't what he'd expected.

"If it isn't Carter, can you think of anyone who might want to impersonate him?"

"No," Eleanor whispered. "I even called his best friend. He thinks Carter is dead. I'm the only one with visions and doubts." She looked up at him. "I'm beginning to think I'm crazy."

"You're a long way from crazy, but the things that are happening around you are enough to make you question your sanity," he said angrily. "And I haven't been the greatest help!"

The night seemed to be closing in around her, and she cast a furtive glance out the window. "It isn't my imagination. He's real!"

"When I was looking around your car after I found you so scared in the garage, the only thing I found was a cigarette stub," Peter said.

"Dunhill, right?" Eleanor asked. There was a hopeless tone in her voice.

When Peter didn't answer she turned to him. "It was Dunhill, wasn't it?"

He nodded. "You really aren't part of the movement that stole those cats, are you?"

She drew back from him. "Of course not." Her eyes widened. "But you never really believed me, did you?"

"I did and I didn't. That isn't important now. Listen, we'll have to resolve this business about your dead husband, but first I need your help. There's a meeting at Pier 27. I'd like you to go." He smiled at her, bending to kiss her forehead. Maybe his scheme would help, after all. There was no telling who might show up for the get-together. Maybe even the person who was trying to drive her crazy.

"What kind of help?"

"We have to get to the bottom of all of this, and I have a really sneaky feeling that once we find out who broke into that lab, we'll find out why your 'dead' husband is wandering around threatening people."

"Do you really think so?" Eleanor's face brightened. "I've tried to make a connection between all of this and Familiar, but so far I haven't been able to."

"It has to be related. And we have to find out how."

He put the car into Drive and they sped toward the river.

"What do you want me to do?"

"Go to the meeting." He filled her in on the flyer someone had planted in her office. "Act like you're one of the people who want to blow up labs. See who's there. Observe everything you can."

"Why don't you go?"

"Someone might recognize me."

"As a vet?"

"Eleanor, my dear, you aren't the only one with a long past." He gave her a rakish grin. "We don't have time for more secrets. We're there and we're late."

He pulled into a parking space by a chain link fence. Pier 27 was a series of connected walkways that made a small marina. Along the river, the lights of Washington shone like a condensed Milky Way. Reflected on the chill water, the boat lights gave the night a festive atmosphere.

"Look—" Eleanor pointed out the window "—it's Christmas!"

Colored lights were strung up the mast of several sailboats, and there were Santas and wreaths and trees on many decks.

"I'd almost forgotten about the holidays," Peter said. "We've had a lot on our minds. But tomorrow, barring any unforeseen disasters, why don't we get a tree and decorate it?"

"A fir?" Eleanor asked, suddenly taken with the idea. The thought of hanging ornaments in the warmth and safety of her own apartment held great appeal.

"If that makes you happy," he said, smiling in the dark. He compressed his lips again as he studied the boats. He picked out the one listed as the scene of the meeting and pointed it out to Eleanor.

"Just look around and listen? That's all I do?"

"And be careful." He leaned across the seat and kissed her. Her lips were as soft as he'd ever imagined. "Be very careful."

The feel of his kiss still tingling on her lips, Eleanor hurried toward the houseboat. The boards of the pier were well lighted, and she ran toward the soft sound of water lapping against the hull. What was it about Peter's past that prevented him from attending the meeting? That was a thought to ponder. She'd been so preoccupied with her past, she'd failed to consider his.

At the walkway to the houseboat she paused. Casting a look toward Peter, she stepped aboard. Something about the boat made her cautious. She didn't want to walk into a room of people she didn't know. First she'd do a little eavesdropping.

The murmur of voices came to her from inside. Inching forward, she strained to hear. A coil of rope nearly tripped her, but she recovered and eased around the deck toward the windows. Peering through the glass, she saw a group of eight people evenly split between men and women. They didn't appear to be desperadoes. Instead, they were earnestly listening to a tall, distinguished woman who was standing at a blackboard.

Eleanor crept closer and pressed her fingers to the windowsill. By holding her breath she could hear.

"Since Magdalena couldn't be here tonight, we'll delay the plans on deciding about the Behavioral Institute. As you know, she was strongly in favor of additional action."

Eleanor slipped down the window and huddled in a small bundle against the wall. Magdalena had lied to her all along. No wonder no one believed her innocence when she proclaimed it! Magdalena, her new acquaintance, was in the thick of everything!

The voices were an indistinguishable rumble, and she had to force herself back to the windowsill. To hear, she had to squat on her toes and cling to the wooden frame with all of her might. She pressed her body to the task, holding her breath once again.

"She's positively identified him," the woman said. There was pride and concern in her voice. "After nearly fifteen years, we have a good chance of bringing him to justice."

"Here in Washington?" a man asked. When his question was met with an affirmative nod, he added caustically, "He has nerve."

"I'm not so certain we should trust this to the authorities," another man said.

Eleanor felt her fingertips begin to tear loose from her hands. She was in terrible pain, but couldn't afford to stop listening.

She sucked in a lungful of air.

"No bombs!" the woman leading the discussion insisted. "I'm sure if Magdalena were here, she'd agree with me. No human, not even him, should be hurt."

"But if we don't stop him, he'll continue with his experiments. No one else will even try to put an end to it. He's working for the government, after all!" There was frustration in the man's voice.

"I know," the woman replied, and there were murmurs of agreement from the other people. "It would give me great satisfaction to know that Evans is permanently...incapacitated. But so much better for us is the idea of a trial and public exposure. Think of it that way. He must survive, so that we can use him to educate the public to the cruel and inhuman treatment one scientist without morality can inflict on helpless creatures."

In the round of applause the woman's words gathered, Eleanor finally had to let her grasp go. She sank to the deck in a huddle, nursing her sore hands, bursting lungs and strained legs. She'd heard plenty.

As soon as she could breath normally, she started inching her way back to the pier. The coil of rope caught her again, sending her flailing to the hard deck. Cursing silently to herself, she scurried back to her feet and aimed for the gangplank.

Movement along the pier caught her eye. She ducked behind a metal cylinder, praying that it was someone late for the meeting. They'd be more interested in getting inside than snooping around the deck.

Chancing another look, she moved so that she could see the figure on the dock. It took something from its coat, a small bundle, examined it for a moment, then leaned back and pitched it toward the houseboat.

To Eleanor's horror, the object landed beside her with a thud, then bounced several feet away. Some primitive instinct for survival shot through her. She knew what it was without even taking the time to look. Crawling toward where she'd heard it fall, she frantically searched the deck. Her hands banged on metal cleats and polished wood, but she felt nothing. She moved forward, fanning her hands in front of her, praying a wordless prayer for deliverance.

Her fingers closed on the bundle. It seemed to be tape and plastic. Nothing much. Surely not a bomb. Stifling a scream that welled unexpectedly in her throat, she threw the object as far into the river as she could. With the sound of the splash, she dropped instinctively to the deck and covered her head with her hands.

The explosion seemed to rumble from beneath the dark water, creating a wave that washed over the deck and sent the boat rocking furiously.

Eleanor grabbed the coil of rope and clung. The deck tipped, and the force of the water tried to suck her over the side. Her hands stubbornly held to the thick rope, and she kicked her legs against the pull of the water.

The boat rocked viciously from side to side several times, and then settled down to a mild keeling.

There was no time to waste. Eleanor scrambled to her knees, then regained her feet. The pier was empty, the figure long gone. A sudden fury gave her legs the needed energy, and she ran across the wet and slippery deck to the pier. Almost jumping the gangplank, she raced toward Peter and the car.

Lights were coming on as other river residents left their craft to see what had happened. Someone would call an ambulance if people were injured. Eleanor didn't have time. She had to catch the person on the pier. He or she was the missing link that would solve the acts of violence that seemed to surround her. With Peter's help she could catch the culprit.

"Hurry!" she panted as she threw herself into the passenger seat.

Peter was leaning back, his head resting against the driver's door.

She touched his shoulder. "Wake up, Peter!" She couldn't believe he'd slept through the explosion. "Peter?"

She reached to touch his face and her hand slipped in the sticky wetness of blood.

"Oh, no!" She gently felt his face, fingers seeking the wound. On the far side of his head she found the gash where he'd been struck.

Near the water the residents of the boats were beginning to create a bigger and bigger commotion. In the distance the wail of sirens split the dark night into fragments of danger. Scanning the waterfront, Eleanor saw that no fires had broken out along the river. She turned her attention back to Peter. He was moaning softly and beginning to move.

"Peter," she whispered, slipping out of the car and dashing around to the driver's side. With a great deal of effort she was able to move him enough so that she could get behind the wheel. The car started with no problem, and she carefully drove away from the pier. She had no desire to be caught in the questioning of authorities, especially not when she'd have to admit that she'd been trespassing and once again in the shadow of some group involving animals.

Peter stirred, sitting up and touching his head.

"Where are you going?"

"The hospital."

"Make it my clinic. I'm not hurt."

"There's blood all over you." She didn't feel in the mood to argue. She wasn't trained to gauge the possible complications of a blow to the head.

"No hospital."

There was no arguing with his tone, so Eleanor changed the subject as she charted a course toward Washington.

"What happened?" she asked.

"I heard an explosion, and I was getting out of the car to go to you when something struck my head. I didn't see the guy until it was too late."

"Did you see him?" Eleanor felt a surge of excitement.

"He was tall. He threw the bomb onto the houseboat where the meeting was."

"He what?" Peter's jerking reaction made him touch his head again. "What are you talking about?"

"I was coming back to tell you what I heard, when I saw the man on the pier. He threw something on the houseboat, and somehow I knew it was a bomb. I picked it up and threw it into the water."

"A bomb?" Peter heard the words, but the full meaning hadn't yet registered. One hand gripped the dashboard and the other touched her shoulder. "Are you hurt? You're dripping wet."

"There was a big wave, but I don't think anyone was really hurt. It couldn't have been a very big bomb." She had to make light of it. Peter was frightening her with the way he was acting. In all of the confusion, she'd never considered that she might actually have died.

"You saved those people's lives," Peter said.

"Only by chance."

Peter's hand tightened on her shoulder. The full implication of what had occurred struck him. Eleanor had been set up, and she could have died. "Was the bomb intended for them—or for you?"

Eleanor felt the wheel wrenched from her hand as the car slipped off the edge of the pavement onto the shoulder. She jerked it back onto the road, but her heart was hammering as the words Magdalena had spoken only a few hours earlier came back to her. The man had said he was going to kill his wife.

"Peter," she whispered, her voice breaking.

"It isn't your 'dead' husband. If he did this, he's very much alive. And whatever he wants, it has something to do with that cat. Let's go see Familiar. I checked him thoroughly, but there may be the chance that something is hidden on him. We'll take X rays."

"I never considered such a thing," Eleanor admitted.

"And all of this has begun since Familiar came into your life." Peter's own excitement began to rise. "The key is

Familiar. If only we can decipher what it is he has, or is connected to, that everyone seems perfectly willing to kill for.''

"This has all seemed such a hopeless muddle to me," Eleanor confessed. "But who would want to kill a boat full of people whose biggest interest is to protect animals? That's insane!"

"I couldn't agree more," Peter said. "But there are a few insane people out there." His jaw tightened.

"Magdalena is a member of that group," Eleanor told him. She couldn't hide her sense of betrayal.

To her complete amazement, Peter laughed.

"That Magdalena, she's a sly fox. No wonder Charles Breck comes at her beck and call."

"What are you talking about?" she demanded. "She as good as lied to me."

"She did lie to me, flatly," Peter said, but he laughed again. "It's just that she's learned to be very cautious."

"I don't find this very amusing. She dragged me down to that lab with her, and I was guilty by association!"

"In that instance she didn't do you any favors," Peter agreed. The humor was gone from his voice.

"She could have planted that flyer in my office."

Peter was silent for a long time. "She could have, but so could anyone else that got hold of it."

"Yeah, great. Did they want to invite me, frame me or blow me up?" Eleanor asked dryly.

Peter leaned over and kissed her cheek. "The first thing I loved about you was your sense of humor."

"Well, if this keeps up, that and everything else about me may get blown to bits."

She pulled into Peter's clinic. Under the bright light of an examining lamp, she could tell that the blow to his head wasn't as serious as it had first appeared. Once the blood was washed away, she was satisfied that he didn't need a doctor. They went straight to her apartment building.

"I can't wait to get out of these clothes," Eleanor said, tugging at the still-damp sweater. She pulled into an illegal parking zone. "Let them tow it tonight. I don't care."

"Look," Peter said, stepping onto the sidewalk and pointing to the doorway of her building. Two policemen were standing guard, and patrol cars were parked on the street.

"I hope there hasn't been an accident," Eleanor said. A sick feeling settled into her stomach. "It's gotten to the point that I can't see a policeman without thinking something else bad has happened around me."

"Paranoia," Peter said.

Dodging traffic, they ran across the street.

"Name and address." The biggest patrolman stepped forward to block their entrance to the building.

"Eleanor Duncan, 919. What's wrong?"

The policemen looked at each other. "The captain is waiting to see you, ma'am. Step this way."

"What is it?" Eleanor asked.

She and Peter found themselves escorted to the elevator. The policemen refused to even look at them as they rode to the ninth floor.

"What's going on?" Eleanor demanded.

"Officer, is there some trouble?" Peter asked.

"The captain will explain it," the patrolman said. He stepped aside so that they could walk down the corridor.

The confusion spilled out of Eleanor's apartment into the hall. Her neighbors were standing in their doorways, murmuring and watching. Plainclothes detectives came and went, and at last an older, grizzled man approached her.

"Detective Jones," he said, rubbing his chin.

"What happened?" Eleanor tried to look past the detective, but couldn't see anything inside her apartment except figures hurrying around.

"I'm afraid there's been a murder." He looked at her sharply. "You wouldn't know about that, would you?"

"Murder? Who?" Eleanor felt Peter's arm slip around her and hold her.

"We're not certain. Maybe you could identify the body for us." He rubbed his chin again. "Middle-aged man, short, wiry."

Eleanor shook her head. "No one should have been in my apartment. I left it locked."

Slowly she stepped toward the door. Peter touched the detective's sleeve.

"What happened?"

"The man was sitting on the sofa. Someone came in and shot him in the heart. Twice."

Eleanor pushed past the officers at the door and walked in.

"Rayburn!" she cried. "Rayburn!" She ran toward the body, which was still sitting on the sofa. "Oh, no!"

Peter hurried after her, crushing her against himself and drawing her away from the terrible sight.

"You'll have to come down to the precinct, Dr. Duncan," Winston Jones said. "Does this Rayburn have a last name?"

"Smith," she mumbled, dazed. "Rayburn Smith."

A stretcher was brought in to remove the body. Peter led Eleanor back to the hallway.

"He's been dead at least two hours," Jones said. "Shot with a .22 pistol, if my guess is correct."

"Familiar!" Eleanor roused herself and looked at Peter with widened eyes.

"Her cat," Peter explained.

"What have you done to my cat?" Eleanor demanded.

"We've poked in every nook and cranny of that apartment. There's no cat," Jones said.

Chapter Eleven

Free at last, free at last. But not exactly the way I had it planned. This is not actually freedom, it's enforced escape. Where is Eleanor? Her pad is getting to be a regular Grand Central Station of disreputable characters crashing in and out. As we speak, there's some yo-yo parked in the middle of her sofa, acting as nervous as a man on a hot tin roof. He practically reeks of trouble. He doesn't seem to be the threatening type, at least not to my Eleanor. He's more the "I've got a big, bad secret" type of trouble. He didn't seem the friendly sort, and he left the door ajar. My instincts told me to strike while the iron was hot. Once an alley cat, always an alley cat. An open door is an invitation to adventure. Well, that was once true, but now it isn't necessarily so. I don't really want to leave her. It's a matter of principle. Right now, though, I've got to concentrate on this road and get across before I become a blot on the pavement of life. At least it's late. Traffic is much slower than it was the other day.

Whew! That little Datsun almost got me. I know it's hard to see a black cat on a black night. But what am I supposed to do? Stand in the middle of the road so that my eyes reflect the headlights? Sure! Then I'd have to change my name to Kamikaze. People! If they could really see at night like us cats, then they wouldn't be such a menace behind the wheel of a car.

Now let's see. Best I can remember, Eleanor brought me this way when we left the university. Yeah, I remember the smell of that little Italian restaurant. I wonder... Naw! no time for gourmet raiding tonight. Besides, I have to confess, Eleanor feeds me so well, I've sort of lost my yen for foraging through ritzy leftovers. Too rich. Not really well balanced. I have to say, the dame takes good care of me. I hope she isn't too upset when she finds I'm gone. She relies on me, you know. She may not know it, but she does. Sometimes when she strokes my back, I feel all this tenderness. I've often wondered why she lives alone, no little rug monsters. I've wondered—and given many thanks. I guess as long as she's got me, she doesn't really need children.

That's one of the things that keeps troubling me. She's going to be devastated when she finds I'm gone. No time for a note, even. I'll just have to take care of business and get back as soon as possible. I know that promise sounds empty to a lot of people owned by cats. See, cats get a bum rap about leaving without a trace. I've heard so many owners moaning and crying, "He just disappeared one day." Well, there's more to that story. We aren't fickle by nature. But a cat has to do what a cat has to do! It's a law of cat physics. The problem is that once we get it done, sometimes we can't get back. Life isn't simple anymore. There used to be dogs, a few birds of prey, other, bigger cats, a handful of rare predators that stood between a cat and his natural behavior. Now, think about it! Millions of cars, billions of people. Those rascals in the white coats that snatch an honest cat off the street and sell him into hell. Getting home isn't as easy as it used to be. But I'll get back here. For the dame I'll do what has to be done, and then I'll come back and devote the rest of my life to purring for her. That's a sol-

emn vow. Running around Washington on a cold winter night isn't what it used to be. I must have covered five miles!

And lo and behold, it looks like the old university campus. My instincts, as ever, are completely correct. From here I can find my bearings and get back to the lab. It'll take some doing, but I'm sure I can get there. And after that? Well, a determined cat knows no boundaries, as my grandmother, this incredible pitch-black feline with a long history of Egyptian blood, used to tell me. Now she was a wise mama. I'm going to rest a while under this shrub and give the old "dogs" a break. Hey, hey! I'm getting pretty good at this pun routine. I wonder if David Letterman is ready for a new segment. Superior Pet Tricks. I'll bet, with a few weeks of training, I could have even him twirling can openers and winding cat toys. Well, that's a challenge to think about during a little catnap.

"I HAVE TO FIND FAMILIAR." Eleanor knew she sounded like an unreasonable child, but as long as she kept hunting, she could hold her emotions at bay. She didn't know what she felt anymore. Not even about Peter.

In the initial questioning by Detective Jones, Peter had blithely lied about where they'd been. He'd told the police they were walking The Mall and a mugger had struck his head. And she'd gone along with it. Why?

Why hadn't Peter told the truth about the houseboat?

"Where do you want to look now?" Peter asked. They'd covered the building from the top floor to the garage. Familiar was gone. They were standing at the front door, scouting the busy street. Eleanor's clothes were still damp, but she refused to go into her apartment to change. At least there were no dead animals on the roadside. Eleanor couldn't have taken that. They both held plastic cups of coffee provided by Wessy.

"I don't know," Eleanor answered. "Do you think whoever...killed Rayburn...took Familiar?"

"It's a strong possibility." And if that were the case, then they might already have what they wanted. Peter was more and more certain that the black feline held a valuable secret.

"What was Rayburn doing in Washington?" she asked aloud, though the question was meant only for herself. "Maybe he was trying to warn me."

"When you talked with him, did he say anything?" Peter asked. Detective Jones had not been able to make a bit of headway questioning her. "Did he say anything about visiting Washington?"

"No." She was distant and withdrawn once again. She couldn't think about Rayburn—about how he'd be alive if she hadn't called him. Code One Orange. She'd forced him to talk about it. Now he was dead. Who had Rayburn told about their conversation? It had to be someone he knew, because she'd told no one about her conversation with Rayburn.

The pieces of the puzzle rattled together in her head like dice in a gambler's cup. The research on animal communication stolen—her office rifled and a flyer on animal activists planted—the reappearance of her "dead" husband—Peter—and Familiar. Always Familiar.

"You think Familiar is dead, too, don't you?" she asked.

"Eleanor, I said I don't know." Peter touched her shoulder. Her face reflected deep misery. "If we were right about the cat, if he carries some secret information, then he may well be dead. And the man in your apartment might have died trying to get that information."

"That's ridiculous," Eleanor snorted. "Rayburn was penny-ante. Besides, he didn't know a thing about Familiar or any of the other stuff."

"So what was he doing in Washington?" Peter turned her so she faced him. "In your apartment?"

She pulled away from him, suddenly furious. "Don't act as if I killed him. Remember, I was with you. Walking around The Mall!" She stalked away from him, not caring that the night was bitter and her clothes clung to her clammy skin.

"What aren't you telling me?" he called after her. "What did you tell him, to motivate him to fly to see you after nine years?"

She whirled, confronting him. "What am I withholding? That's a fine question, coming from you. What is it that you have to gain? You picked up that flyer from my office and didn't tell me. That behavior might have cost me my life, as it turned out." She stepped behind him and started back to her building. She had to get away from him. "I'm going home, and I suggest you do the same."

"You can't go back there." He knew the bloodstained sofa would be her undoing. "Come back to my place and spend the night. Until your apartment can be cleaned."

"Go to hell," she answered, stepping briskly toward the door. "I was a fool to ever think I might—" she turned to look at him "—trust anyone. I mean really trust."

She stepped inside and hurried across the lobby toward the elevator. Peter knew there was no need to follow her. She'd never let him in. She might never talk to him again. And the worst part of it was that her accusations were perfectly justified. He had kept things from her.

He scanned the black night, wishing against all odds that by some dark magic he could conjure up that damned cat. Familiar! There was little doubt in his mind that the animal was dead. That was one feline too smart to voluntarily leave Eleanor's care.

Pulling up his collar against a blast of wind, he went to his car. He couldn't talk to Eleanor, but there were several questions he wanted to put to Magdalena Caruso, and he was willing to bet a hefty chunk of his savings that the short animal rights advocate was not tucked snugly in bed. Not on her conniving little life!

TRY AS SHE WOULD, Eleanor could not make herself enter the empty apartment. No cat, no friendly greetings. She leaned against the wall of the hallway in front of her door and almost gave in to her tears. She'd move! It was that simple. There were other buildings, even other cities, if it got down to it. Once the police were through with her about Rayburn, she'd pack the few things she really wanted and move on. But for tonight? She went back to the elevator, down to the house phone and dialed Betty Gillette.

"I've had some trouble," she said as soon as Betty answered. "Can I come over?"

"Lovers' quarrel?" Betty asked, shaking the sleep from her voice. "This is great. We'll pretend we're living in a dormitory and we can talk about it all night. That way, when school reopens, we'll be better able to communicate with our students."

"I'm sorry, Betty. It's pretty serious."

"Hey, I'm the one who's sorry. I always have to be the wise guy, and you sound really upset. Come on over. I'll put some hot tea on for us."

Eleanor resolved to stop at a convenience store on the way to her friend's house. She had no intention of entering her apartment, not even for a toothbrush.

With her purchases in a brown paper bag, she knocked at Betty's door.

"What is it?" Betty asked, hurrying her inside. "You look dreadful. What'd you do, take a swim in the fountains and then volunteer for Chinese water torture treatments?"

"Almost," Eleanor said. Her voice broke several times as she told her friend about Rayburn Smith's violent death.

"What have you gotten into, Eleanor?"

"I wish I knew. Betty, I needed to talk with you, but I also need to talk with your friend, Alva Rousel. Do you know how to reach him?"

"He's working out of a house not too far from here. It's a cover house, so he told me never to go there."

"Maybe tomorrow?" Eleanor suggested. She was suddenly too exhausted to talk further.

"Absolutely."

Eleanor found herself grinning wryly. "And that's only the half of it. I forgot to tell you about the bomb on the riverboat."

"What?" She saw Betty's face blanch.

"I was checking out this group of animal lovers for Peter, and someone tried to blow up the houseboat. I grabbed the bomb and threw it into the water."

"Eleanor!" Betty grasped her arm tightly. "You could have been killed. All of them could have been."

"I think that was the general idea. But the thing is, I don't know if the bomb was meant to blow up the people on the houseboat or me or both." She felt the tears rising and turned away. "Could I crash on your sofa? I really can't go back to my apartment."

"Let me get a blanket," Betty said. She was trembling. "You've been through it, girl."

"I just need a few hours sleep, and then I'm going to get up and find my cat."

"Familiar's missing, too?"

Eleanor nodded. "But I'll find him. He's a really special cat. Peter thinks he's dead, but I know he isn't. I can sense that he's alive. I'll find him tomorrow."

"You bet," Betty said, tucking the blanket around Eleanor. "You bet."

"WERE YOUR FRIENDS HURT?" Peter stood on the steps at Magdalena's. He didn't wait for her to invite him in. Just as he suspected, she was up and dressed, her coat flung over one arm in her hurry to leave.

"Your timing is incredibly bad," she said, opening the door to admit him. "I expected to see you, but not tonight." She scanned his face, gauging his anger. "You aren't as mad as I expected you to be."

"Oh, I was safely in the car, knocked on the head. It was Eleanor who took the big risk. She was nearly blown to bits." His voice was as cutting as the lash of a whip.

"Eleanor! Is she hurt?" Magdalena grabbed the back of a chair. "How did she get involved in all of this? You said you were going."

"So I'm the one that you thought would get hurt." Peter shook his head in disbelief. "I knew you were an extremist, but I never guessed how far you'd go."

"I didn't think you'd get hurt! Not you or anyone else. Don't be a complete fool." Magdalena pulled him inside and closed the door. "I need to go and check on a few of the AFA members. They aren't hurt badly, just shaken up. How is Eleanor?"

"She saw the man throw the bomb, and she picked it up and threw it in the river. If it hadn't been for her, all of them would be dead."

The coat slipped from Magdalena's nerveless hand to the floor. "I can't believe this has happened."

"Why not? You've clamored for open war for years. Well, now we have it. I only want to know why you wanted me to go to that meeting. Why you lied to me about being a member."

"Because I know who you are, and I wanted the other members to meet you. Some of them still believe you're as guilty as Evans. I wanted you to have a chance to tell them the truth." She took a breath. "But I didn't leave that flyer in Eleanor's office. When you found it, I just didn't try and stop you from making your assumptions."

Instead of an attempt at a frame, she had thought she was giving him an opportunity. His temper dropped several degrees. "How long have you known about my past?"

"Just recently. I put it together when I saw you at Brenniton's. I really wasn't certain then. Almost, but not a hundred percent. Then I checked the old records and easily picked up your trail."

"Why?" He barely breathed the word.

"Arnold Evans has resurfaced."

His breath left him in a hiss. "So you know. Have you located him yet?"

"He's in Washington." Her smile was tight with victory. "I spoke with him recently, face-to-face."

"Impossible!"

"Quite the contrary. Eleanor spoke with him, too. That's what got me thinking about you. Once I saw Evans, then I began to remember the whole story and I recognized you."

"Where is he?" Peter asked. His hands were clenched at his sides. "I want to know where he is."

"So what, so you can beat him up?" Magdalena's smile grew cold. "We don't want him hurt, we want him behind bars."

"Evans nearly ruined my life. He tried to kill me and frame me for horrendous things!" Peter's words were thick with anger.

"I know all of that. But when you start condemning me for using you a little, think what you've been doing. Isn't it the same? You latched on to Eleanor because you thought she could lead you into a group of activists. You had your own agenda to follow. It's true, I used her, too. We're both equally guilty."

Her words were harsh, but essentially true. The last of the anger went out of Peter like a match being snuffed.

"At first," Peter admitted, "I did think she was involved in some of the raids. That cat had a catheter in his leg. The catheter had a distinctive mark, a notch that was exactly like Arnold used. Like a personal brand." He shook his head. "I wanted to find Evans so badly, I willingly used Eleanor. But now it's gotten out of hand. A man was killed in her apartment tonight."

"Who?"

"Some guy from Colorado named Rayburn Smith. He was a friend of her ex-husband. He was shot on her sofa."

"How is he involved?" Magdalena asked. "His name isn't one I recognize."

"Maybe he got caught in the cross fire, sort of like Eleanor. The thing that troubles me now is that we've both been so good at setting Eleanor up, maybe someone out there believes she's really guilty of something."

"If you're right . . ."

"She could be hurt." Peter withdrew his keys from his pocket. "Where is Evans?"

"The Behavioral Institute. I saw him the night I went there with Breck and Eleanor."

"So close." Peter walked away from her. He paced the room, his eyes lowered in concentration. "How could the creep be so close and I didn't even know it?"

"In a sense, Eleanor has been crucial in bringing you to him. If she hadn't picked up that cat and brought it to your office, then you'd never know this."

"That doesn't make me feel any better." Thin lines of anger tightened his mouth. "All of this time Evans has been under my nose. What name is he using?"

"Vrenner. Cal Vrenner. I did a little checking, and I'm sure he must be laughing at us all. The real Cal Vrenner died years ago. He was one of the leading animal activists in West Germany. Evans has not only stolen his name, he's done it to be cute."

"I'm warning you, Magdalena. Keep your group away from Evans. He's mine. And he owes me a large personal debt."

Magdalena approached Peter, raising one hand. "Think about what you're saying. There are several members of ARSA and AFA who want to see Evans disappear. Forever."

"I would like nothing better myself," Peter declared.

"I could get a lot more vivid and graphic in what I'd like to do to him, but we can't afford it." There was an urgency in Magdalena's voice. "We want him punished, publicly. And we can't do anything to risk messing that up."

"So that's why you broke into the lab," Peter said.

Magdalena shook her head emphatically. "We tracked him for years, and we finally ran him to ground. Then an outside agent raided the lab. We didn't expect it, and to be honest, it threw a monkey wrench into our plans. The cats were stolen, several of them in bad condition. Familiar obviously escaped."

"Who raided the lab?" The question had been gnawing at Peter since he'd given up all thought that it was Eleanor.

"We aren't really certain."

"I'm not in the mood for games," Peter threatened. "Eleanor is boxed into a bad position. Who robbed that lab? I'm not going to let her take a fall for something she didn't do."

"We haven't been able to pin it down. I swear, it wasn't someone from ARSA or AFA. A wild-card striker is the best we can figure. I promise I'll tell you when we find out. If we find out. We're running mailing lists to see if we can match a person with the place and time. We have no real idea who did it."

Peter believed her, and it only deepened his worries. "There are a lot of things happening around Eleanor that no one can explain. She thinks that warning you got when you were attacked was meant for her."

"That's impossible. Her husband is dead," Magdalena asserted.

"Tell it to her. She thinks she saw him in her parking garage, and he seems to be threatening her."

"What is going on?" Magdalena walked to a crochet-covered rocker. Gently pushing two cats aside, she saw down. "Dead men walking, labs raided, Evans resurrected and back in business. I'm getting too old for all of this."

"Well, if we don't figure it out, Eleanor won't get a chance to grow much older. I'm really worried about her. When the CIA agent showed up, I honestly believed she was guilty. Now I don't know what's going on."

Acting twenty years older than when she'd first sat down, Magdalena rose. "I have to get down to the emergency room."

"No serious injuries among your colleagues?"

"No, apparently thanks to Eleanor."

"By the way, Familiar's missing. I'm afraid whoever killed Rayburn Smith might have taken the cat."

"Oh, Familiar," Magdalena sighed. "He looked like a perfectly common old tom cat. He's certainly spiced up Eleanor's life, but why would anyone take him?"

"Eleanor and I believe he carries a clue."

"Something that fiend Evans did to him, no doubt!" Magdalena exclaimed. "I was the SPCA worker who was sent to examine what was left of Evans's experiments at International Chem-Co. The carnage was unbelievable." She looked at him. "You were accused of the fire and the atrocities. I saw the news clips where you were led out of the smoldering building, and I hated you."

Her words brought back the past. Peter remembered the lab, the inhumanity he'd discovered. 1977. "When I confronted Evans, he lost his mind. He attacked me, knocked me unconscious and then tried to burn down the laboratory. He'd already changed the records to try and put the blame on me for all of the atrocities done to the animals.''

Magdalena nodded slowly. "For a while it looked as if you were guilty. But you cleared your name. And Evans disappeared underground.''

The stir of emotions created a pounding headache in the back of Peter's head. "I quit vet school for two years after the fire. I couldn't accept what had happened, what Evans had done.'' He paced the room again. "I was almost finished with my degree. I had three weeks left in the summer to work at the chemical company. Three weeks, and I stumbled on Arnold's experiments.''

A worried look crossed Magdalena's face. "Have you revealed any of this to Eleanor?''

"No.'' The word was spoken in a near whisper.

"You have to tell her, Peter. Before she finds out about it from someone else. She must hate me, knowing that I've lied to her. If she finds that you've betrayed her, it might break her heart. I see the way she looks at you. It's something rare and special. Don't lose it.''

Magdalena's words created a sudden panic in Peter's blood that mingled with the pounding in his head. He'd been a fool to leave her alone in her apartment building. If they could find her on a houseboat, then . . .

"I'd better talk with her now,'' he said, heading for the door.

"Good idea,'' Magdalena said. "And ask her to forgive me. My deception was never malicious.'' She had her hand on the front door when the bell rang. She pulled the door open.

"Magdalena Caruso?'' a uniformed officer asked.

"Yes,'' she answered.

"Please come with us.'' He took her arm and signaled to his partner, who appeared from the side of the house.

"What is this about?" Peter asked. He didn't like the way they were hauling at Magdalena's arm.

"You have the right to remain silent—" the officer said, beginning the litany of the Miranda rights.

"What's the charge?" Peter interrupted.

Bewildered, Magdalena looked from one to the other. At last she jerked her arm so suddenly that she was free. "What is the charge?" she demanded.

"First-degree murder of Rayburn Smith."

Chapter Twelve

Peter recognized the tall, slender figure and stepped out from behind a column near The Hub. "Wait up," he called to Eleanor as he started to jog. "I looked all over for you last night. I've been here since eight this morning, waiting for you." With all of the worry about her, it had been the longest night of his life.

"You aren't the only person I know in town," she said, never slackening her pace. He drew abreast and she finally looked at him. "And you're the last person I want to see."

"Magdalena's been arrested for the murder of that man in your apartment."

Those words worked like hydraulic brakes. Eleanor stopped so fast that she nearly fell over.

"Magdalena? Charged with murder? What kind of joke is that?"

She was still wary of him. Peter saw it clearly in her eyes. The brown depths that had once reflected such trust now harbored only suspicion.

"I wish it were a joke," he said softly. "The police checked the murder weapon that was left in your apartment. It was registered to Magdalena. In fact, it's probably one of the few registered guns in town," he added dryly.

"Any fool could see that the gun has been planted," Eleanor said hotly.

"I'm glad you can defend Magdalena, even after she held things back from you." He let that point sink in. "I'm hoping you'll be able to get over your anger at me and let me explain."

"Both of you used me for your own reasons." Mixed with the anger was pain. "It doesn't matter. As soon as I find Familiar I'm leaving Washington."

"Leaving? To go where?"

"Someplace different. Someplace where I can try and start again. I don't know what you got me mixed up in, you and Magdalena, but whatever is it, I can't live in it. I want my own life, my own past." She turned away. "Tell Magdalena I'm sorry, but there's nothing I can do to help her. It's a bitter irony, but I really am innocent."

"I know that." Peter touched her arm, his fingers circling the delicate flesh until he stopped her and pulled her to face him. "Now," he added. "At first I didn't believe you."

"Better late than never." She tried to harden her tone, but it wasn't working very effectively. There was a dangerous crack.

"You can help Magdalena."

"How?"

"Tell me everything that happened the night you went to the Behavioral Institute. What did you observe about the man calling himself Cal Vrenner? What about the facilities? What did Breck say? How did he react to Vrenner? What exactly are they doing in that building?"

"Why is this suddenly so important?" She looked at him and saw his intensity, something had aged him. He wasn't playing games. He was really worried.

"I spent most of last night trying to find you, and the rest of it trying to get in at the jail to talk with Magdalena, but I couldn't. You're the only one who can answer these questions for me."

"Why should I?"

"Cal Vrenner is really a man I knew years ago called Arnold Evans. He tried to kill me, and he framed me for some pretty horrible experiments. I've been actively looking for him for the past three months, after his picture turned up in a pet care magazine."

"I saw that! In your office!" Eleanor's eyes grew luminous. "The man looked like someone I knew, but the name was wrong. It was Vrenner!"

"Let's go to your office. I want you to tell me everything you remember."

"And you'll tell me about Vrenner—I mean Evans."

"I'll tell you everything," Peter agreed. Eleanor was looking at him, doubt still lingering in her eyes. He bent and briefly kissed her lips. The relief at seeing her was tremendous. His arms went around her, and she didn't resist. Her slender body pressed hesitantly against his, and he was suddenly aware of her vulnerability.

"Oh, Eleanor," he said. "I've been so worried about you. Last night I didn't know where you were. After the bomb I realized how much trouble you might be in, and that part of it was my fault."

"It's okay," she managed. She felt her own relief at Peter's return now that he was willing to explain his actions. The feeling of betrayal, which had attacked her all night, diminished slightly. There was still much to be settled, but it was good to see him, to feel his arms and lips.

She pulled back so that she could look at him. "Let's go to my office and get this straight. I do have a cat to find."

Reluctantly he broke the embrace. The chances of finding Familiar were slim to nothing, and he almost told her. Instead, he took her arm and linked it through his own. "Let me tell you about Evans." Arm in arm they walked across the campus, and he told her about the fire.

They had been in her office for several minutes, and he'd finished with his story. In the silence that followed, Eleanor put on a pot of coffee. Soon a rich aroma filled the room, while steam obscured the tall window, fogging the winter view of the nearly empty campus. "I'm ready now to tell you about Vrenner."

Peter took out a notebook. "I'm going to write down what you say, okay?"

She nodded.

"What was your reaction to this Vrenner?"

Eleanor pressed a finger across her lips as she thought. "I couldn't tell what he was thinking about me. Breck thought I was guilty and didn't bother to hide it. But Vrenner, or Evans, was unreadable. I remember his eyes, the way he stared at me. It was unnerving, but I didn't get any sort of animosity. Almost a total isolation, as if I were a different species, something he wanted to study further." A chill raced along her arms and she rubbed them. "He was creepy."

"Magdalena said the place was almost empty, right?"

"There was only the orangutan."

"Tell me about it," Peter prompted.

"It's a female, or at least it curtsies. Anyway, it's being trained by Evans as some gift to a head of state. Breck made the arrangements...."

"You'd think someone like Breck, with all of the surveillance equipment in the world at his fingertips, could break through a phony identity like Cal Vrenner!" Peter almost exploded. He dropped from the edge of the desk to the floor and started pacing. "Evans has been right here in this town, and no one's even bothered to notice. I mean the man is wanted for arson and attempted murder!" He threw himself into the chair. "I'm sorry for the outburst. It's extremely frustrating."

"I understand." Eleanor poured two cups of coffee and handed him a sky-blue mug. "Anyway, Breck hired Evans. I don't believe Breck ever said who the ape is to be given to, but he did say she was being given by some Nottingham person. I remember, because I always loved Robin Hood and hated the Sheriff of Nottingham." She sipped her coffee.

"The rest of the lab was empty?"

"As far as I could tell. There were these horrible, dirty cages. But whoever stole the cats must have gotten all the other animals. I think the ape was in a small back room. We didn't get to see it."

"Knowing Evans, you probably didn't want to see it. There's no telling what he's done to that poor animal. Well, now it's time to get to work." He rose.

"And do what?" Eleanor asked.

"I want you to find this Nottingham person and make an appointment. I'm going back to Magdalena's to see if I can find any clues. I'm certain the man who broke into her house and hit her also took her gun. She said she was pointing it at him when he struck her with the door. It's obvious to me that he took the gun, killed Rayburn Smith and then planted the weapon to frame Magdalena."

"My reasoning exactly," Eleanor agreed. "But what about Familiar?"

"Let's look for a while now," Peter suggested gently. He walked across to her and put an arm around her shoulder. "But please don't get your hopes up."

They searched near the library, where she'd first found the cat. They stopped every person on campus, but no one had noticed a black cat. Walking up and down along the shrubs, Eleanor softly called for the cat. After an hour of searching, she finally conceded that Familiar wasn't going to appear.

"Let's get on with the other stuff. I still haven't given up, though. I just need to think of another place to look. Where would he go if he were free? That's what I have to figure out," she said softly.

"If you can make an appointment with this Nottingham, do it."

"I'll start with a list of ambassadors, things like that."

"Don't call Breck's office," Peter cautioned her.

"Why not?"

"Just a hunch."

"You think he might be—?"

"I don't think anything," Peter interrupted. "Let's just keep our cards to ourselves. You have to admit, that guy he posted at your apartment building isn't very bright."

Alva Rousel had told her about Code One Orange, an obvious violation of CIA procedure. He'd even admitted that he talked too much. "Okay," Eleanor agreed. "I can't believe I'm doing this. I thought I told you when we first met that I didn't like games of espionage and intrigue."

"Well—" he grinned at her "—you obviously lied." Placing a kiss upon her cheek, he left.

Eleanor hustled to the library and went through a stack of governmental reference books before she found Nottingham listed.

"War hero in Vietnam, former CIA agent in Central America, ambassador to Motambu, now a congressman from Maine. Quite an illustrious career," she mumbled as she made notes. Her eyes went back to the CIA notation. Central America! Code One Orange! Rushing to the pay telephone outside the library, she called Peter's office, but he was in surgery.

She had no trouble obtaining Nottingham's office phone number and placed the call from her office, door firmly closed.

"Sam Nottingham," he said when he finally came on the line.

"Eleanor Duncan," she replied, matching his professional tone. "I'd like to see you about a female orangutan. It's vital."

"What?" The cultured voice was startled.

"No joke, Congressman."

"What is this about? I demand to know."

"I'm perfectly willing to discuss this with you. Set a meeting."

A thin edge of anger came into the man's voice. "This better not be some prank. Meet me in thirty minutes, at my office in the Cannon Building."

"I'll be there," Eleanor said. She checked her watch. She could just about make it there in half an hour, if she hurried.

She threw herself into the drive with the fervor of a cabby. Dayton Avenue seemed the most direct and fastest route, and she pushed her accelerator dangerously close to the floor as she drove. With less than a minute to spare, she found herself standing at Representative Nottingham's door.

"He's waiting for you," the receptionist told her with a disapproving look.

Frederick Nottingham was not what Eleanor expected. He was a man of medium height with a shock of prematurely white hair, and blue eyes that were surrounded by a dense web of lines. Another man, dressed in the dark blue suit of an administrative assistant, was sitting unobtrusively in a corner.

"I seldom meet with people who sound like kooks over the phone," he began. "Don't make me regret that I did so today."

"I'm not a kook," Eleanor said flatly. He hadn't offered her a seat, but she took one in front of his desk.

"I know about your gift, the orangutan." She hoped to shock him enough so that he'd listen.

The aide in the chair rose slowly to his feet.

"So?" Nottingham said, but a lot of the anger was gone from his voice. "It isn't a state secret that I intend to make a gift of her. Is there something wrong with that?"

"I don't know," Eleanor said. She leaned forward and placed her hands upon his desk. "I'm not certain of anything, except that the man who's training the ape is a wanted criminal."

"Dr. Vrenner?" Nottingham was clearly incredulous. "Don't be absurd. He has impeccable credentials. I think you should be leaving, Ms. Duncan." He waved at the aide, who appeared at Eleanor's elbow.

"Vrenner is an alias for a man named Arnold Evans. *His* record is anything but impeccable. Check it out." She felt the aide's hands on her arms, lifting her from the chair.

"Mr. Nottingham, be reasonable. Why would I come here and say these things? Why?"

"In the half hour since you called, I discovered that you are mixed up in some behavior that leaves a lot of questions in my mind. I don't know why you have chosen me to torment, but I won't have it. Now get out of my office, and I warn you, leave my orangutan alone!"

"At least check the Vrenner angle," Eleanor said. She was being propelled toward the door. "For your safety, check it," she told him, shooting the words over her shoulder before she found herself in the receptionist's office. The woman gave her a scathing look and pointed at the door.

Eleanor hesitated. She didn't know what to do. She hadn't been able to talk with Nottingham the way she'd wanted to. She had come off as some kind of nut. But where had he heard about her? Breck! That was the obvious connection. And because of Magdalena, Breck believed she was part of it all.

"If you don't leave, I'll call security," the receptionist said, picking up the phone.

"I'm going," Eleanor replied.

The phone on the desk buzzed. The receptionist answered it and turned back to Eleanor. Curiosity filled her eyes. "Representative Nottingham has asked that you meet him with Charles Breck and some others in the Capitol. Breck will be leaving the house gallery. Meet them in the outer chamber."

"When?" Eleanor felt a thrill of victory. Maybe Nottingham had made one call about Vrenner. That was all it would take.

"Immediately. You can take the tunnels and save time," the woman said. "Here." She handed her a pass. "Now hurry!" A note of excitement made her voice sound sharp.

Eleanor eyed the phone longingly. She wanted to call Peter to find what he'd learned about Magdalena. She had to give it a try! Ignoring the frosty glare of the receptionist, she borrowed the telephone. As before, Peter was not available.

"You're going to be late," the receptionist warned her.

"One more call." She dialed Betty Gillette. "Find Peter if you can, and tell him I'm meeting with Representative Sam Nottingham and Breck at the Capitol. We may get to the bottom of this monkey business," she said. "I can't talk anymore," she concluded, not giving Betty a chance to respond. She hung up.

Eleanor left Nottingham's office and took the elevator to the entrance to the tunnels. She'd heard about them, of course, but her one and only visit to Capitol Hill had been strictly as a tourist. There'd been no need to use the underground web of walkways that connected some of the main office buildings with the Capitol.

An aide pointed her down the dark tunnel that would take her to the tram, which ran every two minutes. When the

House adjourned, she could imagine the hustle and crowding of the tunnels, but at midafternoon, the one she walked through was deserted.

Her heels made a soft, crunchy noise on the concrete floor, and overhead the hissing of steam through pipes gave a strange, surrealistic sensation of moving through time. In a moment of sudden panic, she felt as if she'd been swallowed by a snake.

"Eleanor!" The name was a whisper behind her, barely audible above the gurgling pipes.

Up ahead she could hear voices, the quick exchange of greetings and laughter. She moved from one light to the next along the curvy tunnel.

"Eleanor, you can't run away from me." Now laughter floated behind her.

Her hand clutched her purse and she whirled. A tall man walked toward her out of the darkness.

"Who are you?" she demanded.

"It's me, Carter. Don't you even recognize your husband?"

The faint aroma of cigarette smoke tantalized her nostrils, and she saw the man take a long draw. Smoke curled out of his mouth and surrounded his head.

"Carter Wells is dead," she answered, though her heart was nearly bursting with fear. "I'm warning you to leave me alone."

"Give it back, Eleanor." He moved closer. "Just give it back and I'll go away." He laughed softly. "I'll descend back to the grave."

A noise behind her startled her anew. Someone else was coming. She distinctly heard the sound of leather soles gritting on the cement. If she could only keep the apparition talking, then she might be able to trap him.

"What is it that you want? Maybe if you tell me, I'll give it to you."

"What you took from the lab." He threw the cigarette to the ground and crushed it with his toe.

The gesture was so familiar that she felt her heart slip into overdrive. Just when she'd convinced herself that she was being tricked, she started to doubt it. In the poor lighting of the tunnel, the man could easily be her dead husband.

"Listen, whoever you are, I didn't break into that lab. So there's nothing I can give back, because I didn't take anything." The sound of someone approaching came closer. She prayed that whoever it was would hurry. She took a step toward the man who claimed to be her husband. "Come into the light, Carter. Let me see you. It's been a long time. Nine years. Why did you let me think you were dead?"

"It was simpler that way, Eleanor. All of the attention was focused on you. Poor Eleanor, such a young widow. I was able to slip away and leave my past behind me."

Anger made her take two more steps forward. "But I was stuck with your past! You always were a coward."

The man laughed. "So righteous, my dear. Let's just say that I had some people very angry with me, and it was easier to go than to stay. You, on the other hand, had a perfect little record. You couldn't tell anything, because you didn't know anything." His tone grew nasty. "You were always so content to live in your world."

"Come into the light," she challenged him.

"Or what?"

The bravado of his stance and words tripled her pulse rate. If she'd ever doubted it before, she didn't now. Carter Wells stood before her, resurrected from his own grave.

"You jerk!" She rushed at him, not really knowing what she intended to do at all, only intent on seeing his face. He was laughing at her, the sound confident and ugly.

Just as she reached up her hand to brush the hat from his head, something struck her from behind. She found herself falling, falling, a million miles to the hard floor of the tunnel.

"DRAG HER over against the wall," someone said.

"She won't give me the film," the man in the hat replied. "She claims she doesn't have it. I told you the cat wasn't safe!"

"Shut up about the cat! They haven't found anything. She probably suspects, and that's why they're keeping the cat. But all she has is the cat, and we have her."

"Had the cat. Remember, it was gone when I took care of Rayburn."

"What the hell was he doing here, anyway?" the voice demanded. "She must have called him."

"He wouldn't tell me anything," the smoker said bitterly. "Not the first thing, except that she called him and was talking some gibberish about the past."

"And it was your bright idea that we could use the past to frighten her into giving back the cat."

"It may work yet. After today." He laughed softly. "She was really frightened. She didn't know if she was talking to a ghost, a dead man or a husband who'd managed to slip out and leave her holding the bag. None of the choices were very pleasant for her."

ELEANOR HEARD herself moan. She was being unceremoniously jerked up and dragged down the tunnel between two men. Her head lolled back, and she had to force her eyes to open. The lights revolved in a sickening dizziness.

"She's coming out of it," she heard someone say. Without any warning she was slapped on the side of the head. In a loud ringing of bells and total darkness, Eleanor again lost consciousness.

Chapter Thirteen

All sense of time had slipped away from her. There was only the hard floor and a sweet, cloying smell. The odor was disturbingly familiar. Eleanor kept her eyes closed and tried to remember where she'd smelled it before. Someplace bad. That was all she could pull together. She was afraid to open her eyes. The tiniest glimmer of light made her head throb and spin. She couldn't move her arms, and her legs felt weighted. Somewhere in the distance she could hear someone moving about.

What had happened? She'd been in the tunnel—with Carter Wells. He was a distinct presence, alive and mean in a way she hadn't remembered him. But who had struck her? Carter was standing in front of her and the blow had come from behind. There was a vague memory of footsteps. And she'd thought it was someone who could help her!

"Open your eyes, Eleanor," a voice commanded.

She knew that voice! She kept her eyes closed, pretending that she was asleep. The shock of a small electric charge on her leg made her jump with such suddenness that she felt both her stomach and head begin to spin.

"Don't pretend to be out when you aren't," Cal Vrenner alias Arnold Evans informed her. "We have rules here, and like them or not, you have to obey."

Looking into his icy eyes, Eleanor knew now why she hadn't been able to read his thoughts the first time she met him. There was nothing behind the eyes, no sense or emotion. He was a man without a shred of compassion or concern. The word "psychopath" marched before her eyes in bold red letters. She'd managed to get herself trapped by a psychopath.

"Remember me?" he asked. His smile was cruel and more than a little satisfied. "You didn't like my clinic, did you? I'll bet you never thought you'd be coming here to live."

Eleanor looked around, ignoring the spinning sensation that came every time she shifted her eyes. Whoever had hit her, and it was probably Evans, had done a bang-up job of it. The tiniest effort at concentration made her head throb. As far as she could tell, she was on the floor in the small back room of the clinic. The noise of stirring that came from behind her had to be the orangutan, unless Evans had obtained more research animals.

"Where's Peter?" Evans asked.

"Peter who?" She pretended to be woozy. "Can you release my hands?"

The pain of the shock was unexpected. She jumped and screamed, falling onto one shoulder with a painful thud. Her leg was burning where he'd used the shock gun on her again.

"Listen, you sadist...."

"We don't allow temper tantrums in here, Dr. Duncan. You'd better learn to control yourself."

Evans walked around her. "Now once again, where is Peter?"

"I don't know," she answered. She eyed the small gun he carried. It looked something like a stun gun, but perhaps not as powerful. Of course she couldn't begin to estimate the weapon's capacity, and certainly not in the hands of a man like Evans.

"I love my new toy," he said, holding it out for her. "My little pet over there—" he pointed toward the bars of a cage Eleanor could see "—is so afraid of it, she will do anything I tell her. Anything at all. Isn't that remarkable?"

Struggling back to a sitting position, Eleanor ignored him.

"Answer me!" he screamed. "When I ask a question, answer me!"

His face was red with anger, and Eleanor watched the jump of the pulse in his neck. He was beyond any reasoning, a man capable of anything.

"What are you teaching the ape?" she asked.

"Obedience. I am one of the most effective obedience trainers in the world. My attack dogs will kill anyone or anything on command." His eyes seemed to bore through her. "Even their owners. I've had more success in the field than any other scientist. Obedience is a fascinating arena, don't you agree?"

"Absolutely," she muttered, trying to keep her tone level. She couldn't afford to show the loathing and contempt she felt for the man in front of her. What she had to do was find some weakness, some method of making him release her.

"I guess it was your successful career that brought you to the attention of Charles Breck?" She tried to make the question sound flattering, but the words tasted like grit.

"Yes, and he's going to be delighted with my new idea." Evans looked at her and pointed. "You!"

"Me?" She couldn't help the arrow of fear that struck her heart. "What about me?"

"You're perfect. You're the one who's going to present the ape!" He grinned and slowly nodded his head. "Your beauty and the ape's cunning tricks. The whole room will be diverted. And then, should things go wrong, they'll have you to execute. How wonderful, don't you agree?''

Eleanor was too shocked to say anything. She had no idea what he was raving about, but she clearly understood that it was something evil and that she did not want to be a part of it.

"Don't you agree?'' he screamed at her. "Answer me when I talk to you! That stupid ape can't talk, but you can, and you're going to!''

"Yes, yes, it's wonderful,'' she replied. "What is it exactly that you want me to do?''

He ignored her question and walked to the cage. "Come!'' he commanded. The small orangutan came toward him, her entire body radiating fear. "Come!'' He slipped a chain onto her collar.

Working at the knots that held her hands, Eleanor watched in fascinated horror as Evans put the ape through a series of dance steps, curtsies and ingratiating behavior.

"Very nice, right?'' he asked.

"Whatever you say.'' She couldn't afford to irritate him, for her sake and the ape's. "She's the perfect gift.''

"Oh, she's so much more than that.'' Evans put away the ape and came back to Eleanor. He tugged at the rope that held her hands, making sure it was secure.

Eleanor gritted her teeth to keep from cursing him. She had to play along.

"How do you know Peter?'' she asked.

"Well enough to know that he likes to interfere. I've kept my eye on him since I got back to Washington. We're old friends, you know, Peter and I. We go way back.''

"To a fire, I believe,'' Eleanor said. She tried to sound impartial, hoping to draw Evans into some detail.

"Yes, a great conflagration. My work had to be destroyed, such a shame. But now that I have friends in high places, I'll be able to work again. Once the ape is trained and the coup is delivered, I won't ever have to hide and struggle again. I'll have a real laboratory with the best equipment.''

Hearing him ramble on, Eleanor was taken with the change in his personality. When she'd first met him, he'd been quiet, observant, cold. Now he was too animated. Was it possible he was taking some type of drug? When it wore off, would she have a chance to escape?

"I deserve acclaim, and I'll have it soon," he finished.

"Of course," she said steadily. "What great trick is the orangutan going to do? Will she dance at a ball or reception?''

"Something like that." Evans was suddenly cagey. "I hear someone moving around outside.''

"Dr. Evans, wait a moment," Eleanor said quickly. "Do you know my husband Carter Wells?''

"Ah, Carter," Evans said with the biggest smile he'd given all afternoon. "He's an old friend. Older even than Rayburn Smith. Yes, Carter and I go back a long way. Your husband hid me out after the fire, when I was desperate. I introduced him to some useful people.''

"Carter did?" Code One Orange. Evans had to have been involved. And he acted as if Carter were really alive. Was it possible that Carter had helped him, and then the favor was returned?

"We spent a great deal of time together talking, Carter and I. I know many things about you, Dr. Duncan." He smiled. "Many things. Your husband could be a very entertaining man.''

"I'll bet," Eleanor said, unable to hide her sarcasm any longer. "Do you think you might untie my hands? I've lost all feeling.''

"I suppose. There's no way out of this lab. Not even if I were to die. Since your raid, we've improved the security system.''

"I didn't raid this place," Eleanor told him once again. She grimaced as he finally freed the knots.

"No need to lie now. What we want to know is where the cat is. We simply must have him back, you see."

"I don't know where he is, I swear it." Eleanor rubbed her wrists. The feeling was coming back with a vengeance.

"The cat was seen in your apartment. And that wretched Caruso woman was there, too. There's no point denying your involvement. We just want the creature back."

"And then what?"

"You're going to take a little trip. With your interest in language, I should think Africa would be a fascinating continent. The Dark Continent," he said, his eyes glowing too brilliantly, Eleanor observed.

"Linguistics is the science of language. I don't know how things got so confused, Arnold," she said, trying for a personal touch. "I didn't raid the lab. I didn't take anything. I don't know what you're talking about. Carter got things confused when he tried to blame me." She had to turn the conversation back to Carter. Where was he and what role did he play? Evans talked all around the subject but never revealed anything.

"How do you explain the cat?" Evans smiled with forced tolerance, as if she were a stupid child.

When Evans circled her once more, she could see the tiny lines of new skin that ran down both sides of his face. Claw marks.

"You were in the library parking lot. You saw me with the cat, because you were the one who attacked me!" That was why he insisted she'd taken the cat! she realized.

"Pretty and smart," he said, laughing. "We lost all of the other cats but the black one. The most important one. I saw you put him in your coat, and I knew you were the one."

Eleanor thought it pointless to argue with him. He wasn't capable of changing his mind.

"I'll give back the cat under one condition."

"Where is he?" Evans pressed.

Eleanor felt her heart pounding. She couldn't risk saying that Familiar was at her apartment. What if Evans knew differently? "He's in a safe place."

"Is the capsule intact?"

Eleanor knew she had to take a risk. "I don't know. Peter was going to take care of it."

Evan's face flamed with relish. "That's so perfect. Peter has the plan, and I have to get it from him. He never even realized what it was." He stood up. "He always thought he was so much smarter than me. When he found out about the experiments, he was so superior-acting. But he was stupid. I did my research under his nose, and he didn't catch on all summer. And now at last we get to finish what we started so long ago. I tried to get—" He looked at Eleanor and shut his mouth.

"Can I see Carter?" she asked. She couldn't reveal the tremble of fear at the idea. Carter was alive! He'd been involved all along.

"Not today. He'll be by to see you. Don't worry about that. Until he comes, though, I have a carefully planned appointment." He waved the gun at her and began to push her through another door. She found herself in a small room that was little more than a cage.

"What is this?" she asked.

"My observation room. I can see everything you do. And pretty soon, I'll be able to exert some influence over what you think."

Tiny hairs rose on Eleanor's neck in fright. Evans was mad, but he was also intelligent. His whole obedience thing was focused toward more than making apes and dogs carry out his wishes. There was something else, and she had to find out what.

"I'll be back later," Evans said, closing the door. "I have a rendezvous with Peter Curry. Our meeting is long over-due."

"Wait a minute...." Eleanor never got a chance to finish. The door slammed with a bang and she heard the locks click into place. The terrible idea that she'd set Peter up was like something alive in her skin. What had she done? Was Peter aware of how demented Evans had become? Those were questions that gnawed at her as she paced the tiny confines of the prison.

The sound of low crying came again, and Eleanor turned slowly, trying to pinpoint its source. She couldn't be certain.

"Who's there?" she asked in a whisper.

The only answer was more childlike crying.

WELL, ELEANOR HAS gotten herself into a fine pickle this time. She's in there with Dr. Frankenstein, and that ain't going to be a pretty sight. First Zelda, now Eleanor. Do I have rotten luck or what?

These windows are about as useless as a screen door in a submarine. I can get up to them, but I can't really see in-side, just vague blurs of motion. If he's hurt the dame! But I can't clutter my feline brain with such negative thoughts. I have to get in, and I have to get them out. It might even be easier with Eleanor to help. She can at least use her hands. Maybe it's a blessing that she's in there.

Oops! Here comes Vrenner, checking out the back door. He looks demented. Maybe I can just scoot inside. Nope! The door was too fast, and Dr. Frankenstein locked it tight. What luck! They're on the inside and I'm on the outside. Back to the windows.

Eleanor is in the small back room. I can't see clearly, but I can see her moving around. She must be scared to death. Maybe I can get her attention.

Ouch! I might have broken my shoulder against the glass, but it's working. She's looking around. One more time! Eureka! She's looking at the window and waving me away. As if I don't know they're out to get me. She wants me to go away, but I won't. I have to figure out how to get in.

On the other hand, I could go and look for Dr. Doolittle. He could break in and get everyone out.

I don't see a sign of Zelda. She's probably getting some beauty rest, and I'll bet she deserves it. I can remember when he wouldn't let her sleep for days, shocking her and burning her, trying to make her cave in and do those terrible things to my fellow cats! But she fought against him. That Zelda! She used to cry like a child when she was alone. She never wanted to hurt anyone or anything. But I want Vrenner, and I'm going to get him.

Okay, I admit that I'm not going to get inside. I have to have some human help, and the faster I find Peter, the better off we are!

ELEANOR'S BREATH caught painfully in her throat. Familiar was in the window of the lab, sitting perched there as if he were posing for a portrait. There had been a distinct thud—Familiar hurling himself at the window to get her attention? She shook her head. The last place in the world the cat needed to be was at the Behavioral Institute. The cat and the capsule. Evans had as much as said it. So it was Familiar all along. She and Peter had been on the right track, but who would have thought that someone would implant information in a cat? But then again, an animal destined for experimentation and death would be the last place someone would look for contraband goods. She looked again at the window, thinking her eyes might have played a trick on her. But he was there, flesh and blood, and the sight gave her new hope.

Get Peter, she mouthed at him. "I must sound like Timmy on the old Lassie shows," she said aloud. But she went as close to the window as she could and mouthed the words to the cat once more. Familiar had somehow gotten back to the lab, and there was just a chance he could find Peter. If only she could write a note and slip it to him! Hell, if he could carry a capsule, he could carry a note.

"I'm really fantasizing now," she said, leaning her head against the bars that made up one wall of the room. There was a large mirror, which she knew was a two-way glass. Evans could be sitting out there now, watching her talk to the cat! She glanced at the window; Familiar was gone. She was glad, but had never felt more alone.

The only thing she could do was to begin to patch together the things she'd learned, the most notable of which was that her ex-husband and Evans were friends. The idea of Carter alive was almost too much to bear. But he was, and she'd have to deal with him. She could clearly see the link of Carter, Evans and Code One Orange. Rayburn had been caught innocently in the middle of it. By calling him, she'd condemned him to death!

"Oh, Rayburn," she whispered, feeling desolation sweep over her. "I'm so sorry." She paced the small room, avoiding looking into the mirror. She didn't want to give Evans the satisfaction of seeing how upset she was.

Thinking back over the day, she was struck by the possibility that Sam Nottingham had set her up. He'd sent her into the tunnels for a meeting with Breck in the Capitol. Had he known what waited for her in the darkness? After all, he'd first been rude, then had suddenly agreed to talk with her. And Nottingham had a Central American background. Code One Orange.

"Damn!" she whispered. "I should have waited until I found Peter when I called from Nottingham's office." The hard truth was that no one really knew where she'd gone.

No one would even have the faintest idea where to begin looking for her.

Hysteria began to rise like a tidal wave. When she didn't talk with her parents at Christmas, they'd begin to worry. But by then it would be too late. Panic almost overwhelmed her. She gripped the bars and held on, forcing her mind to grow calm, her body to stop trembling. She was underestimating Peter. He was nobody's fool and he wouldn't give up. If she could figure it out, so could he. She went back to the window and tried to look at the outside world. She had no idea what time it was. The only thing to do was think.

What role did Charles Breck play in all of this? Could he really be an innocent who'd happened to hire a psychopath to train a pet ape? What was his connection with Code One Orange? Was he a victim of Nottingham's schemes? She tried to evaluate the situation sensibly. She'd watched the interaction between Breck and Evans. Breck was acting head of the CIA, a tenuous position, at best. His background was in diplomacy rather than counterintelligence. During the meeting at the clinic, Evans had appeared rational. She'd talked with him and hadn't been frightened. He'd been in control of himself, even when Magdalena had attacked him.

She felt her heart skip. And Magdalena *had* attacked him—and invited a physical assault. She wanted Evans to do something so that she could have him arrested. But he'd been too smart! He'd waited and gone to her home to hurt her.

All the blood in her brain seemed to drop into Eleanor's stomach. She'd never felt such fear. She was locked up, a captive of a man who could kill her as easily as he tormented small, helpless animals. Her panic was once again augmented by the sound of low moaning. Somewhere in the clinic there was someone else in serious trouble.

"Where are you?" she whispered, cocking her head for a response. "I'll try and help you, but don't be afraid." She tried to sound brave, but knew her nerve was weakening. When she discovered the moaning person, what atrocity would she find? Her imagination was running away with her, and she felt like curling into a corner and hiding.

"Listen." She forced herself to talk reassuringly. "I'm going to get us out of here. I promise." Something about the sound of the moaning made her think that it came from a child, a young girl. "You aren't alone anymore. Whatever we have to do to get away, we will."

There was the sound of an intercom clicking on. "Save it, Dr. Duncan. There's absolutely nowhere you can go and nothing you can do to save yourself or anyone else. Sleep tight, now."

The lights were snapped off; she was alone with the soft whimpering of the child and the echo of Arnold Evans's hard voice.

Chapter Fourteen

Eleanor's new sofa was a muted blue and still covered in the thick plastic used for shipping. Peter noted the change in furniture as he stepped into her living room, and the emptiness. There was no sign that Eleanor had been home.

"I told you she wasn't here," Wessy said. "The men came this afternoon to deliver the sofa, and Dr. Duncan wasn't anywhere to be found." He gave Peter a sour look. "She's had a lot of trouble since she met you."

"There are a few questions I've been meaning to ask you," Peter said pointedly. "Like how did Rayburn Smith get into her apartment? The police said someone opened the door for him."

"And you're thinking it was me!" Blood suffused Wessy's face.

"I'm thinking you might have had a hand in it." Peter held his ground but kept his voice calm.

"And does Miss Eleanor doubt me?"

Something about the older man's tone gave Peter pause. "I don't know," he said honestly.

"I shouldn't have opened this door," Wessy said, giving Peter a cold look. "You've used me and then set me up to look guilty. Get out!"

"I'm not finished here," Peter said. "Eleanor is missing, and I need to see if I can find any clue as to where she went."

"I have to get back to the door," Wessy said. "I never should have left my post."

"Did you tell this to the police?" A surge of adrenaline pumped through Peter's veins.

"I couldn't," Wessy replied, looking at the tips of his shoes. "I'd lose my job if they knew I let that man in the door—if they knew I'd let you into Eleanor's apartment. But it doesn't matter—" he shrugged "—I'm going to lose my job now, anyway. That man was murdered, right in here." He looked around, but his eyes weren't focused. "Right on her old sofa."

"Wessy, you have to tell me everything that happened. Did the man say why he had to see Eleanor?" An uncomfortable feeling crawled along Peter's spine. Wessy was acting strangely, as if he thought Eleanor was guilty of something, maybe even murder.

"He was talkative, sort of rambling on more than anything else. He really wanted me to open the door, so he talked a lot. He said he never wanted to come here, but that he'd talked with Eleanor and he was worried because of some of the things she'd said." He met Peter's gaze. "The man was afraid he was going to be hurt. He was afraid of Eleanor."

"What things did he say were dangerous?"

"Something about the past and Colorado. He kept talking about her husband." He looked at Peter. "I didn't know she'd ever been married. I never suspected. There's a lot about her that I never suspected."

Peter clearly heard the edge of disapproval in the doorman's words. "What are you implying?"

"I've got eyes and I use them. I always thought she was such a quiet woman, so dignified."

Peter felt his temper ignite. "What are you saying?" He took a threatening step forward.

"That man that watches her. She knows him, though she pretends she doesn't."

"What man?"

Wessy stepped into the hallway. "That one in the lobby, Mr. Rousel. He knows her husband."

"He what?"

"He talks to her about her husband." Wessy shook his head. "She tells everyone her husband is dead, but he isn't."

"That's a lie, Wessy. Her husband was killed in a car wreck."

"That's what you think. I've got to get back to work." He walked backward down the hall, then turned and rushed toward the elevator.

Peter started to go after him, but stopped at the doorway. Something had happened to Wessy to shake his faith in Eleanor. He was truly afraid of her. What could Rayburn Smith have told him? There had to be something in the apartment that would lead him to Eleanor.

Hurriedly scanning the table near the phone, he turned up her address book. He held the book in one hand, weighing it, as if it could determine his next action. He flipped through it. The writing was neat and orderly, the capital letters distinctive with an edge of elegance.

"Just like her," he said aloud.

He was looking for someone who might know where to reach her. Night had fallen on the bustling town of Washington, yet Eleanor was nowhere to be found. He'd already tried the university and Magdalena's. In desperation, he'd even called the police department. She was gone.

Caught between worry for her safety and guilt at prying in her private business, he went through the pages more slowly. Almost none of the names were the tiniest bit recognizable. The addresses were scattered across the globe.

For a woman who led such a quiet life, she certainly had a lot of friends. At last he came to the two numbers in the back. The absence of names made him pause, and out of curiosity he looked up the area codes. One Colorado and one Arizona. Rayburn Smith was from Colorado, and he was dead.

His fingers hesitated over the punch buttons of the phone as his old doubts came back. Could he call the Colorado number? Should he? He put the receiver down. The answer was a bald no. He had no business at all meddling in Eleanor's personal business. Somehow, in the thick of their relationship, he'd grown to trust her. More than that, to love her. There was no room for the tiniest doubt. He turned back to the Gs. Betty Gillette was the place to begin. She knew of his involvement with Eleanor.

"I've been trying to reach you," Betty said. There was breathless excitement in her voice. "I don't have any idea what's going on with you two, but it sure sounds like a lot more fun than my life. I just got home from the university."

"So dedicated," Peter said, checking his watch. Betty did work awfully hard. It was nearly eight o'clock. "Do you know where Eleanor is?"

"Hasn't she found you?" A note of anxiety touched her voice.

"No, I was hoping she might be with you."

"She had a meeting with Congressman Nottingham several hours ago. She called from his office and said there was a meeting with Charles Breck. She sounded very excited and asked me to find you. I called your office, but you weren't there. Peter, what's going on that Breck is involved in it? Sounds pretty high-level to this poor college professor."

He ignored the open curiosity. "I'm worried about her, Betty. She should have been back hours ago. Did she say where she was meeting Breck?"

"The Capitol, I think. What's wrong?"

He knew she could read the worry in his voice. "Maybe nothing," he reassured her.

"Yeah, like a bomb is nothing. You guys need to be horsewhipped. I know just enough to really be frightened, and then you won't tell me any more."

On the verge of asking for Betty's help, he hesitated. The less Betty was involved, the better. "Let me go to the Capitol and look for her. If there's a problem, I'll get back with you."

"In case you haven't noticed, Peter, it's after eight at night. Our dedicated public servants aren't that dedicated."

"Chances are she got involved in a discussion, and they're working out the details. If I don't find her soon, I promise I'll call back and get your help."

"When pigs fly...."

"I promise," he swore. "Now tell me if you can remember any one thing that might give me a clue to why she was meeting Nottingham and Breck."

There was a long pause. "She said something about monkey business. I couldn't make any sense of it, but..."

"Are you sure?" Peter felt a sudden, irrational chill.

"I tried to ask some questions, but she was in a hurry. The meeting was pending, and she'd tried to call you without success. That's why she called me. She wanted me to find you and get you to come, too."

"Thanks, Betty."

"You'll call back? You promised."

"One way or the other." Peter replaced the phone. He stood for a moment, marshalling his plan. Something about Eleanor's apartment disturbed him, and it wasn't the new furniture. He replaced the address book. It was the absence of that damn cat! Familiar had become so much a part of Eleanor that he couldn't sit in her apartment with thinking of him. Where had he gone? Well, the cat would have to wait. If his hunch was right, Eleanor was talking with Nottingham and Breck about the orangutan at the Behavioral Institute. The chill touched him again. Evans! He'd been so busy with Eleanor's problems that he hadn't had time to pursue his own interest in bringing Evans to justice. Maybe, just maybe, the two goals were beginning to dovetail. But if that was the case, Eleanor was in more danger than she'd ever thought possible.

He hurried out of the building to his car. His search of Magdalena's house has been a waste of time. There was nothing there he didn't know about already—a list of ARSA and AFA members tucked away, some notes about future plans for attacks on varying research institutions. Nothing helpful, but plenty that was incriminating. At least he'd been able to remove the lists before the police came to search the place. Magdalena was already under arrest on a trumped-up murder charge. But while he was busy with her, Eleanor had stumbled onto something. And she was alone!

His memory kept flashing the image of Eleanor and Arnold Evans, and his gut twisted at the idea. Evans was the cruelest monster he'd ever met. Even worse, he had delusions of grandeur. He remembered the long-ago days when they'd both been vet students, working their way through school. Initially he'd been impressed by Evans's obvious brilliance. Even as a young student he'd shown tremendous promise and aptitude. His name had buzzed through the Maryland veterinary school, attracting much attention and acclaim. But as Peter had grown to know him better, there had been a disturbing element. None of the research had been done to better the lot of humans or animals. Evans's work had had a peculiar twist—a quest for ultimate control. In the beginning it was a small thing. But as Peter watched more and more closely, it became a flaw that was intolerable. The summer they'd worked for the chemical company, that flaw had expanded into a major earthquake fault. Evans was mentally off, a dangerous man whose brilliance was warped and twisted. He wanted power, control and unquestioning obedience, and he didn't care how he got it.

Peter realized his hands were clenching the wheel. He'd fallen into the vortex of old anger that had been reawakened when he found the cat with the mark of Evans on it. Poor Familiar. If Evans had him again, the cat would be better off dead.

The road was clogged with traffic, but Peter negotiated it with a minimum of trouble. Soon he was parking near the Capitol. The elegant building was bathed in the soft lights skillfully tucked around the grounds. One look at the building, and Peter realized his mistake. He had no pass, and there was no way the guards would let him in at nine at night without some official documentation. As he gazed at the windows, he felt a terrible need to find Eleanor, to see that she was safe. Even a look in a window, to see her seated in an office, would be enough, just to know that she was safe.

He locked his car and stepped along the curb. The realization that he'd never been to the Capitol before struck him hard. The building was enormous. Even if he got inside, where would he find Eleanor?

"Can I help you, sir?" a guard asked.

"Congressman Nottingham, please."

The guard motioned him through a metal detector and up to his desk.

"The Congressman's personal office is in the Cannon Building. I have no record that he's here tonight." He waited for further questions.

"Could you check again?" Peter asked.

The guard ran his finger down a roster of meetings. "No, sir, there's nothing here. As far as I can tell, Congressman Nottingham is gone."

"I have something personal to discuss with him." Peter placed both hands on the guard's desk and leaned forward. "Is he pretty decent to deal with?"

"Well." The guard looked uncomfortable. "He's pleasant enough. He's been here only a few years, not really the kind of time it takes for me to know a man." He shrugged his shoulders. "He's never rude, if that's what you're asking."

"Does he do . . . personal favors?"

The guard pushed his hat back from his forehead and rose. "I don't know what you're asking, but I don't think I like the drift of it. If you're wanting to know if he takes bribes, you'd better ask him. That's not the kind of thing I would know."

"Sorry," Peter said, "I didn't mean to offend you. It's just that I'm desperate."

Appearing to catch the undercurrent of sincere worry in Peter's voice, the guard's tone softened. He leaned toward Peter and lowered his voice. "This place is rife with rumors, and I've heard Nottingham's name mentioned here and there. It doesn't mean anything."

"Can you help me?"

The guard held up both hands, looking around him. "Me, I don't know anything. It's just talk, and I shouldn't repeat it. Do me a favor and forget what I said."

"Of course," Peter said, backing off. The guard was tense; he'd overstepped his limits. "Thanks for the tip, and I'll forget where I heard it. But there is one other thing you might tell me."

"What's that?" the guard asked suspiciously.

"Does Charles Breck maintain any offices here?"

"In the Capitol?" The guard's wariness turned to amusement. "No, sir. That's a little too close for the CIA to suit the taste of some of the people who work here."

"Look!" Peter pointed down the hall. "There went Representative Nottingham now. Could you stop him for me?"

"I didn't see anyone." He gave Peter a funny look.

"I'm sure it was him. Please check it?"

"Wait here," the guard said. "I believe you're mistaken, but I'll be glad to make sure." He strode down the long hallway toward the rotunda.

Peter wasted not a second in opening the files. He memorized Nottingham's address.

The guard returned with a shake of his head. "I don't know who you saw, but no one in that wing even resembled Mr. Nottingham."

"I'm sorry. I thought I saw someone. Just wishful thinking, I suppose. Thanks for your help."

Peter ran down the steps to his car. The address was off Pennsylvania Avenue, one of the nice sections of town where political entertaining was an art. So, the word was out that Nottingham took bribes. It could be truth—or a vicious rumor started by a political opponent.

He found the right neighborhood and drove slowly by the stately homes with their manicured lawns. It was a section of town where appearance meant almost everything, and a poorly thought-out guest list could be the downfall of a career. It was an aspect of Washington he'd never explored, and he wasn't certain he wanted to now.

"Damn!" he cursed as he drew closer to Nottingham's address. The street was swarming with cars, couples and cops. "He's having a party!" Peter exclaimed under his breath as he struck the steering wheel with the base of his hand.

He looked at his clothes. He was still in slacks and a shirt from the office. He didn't even have a tie. And he was going to attempt to crash a Washington soiree. He sighed and got out of the car.

Falling into line behind two older couples, he made it to the butler and the front door.

"Please tell Mr. Nottingham I need to see him about Eleanor Duncan."

"Congressman Nottingham is unavailable for business tonight." The butler looked both ways, then bent his head. "He's having a party." The sarcasm was completely unveiled.

"I see," Peter said, holding back his impatience. "Well, in that case, you'd better tell him to come to the door and talk with me, or I'll make a very big effort to ruin his special little night. Got it?"

The butler drew back in disbelief. "Sir!"

"I'm a man who's worried sick about a friend. Either Nottingham comes out here and talks to me, or I go in there and talk to him. I'd prefer to do it the polite way, but . . ."

"A moment." The butler closed the door.

Behind him, he heard laughter and the murmur of male and female voices. As additional party guests came down the walk, Nottingham opened the front door and stepped outside. He greeted his guests graciously, ushering them into the house. He closed the door firmly and turned in the darkness to confront Peter.

"I don't know what the meaning of this could be, but I've had enough of you people. That Duncan woman was in my office today, implying terrible things about me and my associates. And now you're here, threatening to crash a dinner! I've called the police, and if you aren't gone in the next four minutes, I'm sure they'll be more than glad to take you away."

Peter grabbed the front of Nottingham's tux. "Where's Eleanor?"

"I don't know what you're talking about." He tried to shake himself free, but Peter's grip was too tight. "She came into my office, demanded an interview, hurled accusations at me and then, after I'd gone to the trouble to set up a meeting for her, she didn't show."

"What?" Peter released his grip.

"She didn't bother to come over to the House and meet with Breck herself. We waited for half an hour."

Peter stepped back; it was the moment Nottingham needed to reassert his control.

"Now I'm going to tell you one last time. I've had it with you people. You've tried my patience too far. Get off my property or I'll have you removed. There are security men on the street and inside that front door, highly trained men." He pointed to his house.

"What time did you see Eleanor?"

"This afternoon. Check with my receptionist tomorrow. She keeps a record of all my visitors."

"Dr. Duncan has disappeared," Peter said. "You were the last person to see her, as far as I can tell. Maybe we should call the police."

Nottingham paused with his hand on the doorknob. "What are you trying to imply?" His tone was icy.

"You saw her last, and I'm going to find her. If there's something wrong with her, I'll be back for you, Nottingham. I'll make you think what Evans did to that ape of yours was kindercare."

"Who is this man you keep talking about? What does he have to do with me, my orangutan or that woman?"

"That's exactly the question I was going to ask you," Peter said. "So Eleanor was in your office and you set up a meeting with Breck. I know that much. Between your office and the House, she disappeared. Don't you find that a little strange?''

The sound of more guests arriving floated down the walk. Nottingham gestured Peter aside, behind a hedge.

''The woman said something about Cal Vrenner, my trainer, having another identity. That's impossible. Breck had him checked out thoroughly, and he's a top behavioral specialist. He can make an animal do anything you can imagine.''

''I'm sure,'' Peter said. ''Do you remember when a portion of International Chem-Co burned, back in the late seventies?''

Nottingham thought for a moment. ''Tragic fire. Years of research were lost. I wasn't in Washington at the time, but I do remember. A young man was arrested.''

''I was that man. It took me a long time to clear my name.''

''I'm sorry, I didn't read...''

''You never read about that part. Nor about the man who really set the fire, another student called Arnold Evans. Well, that man is Cal Vrenner.''

''Don't be absurd. The CIA would never let such a thing slip by them. They aren't idiots, you know. Charles Breck is a personal friend of mine. He's taken as much interest in this orangutan as I have.''

''Then you're both inept.''

''I don't have to stand here and take this.''

''No, but you'd better listen to what I have to say. Eleanor told you the truth about Vrenner. Look into it for yourself. Now I'm going over to the Capitol to look for Eleanor. I want the key to your office, and I want whatever documentation I need to get it.''

''Don't be a fool, man. You can't go running around a federal building in the middle of the night.'' The front door opened and the guests entered the house. Nottingham stepped back onto the path. "There's nothing in my office."

"Come with me," Peter said.

"I have guests." Nottingham waved helplessly toward his house. "I can't walk away from this party. Some of my major contributors are here."

"The key!" Peter held out his hand.

"Wait here. I'll get you what you want and come back."

Nottingham let himself through the front door, leaving Peter alone in the dark yard. The noises of the party shimmered around the house, accompanied by blurred laughter and music. It sounded like a large group, a social event. Peter counted the seconds, doubt growing that Nottingham would reappear. He should have collared him and taken him. Each second that dragged by, he felt his desperation grow. It was close to ten. Was Eleanor at home, waiting for him to call? The answer to that frightened him. Where was she?

The door opened and Nottingham came toward him, hand extended. "Leave it in the office, and here's an official pass. It says you're there to pick up something I left behind. I don't know what you think you'll find in my office, but it isn't there."

"I want Eleanor." Peter felt his anger flare dangerously. "If she's hurt, Nottingham, you're in big trouble." He turned on his heel and strode down the walk.

PETER WAS BACK at the Capitol in less than fifteen minutes. Instead of parking near the front entrance, he swung right toward Cannon House. The lot was only a fourth full. All alone, parked at the edge of a lane, was a red Camry. Peter drove to it and got out. Eleanor's car! She'd never left the area!

Nottingham's office was easy to find. So was the receptionist's ledger. Eleanor's name was down for a two o'clock appointment. That was it. No mention of content or disposition of any matter.

Beneath her name was Breck's, with a notation of a meeting in the House anteroom. So that was the meeting that Eleanor had never shown up to attend. He locked the office and returned to the elevator. He started to press Lobby, then remembered the tunnels. If Eleanor was going to the House, she might very well have taken the tunnels!

He descended, his muscles clenching with dread.

The network of tunnels seemed abandoned. The memory of Eleanor's encounter in the parking garage came back to him—along with Wessy's words. She was terrified! Was it possible she'd actually seen her dead husband very much alive?

He took the most direct route to the Capitol, wondering if he were retracing her steps. What had gone wrong? Where was she now? The questions were like brands of fire. He was wasting his time in a dark tunnel, looking for what? A map that would take him to her? When he got out of the tunnels, he was going to call Detective Jones and let the authorities handle it.

The clatter of metal made him freeze. The small noise bounced along the floor, about fifteen yards in front of him. In the erratic lighting he saw a flash of silver, and then a small disc landed near his feet. Scanning the empty distance, he bent to retrieve it. Eleanor's earring. His heartbeat quickened to a dangerous throb.

"Where is she?" he called into the darkness. "If she's hurt, I'll kill you."

His words slurred and repeated, echoing eerily around him.

"If you've hurt her, I'll kill you," he said again.

"Always so rash, aren't you?" Out of the darkness, Arnold Evans stepped around the corner of the tunnel. He stopped twenty-five yards away and confronted Peter.

"You're looking well, Peter. Recovered completely from our little mix-up."

"Where's Eleanor?"

"What makes you think I'd tell you?" Evans laughed. "You never were able to keep a secret."

Peter lunged forward, his outstretched hands circling Evans's throat and squeezing with a sudden pressure that made the smaller man's eyes bulge with unexpected fright.

"I'll choke you," Peter warned. "I should have done it years ago, when I first suspected what a maniac you were. But I've been waiting for you, biding my time."

"The woman," Evans croaked. "Kill me and she dies!"

"Where is she?" Peter relaxed his hold a little, so that the other man could draw a breath.

"Take your filthy hands off me," Evans ordered as soon as he could breathe. "No one touches me. No one!"

"Where is she?" Peter kept his hands on Evans's throat. It had been too many years, and his fingers itched to extract the revenge he wanted.

"She's safe, Peter. Just as safe as you please. She's rather attractive, isn't she? I've never had such a beautiful subject. I've always wondered if the truly beautiful feared losing their beauty more than the average person." He cocked his head. "That would make a fascinating study."

"And how many people would you have to maim and mutilate before you found the answer to that question?"

"It's hypothetical, you fool," Evans snapped. "I won't be able to do any of that type of research until I relocate. In some Third World country, where there isn't such a scramble about a few missing children."

"You are sick," Peter said, almost overcome with disgust. "Now tell me where Eleanor is, or I'll break every bone in your hands and feet. And remember, Evans, I know every single one."

"Love becomes you, Peter. You're quite lost in that glorious emotion of protecting your chosen mate. That's another area that would make decent experimentation. How much are you willing to suffer to protect her?" He laughed out loud, chin tilted toward the damp ceiling of the tunnel. "How much?"

"More than enough." With those words Peter grasped Evans's arm and twisted it behind his back. A scream erupted, echoing through the tunnel.

"I'll kill you," Evans panted. "You're going to pay for this. I'll make her suffer. She'll suffer a million times more than anything you do to me!"

"One last time, Evans, where is she? Tell me, or this arm is going out of its socket. You've watched this kind of pain before, without anesthesia. Remember those animals!" He twisted the arm and sent Evans to his knees. "Tell me!"

"Jefferson Memorial."

"What?" He jerked the arm once more.

"She's there! I tied her there myself. It's cold, and she was crying."

"Is she hurt?"

Evans laughed, a sound that mingled ominously with the groans of his pain. "Not yet, she isn't, but the night is young."

"Why did you come down here?" Peter looked around. He was suddenly aware that Evans had deliberately called attention to himself. He'd practically begged to be caught.

"Because I wanted to tell you in person that I've finally won. Your friend Magdalena is set up for murder. She's gone!" He waved his hand in the air. "And you're next. By the time you find Dr. Duncan, she'll be dead. And the finger will point at you."

Chapter Fifteen

Of all the memorials, Peter preferred the Jefferson. The rotunda was graceful, its symmetry a reflection of Jefferson's personal taste. But as the December wind whipped among the leafless cherry trees, he saw that the monument could easily be viewed as sinister.

Fear for Eleanor pushed him forward in a dead run. He'd left Evans on the floor of the tunnel, his hands bound with his own belt. The knots wouldn't hold him forever, but maybe long enough for Peter to find Eleanor and call the police. When he had to choose between apprehending Evans and saving Eleanor, it had been no contest. Eleanor came first. If Evans got away, he'd catch him again. The years had only magnified the research scientist's insanity. Where once he'd been cunning and brilliant, now he was so far gone that he wasn't even thinking clearly.

Peter skirted the structure, dodging from shadow to shadow around the tidal basin that balanced each side of the rotunda. Brightly colored paddleboats were docked in line for the night. Inside the rotunda, he could catch shadowed glimpses of Jefferson's statue, a bronzed figure, standing tall among the columns.

The back of the memorial was unlighted. His nerves quickened as he moved around, trying to find the place where Eleanor might be tied. Evans had said she was in there, but Peter knew his old opponent could very easily have been setting up an ambush.

He worked his way back to the front, where the floodlights gave a contrast to dark and light that made it impossible to see into the shadows. Attentive to any movement, he mounted the steps. As he approached the top, he saw the revolver lying on the step.

"A .38," he whispered as he bent to retrieve the weapon. He checked the chamber and found three bullets left. Sniffing the barrel, he could tell that the gun had recently been fired. He clamped his jaw at the thought of Eleanor. He made a silent vow that Arnold Evans would pay a severe price if Eleanor was harmed in any way.

Careful to walk silently, he entered the rotunda dome. He held the gun before him with every intention of using it if he had to. Again and again he asked himself why Evans would choose the Jefferson Memorial as a place to leave Eleanor. It didn't make any sense. None at all.

Like an elusive shadow, he slipped from column to column, circling the entire rotunda. There was no sign of Eleanor. "Damn Evans," he whispered tersely, "another of his tricks." But the question why still remained.

He was edging back to the steps when he heard the first wail of the sirens. The cars were coming directly toward the memorial. He counted five, then three more. Whatever had happened, it must have been a major crime wave. He watched as the police jumped from their cars and ran toward the memorial.

He looked around to see more police coming from the opposite direction, straight toward him. Gazing across the water at the approaching cops, he saw that one paddleboat was drifting along lazily, untied. It passed from dark to light, moving slowly in a circle. Something about it captured Peter's attention. With mounting horror he saw a hand dragging the water, and finally the form of a man slumped on his side.

In a flash he had a perfect understanding of Evans motivation and of his last words. There was no time to check who the victim was, no time to answer questions. He looked at the gun he held in his hand. It was a perfect setup. First Magdalena, now himself. And Eleanor? Was she dead or alive?

"Hold it, mister!" a cop called to him.

Peter didn't answer. He dashed into the shadows of the rotunda. Besides the lack of lights, there was a treacherous twenty-foot drop at the back. Peter sprinted as fast as he could and leaped to the ground. Rolling as he landed, he scrambled to his feet and ran. Behind him he heard confused noises from the police; they'd obviously discovered the body and begun to pursue him in earnest.

The gun was still clutched in his hand. He started to throw it aside, then realized that his fingerprints were all over it. Another thought crossed his mind. He might still have cause to use the weapon when he retrieved Evans from the tunnel.

There was no time to get his car. He ran toward the Capitol and the place where he'd left Evans.

Winded and frantic with worry, he finally stood outside the Cannon Building, debating whether to go in or not. The sound of voices warned him to duck behind some shrubs. Evans and Charles Breck came out of the building together. Their voices were low, but audible.

"Why would he go after Nottingham?" Breck asked.

"Your guess is as good as mine. You know how those people are. He was seen at Sam's party earlier this evening, threatening to make trouble. Then Sam got the urgent call to go to the memorial, or his family would be hurt." Evans rubbed his head. "Curry wanted to kill me, too."

"What about the ape?" Breck asked, sounding greatly bewildered.

"Sam would want us to go on with the gift. After all, we've put a lot of time and effort into this project. What happened tonight doesn't change the fact that Issac Demont will enjoy the orangutan."

"I suppose you're right," Breck said. "The ceremony is tomorrow night. Are you sure she's ready? She acted a little unstable to me. I don't understand why she's so nervous."

"She'll be fine," Evans reassured him. "I've added a new little element to the presentation. I'm sure you'll love it."

"President Demont is a very proper man. Nothing in bad taste, I hope."

The scientist laughed. "Trust me, Charles. I know how much you want to become director of the CIA. Bad taste is the furthest thing from my mind."

"I hope so. I certainly hope so. See you in the morning."

"Maybe the afternoon. As I mentioned, I have some polishing touches to put on the orangutan and the . . . addition."

Breck and Evans got into their cars and drove away.

Peter lowered the gun. His hands were shaking. He'd come within an inch of blowing Evans to bits on the walk in front of a federal building. Only the fact that he needed Evans alive had restrained him. He needed him to find Eleanor.

Keeping an eye out for police cars, he circled the Cannon Building parking lot to flag a taxi. With Magdalena in jail, there was only one person he could turn to, Betty Gillette. He settled into the back seat and tried to think.

His suspicions about Breck and Nottingham fell perfectly into place. Those two were involved with Evans in something other than training a monkey to curtsy and grovel. Breck obviously wanted high position and power.

Nottingham had wanted it, too, but in the grand scheme of things, Nottingham had been expendable. He was necessary only as a corpse, a frame for a murder rap.

And Evans? His needs were obvious. Funding and a place to work. What had he said? Some Third World country, where missing children weren't such a big issue? Fury clouded Peter's thoughts for several blocks.

When it finally cleared away, he returned once again to the puzzle of Familiar and Eleanor.

"Here's your stop," the cabby said as he pulled to the curb.

Peter paid the fare and got out. Betty's apartment building was on the other side of the university, but not that far from campus. In a lot of ways it was similar to the building where Eleanor lived, except there was no doorman, only an intercom system, so that a guest could be buzzed inside.

"Betty, this is Peter," he said when she answered. "I need your help."

"Where's Eleanor?" Betty's tone was frantic. In the background there was the sound of two cats squaring off for a fight. "Hush!" she threatened them.

"I can't find her. I'm afraid she's in serious trouble. Can I come up?"

"No." There was a pause. "I'll come down and talk to you. My apartment is a wreck. There's a coffee shop down the block. I'll meet you there in ten minutes. I've been thinking, Peter, and I'm really worried about Eleanor."

"Ten minutes," he said, his own worry accelerating. He hurried against the chill wind to the Java House, a small, cozy specialty shop that featured varieties of freshly ground coffee.

Betty was sitting with him in less than ten minutes. Her features were drawn with worry. "I haven't heard a word from Eleanor," she said as she took a chair. "Where could she be?"

"I don't know," Peter replied. "A lot of things have happened." He didn't know how far to trust her. The truth was, though, that his options were running out. He had to have a confidante and he needed Betty's help. He decided on the truth. "Tonight I was framed for a murder."

"What!" Her eyes widened and she involuntarily drew back. "Who?"

"Representative Nottingham, I think. I only caught a glimpse of a body in one of the paddleboats." He patted his pocket. "But I picked up the murder weapon, and I ran."

"Peter!" she whispered, leaning forward. "What is going on? Where is Eleanor?"

"If my worst fears are correct, she's being held by...an old enemy. Arnold Evans."

Betty's face paled. "Why would he hold her prisoner?" Her hands were trembling so badly that she had to set down her coffee cup.

"I haven't put all of the pieces together yet. But when Eleanor took in that stray cat, she became the focus for Evans and his high-level friends."

"How did they even find out she had the cat? I mean there are about a million stray black cats in this town. What was so unusual about the one she took?"

"It came from Evans's lab. I thought for a long time that maybe the cat carried some information. A clue was a small notch on the tube that reminded me of Evans. If only I could find the person who robbed the lab, they might know." Peter turned the coffee cup in his hand.

"What kind of thing?"

"Plans of some sort. Something of value to Evans, but I don't know what."

"I think you're jumping to conclusions." Betty picked up her cup and finished the coffee. "I have to go."

"Can I borrow your car?"

"Sure." She reached into her purse and pulled out the keys. "It's around back, a blue Tercel." Fear danced in her eyes. "Be careful, Peter. This Evans character, he must be a real SOB."

"He is," Peter agreed. "You don't even know him and you suspect what type of person he is."

"Yeah," she said, putting a bill onto the counter as she walked away.

Peter sat a moment longer, watching the night outside the café window. Each moment that passed might bring additional danger to Eleanor. His gut instinct was that Evans had her and planned to use her in some way. But how? And where? If only he could lay hands on Familiar. The more he thought about it, the more he believed the cat held all the answers. Or at least a lot of them.

If Evans had Eleanor, then the most logical place would be at his lab. Peter bolted from the table. The lab! Cold fear nearly locked his knees as he paid for the coffee and ran out of the café into the night. What was Evans doing to Eleanor if he had her in the lab?

He found Betty's Tercel and roared out of the parking lot. He had a clear memory of where Eleanor told him the Behavioral Institute was located. It was about five miles from her campus, tucked back on a dead-end road that looked deserted. Eleanor! She had to be safe. She had to be!

By the time he arrived at the institute, his head was clearer. The race of fear and emotion had calmed, giving him time to plan. He parked the car half a mile down the road, wondering how, in a city as crowded as Washington, Evans had found a place so isolated and remote. But then, the work Evans did wouldn't bear the close scrutiny of neighbors.

No cars were parked in front of the brick building, and there was no sign of life. Peter hugged the surrounding growth of small shrubs and wild bushes as he made his way toward the front door. He saw the small wires of the electric alarm that were glued to the windows. It would be like Evans to have a highly sophisticated burglary system.

At the front door he peered through the tiny square of reinforced glass. The hallway that came into view was empty. The interior walls were a dull institutional green. Gloom and depression seemed to swell from the dirty, brownish floor.

It was the same scenario he remembered so well. Evans was oblivious to his most basic surroundings. As a young researcher, he'd often worn the same clothes for days at a time. He'd never seemed to notice the need to wash or change. He could work in a hole in the ground and never feel the dirt or damp.

The Behavioral Institute wasn't quite that bad, but there was a pervasive atmosphere of hopelessness. Peter had a sudden urge to destroy the building, brick by brick. He wanted to put an irrevocable end to Evans's work.

He moved from the front window to the east side of the building. The windows were high slits, further protected by thick iron bars. Jumping, he grabbed two bars and pulled himself up. He could see a large, empty room. He spotted the empty cages where Familiar and the other felines had obviously been contained.

"Where is that damn cat?" he asked.

"Meow!"

The sound at his elbow was like a jolt of electricity. His body tensed, he dropped to the ground and rolled.

"Me-ow!"

Looking up at the next window, Peter couldn't believe his eyes. The inky silhouette of a black cat could barely be detected there.

"Familiar!" he exclaimed, the word coming out on a big sigh of relief. "We've been worried sick about you."

"Meow!" The cat jumped to the ground beside him and rubbed against his leg.

WELL, IT'S ABOUT TIME *Dudley Do-Right got here. I've been hanging out in that window for the past three hours. Eleanor is fine. She's sitting on the floor in a corner. At first I was worried about her. I thought maybe Dr. Frankenstein had given her something. But naw, she's okay, just furious. She looks up at me, and those brown eyes of her are blazing. I'd like to be a witness, if she could lay her hands on Dr. Frankenstein's neck!*

It's Zelda I'm worried about. I can barely catch a glimpse of her, and she's almost in a state of shock. Sometimes she shakes uncontrollably. Whatever he's done to her, it's hurt her bad!

Now I've got to get old Dr. Doolittle-Dudley Do-Right up and going in the right direction. I've checked this place out pretty thoroughly, and there's only one way he could get in. And then, I don't know, it's going to be a tight squeeze.

Well, he's off the ground now and following me. Good! That's progress. He keeps calling me that ridiculous "Kitty! Kitty!" and acting as if I should come to him. Those veterinarians. They are certainly slow to catch on to the order of things. Cats don't obey anyone! Well, I'll give him a lesson in feline-human etiquette at a later date. I want to get the girl, get the ape and get out of here. Yaba-daba-doo! Come on, Dr. Doolittle, there's a back door just over here, and I think I've been able to work the latch up a little. Being small, sleek, agile and brilliant does have its tremendous assets. We have to work fast, while Dr. Frankenstein is distracted.

"HEY!" ELEANOR WHISPERED. "Hey, little monkey!" She waved her hand and tried to attract the ape's attention. The orangutan was completely lethargic. She sat in a corner of her cage and looked at Eleanor, then her entire body began to tremble as if she had a fit of the ague.

"It's okay," Eleanor said. A surge of compassion for the creature touched her. "If I had my way, I'd get us both out of here."

She talked to the ape to pass the time and to keep her own nerves from snapping. She was afraid, and there was nothing she could do about it. No one knew where she was, except for the people who held her prisoner. Sam Nottingham! The man had set her up perfectly. And Evans! He was a monster, and now she knew why Magdalena Caruso felt no qualms about attacking him.

"I'd give a lot to see Magdalena walk through that door," she said aloud, hearing the note of wistfulness in her voice. She looked at the window again. The cat had vanished. "At least Familiar is free."

She studied her prison for the hundredth time. The room was small with bars on two sides, a wall with a mirror on the third, and the entrance on the fourth. There was a simple cot and nothing else. As far as she could see, the ape was confined in a similar cage.

Glancing back at the ape, she saw that it was standing by the bars, staring at her.

"Hey, girl," she said. "You're going to get out of here soon. You're going to be free, a pet of a nice man. Thank goodness for you." She sat down on her cot. "But what's going to happen to me?"

"You're going to help me." Evans's voice came to her through the speaker by the mirror. "Make friends with the ape. You'll be working together, and she could use a little support."

"I wouldn't help you across a busy street if you were blind," she said hotly. All of her self-imposed restraints suddenly burst. "You're sick, Evans, and *you* belong in this cage."

"I warned you once about those outbursts of temper." His voice was soft, its tone gleeful. "Must I come back in there and make you behave?"

Eleanor's hand involuntarily went to her leg. The shock had hurt!

"Answer me!"

"No," she said more carefully. Temper was great, but at this time she couldn't afford to exercise hers. Silently she vowed that when she had the chance, Evans would feel the full power of her wrath.

"Tomorrow is a big day for us at this lab," Evans said. His disembodied voice sounded eerie. "Tomorrow we present the orangutan to her new owner."

"I'm glad for her," Eleanor answered, unable to completely hide her sarcasm.

"With her impressive repertoire of behavior, she will demonstrate that an ape can be trained to follow a series of very complex orders." He laughed. "I'm coming in to show you."

Remembering the ape's terror, Eleanor jumped up. "That's okay. I'll take your word for it. I'm sure she's perfectly trained to carry out the most explicit social orders."

"It's a little more than than, Dr. Duncan. You'll see."

She heard the click of the lock, the turn of the bolt, and Evans entered the room. To her surprise he was dressed in a tuxedo, though his hair was still damp and glistening from a shower.

He opened the cage, and the monkey reluctantly walked up to him. "This is your final dress rehearsal, Zelda. Do it right tonight and then tomorrow, and you'll never be hurt again." An edge of softness had crept into his voice.

"Most animals aren't violent, and to train one to commit violence on command is often one of the most difficult obedience challenges."

"What are you talking about?" Eleanor was intrigued despite herself.

"Zelda here is going to perform an assassination tomorrow at a full state banquet. And you, Dr. Duncan, are going to be holding her leash when she does."

Chapter Sixteen

Peter leaned against the back door of the laboratory and stretched. He'd worried a small hole in a rotted portion of the door, about two feet from an ancient slide bolt that held the door shut. If he could only force it up, he could get inside. His fingers almost reached the lock. He pressed his face against the wood and stretched harder. The tip of his forefinger touched the metal, but he couldn't reach far enough to move it.

"Meow," Familiar said, pressing against the door.

"You open it if you can," Peter said in disgust. Withdrawing his arm, he sat back on his heels.

The door was of solid wood. It would take a stout fireman's axe to chop through, and he didn't have one. The old slide bolt tantalized him.

The cat had crept into a hole and was moving silently inside what was apparently a storage room. Peter got up and began to check the ground for a flexible stick. Maybe he could rig some type of lever so that he could exert pressure on the lock.

He found a maple tree and twisted off a low-hanging limb. Walking back to the door, he almost fell over the cat. Familiar was next to invisible in the darkness.

"Watch it," he cautioned, lifting his leg high to step over the cat.

"Meow!"

Familiar's claws dug into his leg.

Peter jumped backward, but Familiar clung to him. The cat was literally dragging him away from the door. Familiar stopped near the window and leaped onto the ledge.

"I feel like a fool," Peter said softly. "Dogs are supposed to do this kind of thing, not cats."

"Meow," Familiar said softly, then turned to look into the building.

Jumping for the window bars, Peter grabbed hold and pulled himself up. Through the narrow glass pane he saw Eleanor, the ape and Arnold Evans. While he'd been trying to break down the back door, Evans had returned. Peter's anger was so intense, he felt as if he could pull the bars loose and hurl himself through the window. As he watched, he saw Eleanor shake her head vehemently. The ape clutched its head and doubled over, apparently in great pain. Eleanor bent to the ape, then her hand lashed out to Evans's face. Peter looked on in helpless horror as Evans slapped her so hard that she stumbled backward.

He shook the bars, but they held steady. Enraged, he dropped to the ground again. In desperation he found another stick and went back to the wooden door. He had to get inside before Evans did anything worse. He was going to get inside, if he had to take the door down splinter by splinter.

Reaching through the small opening, he struggled to place the stick on the lock. To open the door he had to raise the lever of the lock, and then push it away from himself. The stick gave him the extra leverage he needed, but it kept slipping. The lock required a delicate touch. Gritting his teeth, he replaced the stick and started to lift the lock.

Sweat collected on his forehead as he worked. When he heard the crack of a branch only inches from his back, he tried to pull his arm out of the opening and turn around, but before he could see who was behind him, he felt a blow. Thunder echoed in his head, then there was nothing.

"I DIDN'T really want to do that," Joey Knight said. He knelt over Peter's body and felt for a pulse for the tenth time. "Are you sure he's okay?"

"Perfectly," Betty Gillette answered. "Thanks for coming with me, Joey. He was going to try and hurt Dr. Duncan. You were the only person I knew I could call."

"Where is she?" he asked, rising and shifting anxiously from one foot to the other. "Let's get her and get out of here. This place is creepy."

"Meow!" Familiar came through the hole in the back door. Wide green eyes held Betty.

"So, here's the elusive black cat," Betty said with a note of satisfaction. "We can get Eleanor and the cat. Sort of kill two birds with one stone."

"Let's do it." Joey looked around. "This place is awful. What do they do here?"

"Animal experiments. Basically whatever they feel like doing. Let's tie him up before we go."

"I don't know," Joey said. "He may be hurt. Why don't we leave him, get Dr. Duncan and then call an ambulance? I might have hit him too hard."

"He's fine," Betty said. "Here." She handed the student a length of rope she had wound around her waist. "I thought this might come in handy. Tie him good. I promise you, he isn't hurt. He'll come around in a few minutes, and I want him tied and gagged so he doesn't interfere."

"Yes, ma'am." Joey reluctantly took the rope. He bent to tie Peter's hands behind his back.

"Tighter!" Betty said, jerking the rope. "It's for his own good, Joey. If he gets in the middle of this, he could get us all killed, especially Dr. Duncan."

Joey pulled the rope tighter, then took the bandanna she offered him and fashioned a gag for Peter's mouth.

"He'll be fine," Betty said. "Let's get that cat. Here, kitty," she called, bending and reaching into the dark bushes. "Remember me? I'm your friend. Of all the cats that escaped, you were the one. That's fate, isn't it, big, black kitty? Where'd the damn cat go?"

"He was by the bush," Joey answered. He felt along the dark roots. "But he's gone now."

They'd searched for five minutes when Peter's moans finally drew Betty to his side. Catching the worried look on Joey's face, she checked Peter's pulse. "Slow and steady. I promise he isn't hurt," she said.

"Forget the cat for now. Let's get Dr. Duncan," Joey insisted.

"I guess you're right." Betty straightened. "We'll get him later."

"What's so important about an old black cat?" Joey asked.

"Oh, I don't know. It just seems that a lot of people want to get their hands on him, so that makes me believe he must have something pretty special to offer. We'll get him later. Can you give me a boost up to the window? I'd better check this out, before we go crashing into the building."

Using Joey's leg as a step, Betty forced herself up the wall. Her hands tightened on the bars as she caught sight of the interaction between Eleanor and Arnold Evans.

"Listen, Joey," she said, sliding to the ground again. "Drive back to the university and call the police. Don't stop around here, just get back to the campus, okay?"

"What's wrong?" he asked, panic in his voice. "Is Dr. Duncan in trouble?"

"There's no time to talk about it." Betty's voice was terse. "Go call the police. Tell them to get here as quickly as they can. Go!" she pushed him hard. "Run!"

As soon as he had disappeared into the night, she walked to the front door and rapped sharply. "Hey, Vrenner, open up! It's Betty Gillette."

In the back room, Evans paused before jerking on the ape's leash. He cocked his head, listening.

"Someone's at the front door," Eleanor said. The pounding of her heart was so loud that she could barely hear above it. She didn't know whether to be afraid that it was or wasn't Peter. Somehow she'd held on to a sliver of hope that he'd be able to figure out where she was and come to her. Part of her wanted him there, and another part feared for his life. Whenever Evans mentioned Peter's name, all the venom in his soul was exposed. He hated Peter, despised him. Evans wanted Peter dead.

"Wait here," Evans ordered her as he handed her Zelda's leash.

He left without a backward glance. Eleanor quickly moved around the door, trying to find a way to escape. The orangutan clung to her side, tentative fingers reaching for her hand.

"It's okay," Eleanor said, stroking the ape's coarse hair. "It's okay." If only Magdalena would come bursting through the door with an army of AK-47's and the desire to press Evans against the wall.

"I should have listened harder to that woman," Eleanor said as she continued to soothe the ape. "Magdalena may not be right about everything she does, but in some cases I fully understand how she's been pushed to the extreme. Under cover of the law, under the guise of medical advancement, Evans has tortured innocent animals." She picked up the ape's hand. The scars were deep. "One day he'll pay, Zelda."

There was some confused noise from the front room, and Eleanor pressed herself against the door to hear. There was the sounds of a struggle, someone falling against a desk or table. Books crashed to the ground, and metal screamed as it was dragged across cement.

"It's Peter," she whispered, her hopes rising. "He'll get us out of this mess." She held the ape's hand, amazed at the trusting way the fingers curled around hers. Like a child's, she thought.

The sound of the struggle drew closer to the door, until a body was thrown against the metal. Eleanor jerked back, just in time. The door opened and Betty Gillette came flying into the small prison. She landed on her back with a thud that knocked the breath from her.

"Betty!" Eleanor was at her side, helping her to sit up. Zelda approached slowly, putting her long fingers into Betty's red hair.

"I thought I could get you out," Betty said, her face marked with anger and fear. Her words came in short gasps as she struggled to get air into her lungs. "That degenerate Evans! I should have known who he was, but I didn't recognize him. Who would have thought he'd be right here, right in Washington under our noses?"

"What are you talking about?"

"Yes, Dr. Gillette. Why don't you tell your friend how you set her up so successfully?" Evans stood in the doorway. "To be honest, I found this out only a moment ago. Such a delightful twist."

"What's he talking about, Betty?" Eleanor helped the other woman to her feet.

"I didn't mean to—"

"Tell her!" Evans ordered.

"I took the cats from here," Betty said, staring defiantly at Evans. "If I'd had any idea he was involved, I'd have set up some kind of trap to blow him to the ends of the earth."

"Such emotion," Evans said, allowing himself a chuckle. "The bottom line is that Dr. Gillette took the animals and then allowed you, Dr. Duncan, to take the blame. Betrayal is such an interesting duality of emotion," he continued. "Are you ladies aware that animals feel betrayal? There was an experiment where mother cats—"

"Stop it!" Eleanor put her hands over her ears, a gesture which Zelda imitated perfectly.

"I didn't mean to involve you like this," Betty said. "You have to believe me." She touched Eleanor's shoulder.

"Now's a great time to think about it," Eleanor responded as she went to stand beside Zelda. "What are you going to do with us now?" she asked, directing the question to Evans. "Peter will get here anytime."

Betty shot her a look that signaled despair.

"My plans are magnificent," Evans said. "Tomorrow I topple an administration and gain the laboratory, funding and isolation I so richly deserve. After tomorrow I won't care what happens in this country."

"How are you going to topple an administration?" Betty had moved around the room, putting space between Eleanor and herself.

"Zelda here, accompanied by your charming friend, is going to pull a loaded gun from inside a gift box and fire at point-blank range." Evans smiled, shrugging his shoulders as if he were discussing a television show. "President Issac Demont will be dead. The Republic of Motambu will fall, and well, the rest will be history."

In the horrified silence that followed Evans's statements, Eleanor's voice seemed to crackle. "Why? Why are you doing this?"

"To demonstrate that I can train an ape to do anything. With the proper incentives, fear and pain, I've created the perfect killing machine. She looks so sweet and innocent. She grovels so sublimely. But on a given signal, she changes into the most savage, unstoppable creature ever imagined. And you, Dr. Duncan, will give that signal."

"I won't," Eleanor whispered. "I won't."

"Oh, yes, you will, or your associate here, Dr. Gillette, will die a very painful, unpleasant death. Now that doesn't sound good, does it?"

"You can't force me or Zelda to kill." Eleanor backed against the bars, trying to give Betty the opportunity she needed to get out. Eleanor wasn't certain what role Betty was actually playing, but her colleague's escape might be her only chance.

"Don't try it!" Evans rounded on Betty. His hand lashed out, striking her across the face with such force that she fell into Eleanor. "Now, let's go." He drew a pistol from his pocket. "And don't try anything. Remember, neither of you are so highly trained that you aren't disposable. I have the necessary clothes for you, Dr. Duncan. And Dr. Gillette, you're going to be my safety precaution. If Dr. Duncan doesn't do exactly as she's told, I'll use you for some of my more advanced experiments. I've always wondered what damage the human brain suffered from repeated blows to the head."

Betty started to say something, but Eleanor touched her elbow. She shook her head in warning. When she was certain that Betty would be silent, she held out her hand to the orangutan. Zelda walked up to her and put her hand into Eleanor's. Together they followed Evans out of the lab and into a waiting van. Before he slipped into the driver's seat, he handcuffed them.

"The Mayflower," he said aloud, smiling. "A final night in the lap of luxury before you go to work."

PETER CAME BACK to consciousness slowly at first, then with a start. Sandpaper was being dragged across his face, rubbing the skin away.

"Meow!" The rubbing stopped and there was the sound of loud purring.

"Familiar," he said. "You always show up when I least expect you. Someone slugged me, hard."

"Meow." The cat rubbed against his arms.

Slowly Peter forced himself to a sitting position. He worked his hands, relieved to see that whoever had tied them had done a halfhearted job. It would take a little time, but he could free himself. Time, though, was the one thing he didn't have a lot of. Eleanor was trapped in a building with a madman, and he had to get her out.

He struggled with the ropes for ten minutes, finally loosening the knots. As he slipped from the coils, he heard the sound of sirens wailing.

"Thank goodness," he said as he scooped Familiar into his arms and ducked into the shrubs. "We'll hide here while they free Eleanor. Don't tell anyone, Familiar, but you're hanging out with a wanted man."

Pushing backward, Peter lost himself in the dense shrubbery. From his vantage point, he watched the law officers force their way into the lab. He wanted to rush forward and grab Eleanor, but restrained himself. He had to wait until he could clear himself from the charge of murdering Sam Nottingham. As long as he knew Eleanor was safe, he'd be able to concentrate on his own problems. It would also delight him to see Evans led away in handcuffs.

"They're gone!" A cop shouted from inside the building. "The place is empty."

"The kid said someone was in danger, a university professor," another cop called back. "Boy, this place looks like some kind of torture chamber."

"Seal the door," the first cop said as he came out into the night. "The kid who called in wouldn't leave a name or anything. What should we do?"

"Call the lab guys and have them come down to take a look. That spot on the floor looks like blood. I suspect some crime has been committed in this place. Let the lab check it out."

"Right," the first cop said as he went to the patrol car. "I wish I could get my hands on that kid. He sounded terrified."

Peter crept backward, moving away from the building. Eleanor was gone! Evans had moved her and the ape! Where?

He put Familiar down so he could move easier, and the cat followed him without any hesitation. When they were a good distance away, Peter scooped up the cat once more and circled toward his car.

At last he got back to Betty's Tercel. When he was in the front seat, he realized he had no idea what to do next. Where could Eleanor have gone? Who had struck him? And what kid were the cops talking about? The questions came at him faster than he could begin to answer.

"Meow," Familiar said, rubbing against him.

Peter absently rubbed down the cat's spine, then moved to scratch his belly. It was one of Familiar's favorite places. His fingers found the small lump that moved freely with the skin. "Meow," Familiar said, pushing his body harder at Peter. "Meow!" He grew insistent, digging his claws into Peter's legs.

Peter started to push him away, then his fingers brushed the nodule again. "Wait a minute." Deftly he picked it up, a free-floating lump between the cat's skin and muscle. It could be a pellet, as he'd originally thought—or something else.

"Let's go," he said, throwing the car into Reverse. "I think you need to take a little nap, Familiar."

"Meow," the cat replied, curling into the seat and closing his eyes as if he agreed with everything Peter had said.

UNDER THE INTENSE LIGHTS of his office operating room, Peter studied Familiar's skin again. There was the site of a small incision that had healed perfectly. He patted Familiar's head. The cat had been fabulous about being shaved. He'd hardly batted an eyelid.

"Now comes the easy part," he said, slipping the needle into the cat's vein. "Just a few moments, and you're sound asleep."

Working with precision, he reopened the original scar. A few seconds of careful probing revealed the stainless steel container that resembled the shot from an old rifle. Peter carefully extracted it, then neatly restitched Familiar's stomach. The cat would be as good as new in a matter of days.

"And for your own safety you can stay in the kennel," he told the sleeping cat, gently carrying him to a recovery cage.

Back in the operating room, he grasped the metal cylinder with a pair of forceps. He washed it thoroughly, uncovering the mechanism that held it closed. It opened with a snap, and a sliver of microfilm was revealed.

"All along it was the cat," he whispered. He took the film to his microscope. Using tweezers to hold it, he placed it under the scope, then turned on a high-powered lamp. Reaching behind him, he flipped off the overhead light. Now he could see a definite picture on the white tile counter.

The focus was distorted, and he carefully began to make an adjustment. In a few seconds he could make out the numerals of a seven-digit code. Grabbing a pad, he wrote them down.

He moved the microfilm slightly, and a new frame came into focus. "Code One Orange XX to Code Two Blue." He noted down the exact letters and moved to the third frame, a series of numbers that indicated a Swiss bank account and possibly two passport numbers.

Although he didn't have the specifics, Peter understood the text he was reading well enough. He knew from Eleanor that Code One Orange had been the terrorist group her husband had been involved with. That could only mean subversive activities.

A pounding at his door made him start, so that he almost dropped the film. Recalling that he still had the gun he'd picked up at the memorial, he pulled it from his pocket.

The pounding came again. He walked silently to the door.

"Dr. Curry!" Joey cried. "Let me in! Something terrible has happened to Dr. Duncan!"

Peter threw the door open, and the young man nearly leaped into the room, gasping for breath. "They've got Dr. Duncan, and Dr. Gillette, too."

"Where are they, Joey?"

"I called the police like Dr. Gillette said. She acted so funny, though, that I went back. I saw that man loading them into a van, Dr. Duncan, Dr. Gillette and this monkey, and they drove away."

Peter's hopes sank. "They drove away?"

"Yeah, and I followed them to the Mayflower Hotel."

"Let's go," he said, grabbing Joey's arm.

"He had a gun on them," Joey added. He was shaking violently, but Peter heard him pull in a calming breath. "I got pretty close, and I heard him say that he would kill them all."

Chapter Seventeen

"I stole the cats because I believe it's wrong to use them in unnecessary experiments," Betty said as she slumped onto the plush bed. She and Eleanor were securely handcuffed to the bed frame, while Evans was busy in the adjoining room with Zelda.

"Why didn't you tell me?" Eleanor started to get up and walk, but the handcuffs jerked her back to the mattress.

"How was I to know that damn black cat would escape? I had all of them in the car, and when we went by the campus, he jumped out the window like a streak of lightning. I hunted everywhere for him, but he was gone."

"And I had to pick him up," Eleanor said. "Well, at least he's still alive. And Peter, too, if you didn't give him brain damage."

"He isn't hurt," Betty emphasized. "I thought Joey and I could break in, release you and we could all get away. I didn't want anyone to know I was the one freeing the lab animals around town. Especially not Peter. I recognised him from that chemical plant disaster years before. He was originally accused of the atrocities. Even though he was cleared, I wasn't certain about him."

"And you didn't try to warn me?"

"You may not realize it yet, but I saw the way you two looked at each other. Fools for love! What was I supposed to do? Rush up and say that the man you were falling in love with might torture small animals? I'm sure you'd have listened.''

"Great!'' Eleanor said dismally. She looked again at the telephone by the bed. Evans had pulled the cord from the wall. More than anything in the world she wanted to hear Peter's voice. If she could just talk to him, she could endure almost anything. "Are you sure you didn't hurt Peter?''

"Positive. He's probably come round and gotten untied by now. He's looking for you . . . if the police haven't found him,'' Betty said, suddenly remembering that he was wanted for murder. She gave Eleanor a hesitant look.

"What is it now?''

"The police think Peter killed Sam Nottingham at the Jefferson Memorial.''

"Nottingham! I thought he was part of this.'' Eleanor dropped her head into her hands. The handcuffs rattled like cheap jewelry. The only person who might possibly rescue them was more than likely in jail. "We need a plan.''

"No one will ever think to look for us in the Mayflower,'' Betty said, leaning back on her elbows. "We may as well wait it out. The banquet is tomorrow at six. By then, surely we'll have thought of something.''

"If we don't, someone is going to die.'' Eleanor felt a new surge of desperation-inspired energy. "Maybe we . . .''

The door to the adjoining room opened and Evans entered, carrying two evening dresses. He pointed to one. "For you, Dr. Duncan,'' he said. "You look like a woman who looks good in red. I thought you two would appreciate the idea. The old story of the lady in red.'' He laughed. "Demont will be so busy looking at you, he won't even see Zelda pull the gun. Did I mention that she was his pet before my associates stole her? Isn't that ironic?''

"What will happen to Zelda when this is over?'' Eleanor hoped for some trace of compassion.

He shrugged. "She's served her purpose. I'm sure the security guards will kill her on the spot. More than likely you'll be killed, too."

"Don't do this," Betty said. "Eleanor was never involved. I did it all." She looked at Eleanor and hung her head. "I even set you up for that AFA meeting by breaking into your office and leaving that flyer."

"Why?"

"You were already a suspect. I figured you'd eventually clear your name, and I'd be free to continue liberating animals. The thing I didn't count on was running into Arnold Evans." She spoke the name as if it had a vile taste. "Subhuman, torturer..."

"Enough, Dr. Gillette," Evans said. He was completely undisturbed by her disgust. "Now, both of you ladies have a good night's rest. We have a busy day tomorrow." He came toward them, two pills on his palm. "Take one."

"What about Carter?" Eleanor picked up the capsule and held it. "When can I see him?"

"Sooner than you wish," he said, laughing.

"Does he know you killed Rayburn?" She held her breath.

Evans's face hardened for a brief moment, then relaxed. "Too bad Rayburn didn't keep his mouth shut. As soon as he hung up talking to you, he called us. It was a simple thing to lure him to your apartment and eliminate him. It was our misfortune that you evaded the suspicions."

"Where is Carter now?" Eleanor held her breath again. If he was indeed alive, she might be able to sway him to help her. He'd never really loved her, but surely he didn't hate her enough to want her to die. "Where is he?"

"Well, after the number my associates did on his brakes, I sincerely hope he's a heap of bones at the bottom of a canyon."

"You killed him! And all of this has been a trick!" Eleanor felt relief, anger and the destruction of her last, fragile hope.

"Yes, pretty good, huh?"

She could never let Evans know how frightened she was. He fed off the fear of others. "That's pretty clever. The person who pretended to be him—he sounded exactly like him, moved like him," she agreed matter-of-factly. She saw Betty's openmouthed astonishment. "You really had me going, Evans. I believed that Carter had come back from the grave." An eerie sensation moved across her skin. "When he came to the parking garage . . ."

"What parking garage? We never set you up in a garage." Evans looked baffled, then angry.

"That first time he 'appeared' in the garage of my building." Something was wrong. "What is it?" she asked. Watching Evans's eyes, she felt the return of her darkest fears. Evans had never sent the man playing Carter to her building. She could read it in his face.

"I've had enough of this foolish talk. Take it!" He thrust the second pill at Betty.

Neither woman had a chance to spit them out; he kept too close an eye on them.

"Now sleep," he said as he flipped off the light. "Tomorrow you're going to need to be rested."

"I wish I could get to a phone and call Alva Rousel," Betty said angrily. "He'd show you a thing or two."

Evans's laughter rang across the room. "Yes, I'm sure he would. He isn't anything if he isn't Mr. CIA, is he?" He laughed again.

"WE MUST bide our time and wait," Magdalena said. She was back in her own living room, bundled in a comforter. A line of pain was etched on her forehead.

"Why can't we go now?" Peter asked. "Eleanor's life may be at stake."

234 *Fear Familiar*

"Patience, Peter," she said softly. "There's a lot more at stake here than Eleanor's life, as much as I value it. Evans has slipped through our fingers too often before. When he tries to pull this scheme off, we'll have him cold. Besides, if he were going to hurt her, he'd have done it at the lab." She looked at Joey. "You have the waiter's uniform."

He nodded. "I can do it. I know exactly what I'm to do."

"And you, Peter? Will you be able to hold yourself in?"

"Yes," he said. "But Evans is mine when this is over. For old times' sake."

"Thanks for making my bail," she said, shifting so that he could prop up her injured ankle. "They know I didn't kill that man, but once you get on the wrong side of the law, they like to make you pay."

"Thank Joey for bailing you out," Peter replied. "I couldn't go inside, because they think I killed Nottingham in the tidal basin. Let's try to get some rest," he added, standing up and stretching. "We'll need it tomorrow. Issac Demont." He said the name slowly. "How did you know, Magdalena?"

"I should have thought of it sooner, actually. The orangutan is such an obvious clue. Demont has worked hard to preserve species in Motambu. His love of apes is not exactly a secret, and he and Nottingham worked closely together. The microfilm was conclusive. Code One Orange," she said. "All of these years and they never gave up. If it couldn't be Central America, Africa would do. As soon as we have Evans, we can get the professionals to run down those numbers. If I were guessing, I'd say foreign bank accounts."

"To fund Evans and his criminal plans," Peter said bitterly.

Magdalena's voice was suddenly tired, disillusioned. "I need to go to bed. Talking about this won't change it, or bring tomorrow any faster."

Peter and Joey stood up when she rose. "It won't be long now," Peter said. He checked his watch. Less than sixteen hours.

THE ZIPPER sealed the red sequined dress up her back, and Eleanor felt her heart skip. It was a perfect fit. Even the makeup that Evans had brought for her was perfect. She felt like a mannequin, some dressed-up killer doll. The tears threatened and she thought of Peter. She wanted to speak to him, to at least tell him what she felt for him.

"Don't think about it," Betty warned her. "Our plan may not be the most sophisticated, but it might work." She tugged at the bodice of the emerald gown Evans had provided for her. The dress was attractive, but not as stunning as the one Eleanor was wearing.

"He says he'll be holding a gun at your back," Eleanor said. "What if he kills you first?"

"Not much chance on that." Betty grinned, bringing back the dancing light in her blue eyes for a moment. "My mother always told me I was tougher than any girl had a right to be."

"I hope she was right," Eleanor commented. She picked up the silver leash and Zelda rose slowly. There was no sign of life in her big, brown eyes.

"Whatever he gave her must have been strong," Eleanor said. "She doesn't really know what she's doing."

"Thank goodness," Betty said. "Thank goodness."

The door opened and Evans walked in, his tuxedo smudged and rumpled as if he'd slept in it. "They're waiting for the presentation." His eyes roamed approvingly down Eleanor's sleek, glistening form. "You look perfect."

"If I could kill you, I would," she answered. When he tried to take Zelda's leash from her, she jerked it away.

"Suit yourself," he said. "I have no fondness for that creature. And I'll have Dr. Gillette to keep me company."

He took Betty's bare elbow, digging his fingers into the tender flesh of her upper arm until she winced. "Just remember," he told Eleanor, "your friend will suffer if you make one false move."

They walked through the hotel, an eye-catching foursome of man, women and orangutan.

"Isn't that little ape darling," one woman gushed, coming over to visit Zelda.

"Stay back!" Evans commanded sharply. "She's extremely valuable."

"I'm sorry," the woman said, withdrawing. She cast a strange look over her shoulder at Evans, but moved away, nonetheless.

Wait! Eleanor's mind screamed at her. *Can't you see something is wrong?* But she remembered the metal pressed into Betty's back and kept moving. Zelda walked like an automaton at her side.

They went through the lobby and down an elegant hallway with beautiful carpets and large vases of fresh flowers. At the Chinese ballroom they were stopped by several security officers.

"No handbags, no weapons," the officer said, giving them a professional smile. "And you have an invitation?"

Evans gave him the embossed card, and they were ushered into the room.

A swirl of hunter green and rich burgundy seemed to stretch across the white marble floors and walls. Tiers of starched linen tablecloths folded out on all sides. Sparkling chandeliers shimmered with golden points of light.

Eleanor felt herself being pulled into the room, moving past a line of people whose names and faces were only a blur. At the end of the line she saw Issac Demont, a tall, smiling man who bowed to her with the most courtly of manners. His eyes seemed to hold some special promise for her, and she felt her knees begin to buckle.

Evans's arm went around her waist, and his fingers dug into her ribs. "Make a scene and I'll kill you all right here," he whispered.

Eleanor forced her body to move forward. The presentation of Zelda would come in only a few moments, as soon as the official receiving line was closed and Demont took his place on the podium.

"Good luck," Betty whispered.

"You're on your own, and your friend's life depends on you," Evans said as he pushed Betty away. Eleanor stood stock-still, Zelda's leash in her hand. Her eyes caught the movement of additional guests taking seats in the back of the room. Balconies extended from the mezzanine, and tables were already filled with expectant guests. Little did they know they'd come to see the man who held the key to peace in a large segment of Africa die.

She felt the tears sting behind her eyes, then suddenly the ape's hand clutched hers. Looking into the depths of those warm, brown eyes, Eleanor saw a spark of the old life.

"Zelda," she whispered.

The ape's fingers closed tighter on hers.

"We can make it. We'll outfox that maniac," she whispered, feeling a moment of hope for the first time all day.

There was the official fanfare of trumpets as Demont made his way to the dais. Eleanor took up her position with Zelda. A procession had formed, and she was the center of it. She looked around, surprised to see that Charles Breck was not in evidence. Surely he'd want to see his handiwork come to pass, she thought. It struck her suddenly that Nottingham had been as thoroughly set up as she had herself. Breck was arrogant, intolerable, but he obviously knew nothing of this plan. He wouldn't want to be the man whose gift backfired so tragically.

Her attention was called to the head table, where Issac Demont had risen.

"We all gather here to express our sympathy," he began in a deep, melodious voice. "I have known for months of the work the Honorable Sam Nottingham has undertaken in order to provide me with such a special gift. I grieve for him today, and my sympathy goes to his family in their hours of mourning. Sam and I saw many things in many distant lands. I learned much from him, and I believe I can say that I taught him a few things. We were good friends. I know the police will apprehend his murderer, and some degree of solace will come for his family. He was a man with a hot temper, who knew the value of a cool head and the need for peace. I am prepared to accept the gift he worked so hard to prepare for me."

Stunned that the moment had arrived, Eleanor failed to move forward. She felt a nudge at her back.

"Go ahead," a woman urged her. "Everyone's waiting."

Eleanor stepped forward and down the aisle made by the spectators. Something was wrong with Zelda. At the sight of Demont, she had suddenly grown agitated. She shook the gift box as she twisted and capered against the leash. Eleanor held it tight, using all of her strength to keep the orangutan from rushing down the path to the man who waited for her with such open pleasure.

When they were only five feet away, Eleanor stopped. Now was the moment. Hand sweeping the floor, Zelda curtsied. Demont and the whole room thundered applause.

Helpless, Eleanor held the leash as Zelda lifted the lid from the gift box. In one fluid motion Zelda pulled the gun from the tissue and pointed it directly at Issac Demont's head. The scream she uttered was anguished, unearthly.

Eleanor's hand lashed out swiftly and struck Zelda's forearm. The gun exploded into the marble floor, sending the bullet ricocheting into the roof. A second shot was fired from the back of the room, followed by a third from one of the balconies.

Too late, Eleanor reached out to Demont. There was an amazed expression on his face as he fell back, propelled by the blast of a shot into the arms of his security men.

Completely out of control, Zelda screamed and jerked forward. Her lurch was so sudden and so strong that she pulled free from Eleanor's grasp and ran to the stricken man. Her voice was that of a sobbing child as she cradled Demont's head against her hairy chest.

Stupefied by the turn of events, Eleanor swung around slowly. Betty Gillette was standing by Evans's fallen body. Rushing across the room toward her was Peter, dressed in the garb of a waiter.

"Peter," she cried, staggering toward him. "Peter!"

The crowd parted for them, Eleanor flung herself into his arms, the pent-up tears finally flowing. "I tried to stop it. I tried. But he's dead! Evans shot him."

"It's okay," Peter said, holding her, crushing her against himself. "It's okay. Really, Eleanor. It's not as bad as you think. Listen to me." He drew her aside as the commotion near the fallen leader seemed to thicken and swell to a mild uproar.

"Demont's okay. He isn't hurt. I promise," Peter said. He stroked her hair, her cheek, he held her and talked to her. He wanted to pick her up in his arms and carry her out of that room, away from the nightmare she'd been forced to endure.

Very gently he took her to the dais, where a small cluster of dark-suited men stepped back. Issac Demont rose on one elbow and held out his hand to Eleanor. Zelda was at his side, patting his shoulder.

"I am not hurt," he said. "Your friends warned me." He pulled back his jacket to reveal the outline of a bulletproof vest.

"I'm taking that orangutan out of here," a loud, female voice proclaimed. Pushing her way through the crowd, Magdalena Caruso limped toward Eleanor.

"Peter and I argued all morning on account of you," she said to Eleanor, ignoring everyone else around. "He wanted to storm the Mayflower and rescue you like some old-time damsel without a brain. I told him not to bother, that you were smart enough to handle things for yourself, and I was right. Zelda didn't want to kill her old master, but you knocked the shot down, anyway."

"Breck?" Eleanor felt as if she were hearing an unknown tongue. "He was behind this. He's the one who hired Evans to train the monkey. He's..."

"I never knew anything," Charles Breck said. He assisted Issac Demont to his feet and helped steady him.

"He was a tool of Evans," Peter agreed. He pulled Eleanor closer, delighting in the feel of her body against his own. He'd been worried sick about her.

"And Evans?" She swung around to find her colleague at the end of the room, a wide smile on her face. She held a deadly looking weapon trained on Evans, who sat holding his wounded arm.

"He's going to a place where he may come to understand the sensations of being caged," Magdalena said with pleasure. "Of course, if our system gets tired of holding him, we can always send him to Motambu to stand trial."

"Who shot him?" Eleanor asked. Events had transpired too fast.

"I did," Peter said softly. "He fired at Demont, and I shot him. He set me up for Nottingham's murder."

"And me," Breck said.

"And me," Magdalena added. She turned to Breck. "When will you learn not to trust people who mistreat animals? We've been through this again and again...."

"A very wise and valuable lady," Issac Demont said, taking Magdalena's arm. "Let me talk with you about a job in my country. Perhaps as Minister of Small Creatures." He smiled at her and for the first time in her life it appeared Magdalena was at a loss for words.

"And Zelda?" Eleanor asked. The orangutan was following closely at Demont's heels as he walked to a corner with Magdalena.

"We thought at first she'd have to be destroyed," Breck confessed, "but Issac absolutely refuses to consider it. He's going to take her home and love her. You know she was his, and Evans had her stolen. It's one of the sickest plots."

"Why?" Eleanor asked. Pressed against Peter, she felt isolated from all the terrible things that had happened to her. He was strong, safe, and he held her as if he'd never let her go.

"Because he's a sick man," Peter said softly. "I've hated him for years, but I guess I never fully acknowledged that he isn't evil. He's merely sick."

"And he will be put in a place where he can never harm another living thing again," Breck assured her.

"What will happen to Betty?" she asked. She sought her friend's gaze across the room. Betty grinned and nodded at her.

"We'll see," Breck said. "We'll take everything into account."

"Champagne, *madame*?" A waiter came up to Eleanor and held out a glass.

"No, thanks," she said, shaking her head. It wasn't until she saw the laughing eyes of Joey that she laughed herself. "And you were in on this, too?"

"As much as Dr. Curry would let me," he said. "We wanted to rescue you, but Magdalena made us wait."

"A wise woman," Charles Breck finally agreed. "But don't tell her I said so," he whispered to Eleanor. "Now I'd better take Evans to the local authorities, so we can begin the process of ending this mess."

Chapter Eighteen

"Home at last, Eleanor." Peter opened the door to her apartment building for her and handed her into the lobby.

A wide-awake Familiar was clutched to the bosom of her red sequined dress. Eleanor held the cat as if he were her last friend.

"You need a hot bath and some rest." He continued talking to her, soothing her. "You look positively haunted."

"I'm okay," she said, finally hearing the worry in his voice. She'd been lost in her own thoughts. So much had happened so quickly, it was still hard for her to grasp that it was all over. Evans was under arrest, and everyone else was safe. Everyone but Sam Nottingham.

"Don't think about it anymore," Peter said.

His hazel eyes were fiery with determination, and Eleanor felt them transfer their warmth to her chilled bones. And those eyes held a promise that at last made her emotions begin to thaw.

"Dr. Curry, Dr. Duncan!" Wessy came up to them. "Is everything all right?"

"Yes." Peter patted the older man's arm. "At last everything is okay. And I owe you an apology. I thought you were mixed up in all of this."

"No problem," Wessy said. "As long as Dr. Duncan is safe, there's no problem at all. I'm glad you worry about her."

He turned to Eleanor. "Hey, you've got a present. Some kid left this for you," he said, reaching into the doorman's room and coming out with a bottle of wine. "He said to tell you to celebrate your victory—and your future together. Those were the exact words."

"Joey," Eleanor said, taking the bottle. "I'm glad he escaped any serious injury." She looked at Peter and felt an irresistible desire to kiss him. Fate had kept them apart, but now it was time to explore the delicious feelings they had for each other. It was a risk as big as any she'd ever taken in her life. "Let's go upstairs and uncork this bottle," she said.

Twenty minutes later with a purring Familiar curled on her lap and a glass of the delicious burgundy in her hand, Eleanor felt the knots in her stomach loosen. There was only one thing left to do—to bury Carter Wells and her past. Peter was her future, and she wanted to start clean, without any misunderstandings.

"Let me say one final thing," she said slowly. "My life with Carter was hell. I suppose it was worse than I remember, because I monitor my memories. I should have left him a million times. But my family disapproved of him—disapproved is too mild a word. When I married Carter, I severed all ties with my family. I call them in Arizona at Christmas—" she paused to push back her hair "—but I'm going to change that this year. Anyway, they forced me to the choice, and I guess I was so headstrong I couldn't admit I'd made a serious mistake. So I stayed with him."

"You were a very young woman," Peter said. "I'm sure you were scared."

She nodded. "Very scared. If I was wrong about Carter, then I'd ruined my own life for no good reason. So I hung on, hoping each day that he'd change, or that something would happen to free me. And it did. The car accident."

"You can't feel guilty because Carter's death brought you a measure of relief. You were trapped in a bad situation, but you didn't do anything wrong."

"I know I didn't, and I honestly hadn't thought about him in years. But when I saw the man Evans had hired to pretend to be him, when I heard that voice, I believed he was back. Logically I fought it, but emotionally it was my nightmare come true. I didn't tell you right away, because I was afraid I might have been hallucinating."

She filled both of their wineglasses again before she had the nerve to continue. "I haven't felt anything—allowed myself to feel—for a man since my feelings for Carter died. I guess I was afraid of my reaction to you. I do feel something for you, Peter. Something real."

"I know," he said.

"And I was afraid that I'd brought Carter back in my mind, to punish me for wanting you."

"Oh, Eleanor." He put his glass aside and drew her into his arms. "What have you been going through? Whatever happened, just remember that you're not alone. Whatever happens in the future, we'll solve it. Together."

His fingers traced along her back, delicious swirls of pleasure following each light touch. The pressure became stronger, more insistent, and she moved toward him in response. Lifting her face, she smiled at him, then initiated a kiss.

Peter's response was restrained, but hungry, relishing her suppleness. She pressed her lips eagerly to his, demanding a longer, deeper kiss.

Throwing caution to the wind, Peter kissed her with a devouring need. A quick memory of his first sight of her came back to him. She was standing in his examining room, black cat in her arms. He'd wanted her then. When he'd examined her face, he'd been drawn to her eyes. Brown and wide, they'd surprised him with their innocence. He'd been sure she was trying to set him up. He smiled slightly, and Eleanor drew back.

"What is it?" she asked, breathless.

"Sometimes I amaze myself with my cynicism," he murmured. "I saw many things I admired when I first met you. Yet I couldn't accept that right away. It took time for me to believe you were real." He closed off further conversation with another kiss, one that grew quickly to an unspoken agreement. He helped her to her feet, and they walked to the bedroom.

The moon was a silent witness as Peter removed her clothes. When she was nude, the red dress a shimmer of fallen stars around her feet, she began to unbutton his shirt. His hands explored the contours of her back as she worked quickly.

Stepping free of the last restraints of his clothing, he pulled her into his arms yet again and kissed her with a possessive force that tipped back her head against his arm. Locked in an embrace, they moved to the bed.

Later, lying in the silvery light that filtered through the blinds, she kissed his cheek. The moon was high, unblinking. Her voice was barely louder than a sigh when she spoke. "When did you make me fall in love with you?"

"Oh, about two hours ago. It was the magic of my kiss." He grabbed her hand and kissed her fingers. "Up until that time, you were only moderately interested."

She laughed at him, kissing his nose and chin and chest. The dark hairs were soft and cushiony to her fingers. She traced patterns through them.

"Are you sleepy?" she asked.

"I'm too satisfied to sleep." He kissed her neck. "Why don't we finish that wine?"

He rose, taking a moment to give Familiar, who was curled at the foot of the bed, a friendly stroke before he went to the living room and retrieved the wine and glasses.

"Do you think Familiar is jealous?" Eleanor asked. She meant the question to be a joke, but Peter gave her a long look before he poured the wine.

"Don't take it too lightly. He might be. So we'll just have to give him some extra affection and reassurance. Remember, you belong to him. I'm a visitor, until he comes to accept me into his family. And I believe he will. Familiar is a smart cat, and animals often understand the dynamics of a relationship long before the people involved do. Familiar has been aware of my evil intentions to seduce you." He waggled his eyebrows and grinned.

Eleanor lifted the cat into her lap, adding another contrast to those of the blue sheets around her legs and the pale ivory of her skin. "I can't believe the way this rascal has won my heart," she said. "I must be a real soft touch for hairy mammals."

"And I can't believe the way you've won mine," Peter answered, handing her a brimming glass. "I have to tell you, Eleanor. I've fallen deeply in love with you. I want to become a part of your life."

"Peter," she said, suddenly overwhelmed by what he was saying. "This is happening so fast."

"Take your time. We have the entire future to work it out. But know that I love you, and that I want to share my life with you. There's no obstacle we can't overcome, if we attack it together."

Eleanor stroked the purring cat. Peter's words affected her deeply, touching a place in her heart that she'd never allowed anyone else to touch. She'd never had a real marriage. She and Carter had been at odds from the first. But now she felt the pull of Peter's love.

"We'll talk. Tomorrow," she said, her voice husky with emotion. "I have to ask Familiar what he thinks."

"You've got it," Peter said, sitting on the bed. "Now drink your wine and tell me when you'll be free of all university obligations this coming spring. I want to plan a trip.

Ve'll go somewhere with sun and sand and water. We'll put
ll of this behind us and simply relax."

"I could learn to love this way of life," Eleanor told him,
nuggling into the covers. She sipped her wine and let her
and scratch and tickle the sleeping cat. "I have this feel-
ng that life with you could be close to perfect."

They talked for another half hour, finishing the last of the
vine. The intimacy, the physical release and the wine began
o act on Eleanor like a powerful potion.

"I feel like Sleeping Beauty, ready to go down for the
housand-year count," she declared, sliding farther into the
ed.

"I feel absolutely drugged," Peter answered. His wine-
lass rolled from his fingers and fell to the carpet. He made
n effort to grab for it, but fell back half a foot short. "I
an't even judge distance anymore," he said, amazed.

Eleanor reached for the bedside light switch, but her hand
truck the table with enough force to bruise. Oddly enough,
he didn't feel anything. A singing wire of panic flashed
hrough her brain.

"Peter!" She spoke aloud, but the word came out as a
vhisper. "What's happening to us?"

"I don't know," he answered. "I feel . . . helpless."

She tried to struggle from the bed, but her limbs refused
o cooperate. She had to get up, to move. She felt as if her
ife depended on it, but her body refused to budge. Turning
o Peter for help, she found him already asleep, his dark
ead pressed deep in a pillow.

"Peter!" She shook him. "You have to wake up!"

He flailed at the bed, but his eyes never opened.

"Peter!" Hysteria grew in her, but she could barely move.

"Peter!" She cried his name as if she could pull him from
is deep sleep by her need.

"Eleanor!"

The voice came from somewhere outside the bedroom "Yes, Eleanor, it's me. Peter can't help you now, you're mine!"

It was impossible. Evans was behind bars and Carter was dead! She struggled against the sheets and blankets. They pressed on her like some constricting device. She had to get up, to save Peter and herself.

"Don't struggle, Eleanor. There's nothing you can do I've come for you, to take you back with me. Back to the grave."

Carter Wells's body materialized in her bedroom doorway. Backlighted by the lamps in the hall, he was as tall, as broad-shouldered as she remembered. His facial features were once more shadowed by the wide-brimmed hat. The reek of his cigarette made her want to choke.

"Carter," she cried, "leave me alone!" The nightmare sensations so well remembered from the garage spun across the room, trapping her in a web of fear. No matter how often she told herself that Carter was dead, he was standing before her. No trick this time. Carter was real and he was angry.

"Eleanor, you're my wife."

"I'm not. You died. And I made a new life. Leave me alone!"

"I'd like to, Eleanor. But you have to give back what you took from the lab. Give back the microfilm that your lover took from the cat, and I'll leave."

The figure stepped closer to the bed. It was indeed Carter Wells. He'd fooled everyone, including his own enemies.

"No!" Eleanor tried to rise from the sheets, but couldn't force her body to move. She knew she was drugged. The wine! How could she have been so stupid? Beside her, Peter, who'd drunk more than she, was deeply under the influence of the drug.

"Give it to me, Eleanor. Or I'll have to hurt your lover. I have a perfect right to kill you both."

"Leave us alone, Carter. I don't have any microfilm. Peter must have given it to one of the CIA agents."

"You have it!" The figure turned on her, an angry finger jabbing in the air in a long-remembered, authoritative gesture. "Otherwise, they'd be looking for me already. You see, that little bit of film can implicate me. I foolishly put my code on it. It's so much more convenient when people think I'm dead. I don't want them to know that I'm actually very much alive."

"I don't know what you're talking about." A tiny portion of her brain was struggling to function clearly. She had to pay attention. The figure rushed to the bed, lifting her by her hair into a sitting position.

"Don't tempt me, Eleanor!"

She struggled to free herself, but still couldn't make any of her limbs obey. The smell of Carter's favorite cologne made her twist away from him. Beside her, Peter lay as if he might be dead.

"Okay," she agreed. "I'll give you the microfilm." She had to do something to make him leave. "Peter hid it in his clinic. He said it was in a file. My file," she amended, trying to make it sound convincing.

"You'll come with me to get it," he said. "Get dressed."

"Yes," she agreed. Her hair felt as if it were being pulled from her scalp.

"Don't try anything stupid." He reached down and jerked the phone from the wall.

"I promise," she said. She fell to the mattress when her hair was released. "Wait for me in the living room."

Carter hesitated a moment in the doorway—was he reconsidering? Eleanor wondered—then disappeared down the hall. As soon as he was gone, she fought her way to a sitting position. The drug was powerful, but she managed to hold herself erect.

"Peter?" she called.

There was no answer, only the darkness.

*WHO THE HELL is this guy, rummaging through here? He had
a key to the door, and he came in like he knew where he was
going. Thank goodness, I'd taken a little run to the kitchen
to see if Eleanor left anything good to eat on the counter. No
dice on the food, but it gave me the drop on the guy when
he zipped through the door. A healthy human specimen, I
have to give him that. Not as big as Dr. Doolittle, but the
two of them would be a match. Somehow I get the distinct
impression that they are adversaries. I'd better follow this
guy to see what he's up to.*

*The guy moves like he's upset. He's headed straight for
Eleanor's bedroom, and he's no friend! Who the hell is he?
Eleanor knows him! She's talking really strange, but she
knows him! Rat litter! She's afraid of him, and he's not
doing anything to remedy that situation. He's pulling her
hair and threatening her! I know him now! He's been lurking around here like somebody's lost shadow!*

*Hey! Dr. Doolittle! Snap out of it and defend Eleanor!
What's wrong with the two of them? She sounds like a record on 78, and the good doctor is out cold. From one bottle of vino! What pantywaists! They'd never make the
Washington party circuit that I grew up in. But all of that
aside, I have to do something to get the tall, blond stranger
out of here. It's just that my resources are limited in this
apartment. Give me a dark alley and I'd have that sucker on
his knees, begging for mercy. But, hey, I've got to work with
what I've got.*

*Wait! Here he comes! He's striding out of her bedroom
like a king. Now it's time for a little fancy, furry footwork,
if you don't mind unnecessary alliteration.*

*A direct attack is too risky. Don't ask me how I know this
guy's here because of me, but he is. Following the example
of the best fighters ever known, I'm going to initiate the old
ambush plan.*

*Timing is all in this situation. Timing and an intense de-
sire to inflict pain. I do believe he hurt the dame. Not bad,*

*but nobody hurts my Eleanor and gets away scot-free. So
here goes!*

ELEANOR was pulling on a pair of sweatpants when she
heard the enraged scream of the cat. She staggered down the
hall, leaning against the wall for support, then hit the light
switch and flooded the room with brightness.

In her living room, Carter was spinning in a circle, Familiar riding his head, clawing and biting with every ounce
of his twelve pounds. Calling on her last reserves, Eleanor
picked up a lamp and swung it sideways into Carter's face.
The lamp shattered, and the man fell to his knees, then
crashed into the wall. Familiar leaped to the safety of the
sofa. For a moment there was silence. A tiny trickle of blood
oozed down the wall and into the fibers of the muted gray
carpet.

Familiar sat on the arm of the sofa, his golden-green gaze
focused intently on the unconscious man. He seemed to take
in every detail of the man's features. Only a few feet away,
the hat had fallen against the wall.

Eleanor stumbled closer. Something was wrong. It wasn't
Carter. With the hair slicked back, a fake nose and a little
makeup, he resembled him a lot, but it wasn't him.

"Alva Rousel," Eleanor said, standing over the unconscious form. "All along it was you." A very distant memory came back to her of a tall, blond man who'd come to her
home the day Carter died. He'd said he was there to inspect
the swimming pool, and she'd left him unattended in the
yard. He'd borne a simple resemblance to Carter then,
something she'd noted but never thought about again.
Strange coincidence, she thought, recalling that she'd
learned Carter's brake line had been cut. She'd never connected the two until now. So Carter had been involved in the
CIA plot with Rousel, and then Rousel had killed him.
While they were working together, Rousel had gotten to
know Carter well enough to imitate him perfectly.

"Meow," Familiar said as he sprang from the sofa. He brushed against her leg, using his soft claws to nudge at her feet.

Eleanor responded, moving to the telephone and dialing 911. Then she went back to the bedroom and this time managed to rouse Peter.

"HE WAS TERMINATED in 1982, or at least that's what we thought," Charles Breck said, shaking his head; the police were leading Rousel away in handcuffs. "Our last report was that he was killed in Beirut, in an attempt to provoke some international trouble there."

"Terminated?" Eleanor asked. Her head was pounding from the aftereffects of whatever drug Rousel had put into the wine, but she had to know the truth.

"Our reports indicated he was blown to bits by a faction of Black September. We heard that he betrayed the wrong people, and they killed him. Even though we tried to find his CIA credentials, we never did. We thought he was dead." Breck ran a hand through his hair. "Now that I'm going to be director, I promise you such slipshod methods won't be tolerated."

"Spoken like a true politician," Peter said, but there was more humor than malice in his words. "So Rousel was actually the brains behind the whole plot. Evans was simply a tool. Incredible." He shook his head. "All of this was designed to ruin Sam Nottingham."

"Because Nottingham blew the whistle on Rousel in Central America," Breck told them. "I don't believe Rousel intended to kill Nottingham, but it was the perfect setup for revenge on you, Peter. Evans was out of control." He sighed deeply. "Maybe I'm not cut out for this business, after all."

"Poor Betty," Eleanor said, thinking of the way her colleague had been tricked by Rousel. Peter's arm circled her shoulders.

"You'll be relieved to know that there are no official charges against Dr. Gillette or Magdalena Caruso," Breck told them. "Maybe a few stern lectures, but no charges. And our people are now thoroughly checking the trade in research animals. As we've discovered, a lot of information can be illegally passed in innocent cats and dogs. Those Swiss bank accounts were very lucrative."

"Thanks," Eleanor said as she and Peter walked Breck and the policemen to the door.

"And Merry Christmas," Breck wished them in farewell.

Peter closed the door and locked it. His strong arms reached out for Eleanor and drew her close. "If it isn't too late to make a special request to Santa, I know what I want this year."

"What?" She held back the laughter that tickled her throat.

"I have her right here in my arms. So that part is simple. But I want her for the rest of my life."

"And her little cat, Familiar, too."

"This ain't Kansas, Dorothy."

"Meow!" Familiar interjected from his perch on the mantel.

AREN'T HUMANS RIDICULOUS! I just hope with all of this mooning around, they don't forget to leave a good snack out for old Saint Nick. Something along the line of tuna or sardines. After all, if it wasn't for me taking care of them, where would those two be now? Ah, well, time for a nap. It never hurts to be good and rested, because we know a human may toil from sun to sun, but a cat's work is never done. Good night, Clotilde, I'll see you in my dreams.

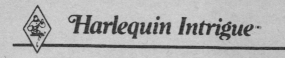

Harlequin Intrigue

COMING NEXT MONTH

#135 SWITCHBACK by Catherine Anderson
When kidnappers stole Mallory Christiani's little daughter Emily, she was warned not to tell anyone. Mallory desperately wanted to meet the kidnappers' demands and make the switch but, despite her efforts, she couldn't keep private investigator Bud Mac Phearson out of her life. Mac and Mallory were strangers, with no one to turn to but each other... and their future and happiness depended on holding nothing back.

#136 UNDER THE KNIFE by Tess Gerritsen
When a patient perished on the operating table during routine surgery, Dr. Kate Chesne was accused of malpractice. Had she misread an EKG... or was something, someone else the cause of death? Prosecutor David Ransom certainly didn't believe in her innocence despite his admiration for her. He only hoped she was wrong. For if murder had been committed in OR 7, Kate was the next target of a fiendishly clever psychopath.

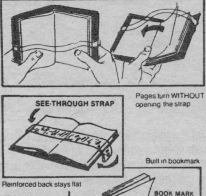

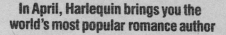

In April, Harlequin brings you the
world's most popular romance author

JANET DAILEY

No Quarter Asked

Out of print since 1974!

After the tragic death of her father, Stacy's world is shattered. She
needs to get away by herself to sort things out. She leaves behind
her boyfriend, Carter Price, who wants to marry her. However, as
soon as she arrives at her rented cabin in Texas, Cord Harris, owner
of a large ranch, seems determined to get her to leave. When Stacy
has a fall and is injured, Cord reluctantly takes her to his own ranch.
Unknown to Stacy, Carter's father has written to Cord and asked
him to keep an eye on Stacy and try to convince her to return home.
After a few weeks there, in spite of Cord's hateful treatment that
involves her working as a ranch hand and the return of Lydia, his ex-
fiancée, by the time Carter comes to escort her back, Stacy knows
that she is in love with Cord and doesn't want to go.

Watch for *Fiesta San Antonio* in July and *For Bitter or Worse* in September.

JDA-1